Avery the Dogless Orphan and the Interdimensional Stray

Prim Pawn

CHICKEN SCRATCH BOOKS
WWW.CHICKENSCRATCHBOOKS.COM

Chicken Scratch Books
PO Box 104
Wisdom, MT 59761
www.chickenscratchbooks.com

First Chicken Scratch Books Printing, 2022
ISBN 978-1-953743-22-0 (paperback)
ISBN 978-1-953743-23-7 (ebook)

Printed in the United States of America

For Onion and Cadence

CHAPTER 1

A Fur Friend of Her Own

In the garden shed of Slug Brook Academy, rusty tools hung from a crooked shelf, a lawn mower leered from the corner, and Avery brushed the black-and-white critter curled in her lap. Besides shadows, Avery and her new fur friend, Rosie, were all alone.

Strands of Rosie's fur clung to Avery's staticky wool skirt. She didn't mind. Her school uniform looked better with a touch of animal hair, at least in her opinion. Headmistress Bunhead might think otherwise. But what could the Headmistress do? Give Avery a detention for a dress code violation on the last day of school? Really?

Fifth grade was nearly over, and Avery had almost gotten through the year without a major incident of schoolwide embarrassment—*almost* being the key word.

Avery nuzzled her nose against Rosie's, wet and cool. "Rosie, you're the cutest pet ever. We're going to be best friends, I just know it. Nothing will keep us apart. Not even my Aunt Laurel."

Aunt Laurel had taken care of Avery, acting as both mom and dad, for most of Avery's life. And while her aunt was younger than her classmates' parents—so you'd think she'd be cooler, maybe even relatable or laid back—in actuality, Aunt Laurel was the strictest and most unreasonable adult Avery knew. Cautious, careful Aunt Laurel. Ridiculous rule-follower Aunt Laurel.

Fabricator-of-the-worst-excuses-in-the-history-of-excuses-for-not-getting-a-dog-Aunt-Laurel.

"Auntie L says that dogs shed and drool, that they're too expensive and a lot of work. That they give her allergies, bark at cats, chase after squirrels, and even eat their own poop if you don't watch them carefully enough." Avery's cheeks reddened with anger at the injustice of it all. "It's not fair! All I've ever wanted is a fur friend of my own!"

As though startled, Rosie dug her claws in Avery's wool skirt.

"Oh, I didn't mean to upset you, Rosie." Avery caressed the creature's mane, trying to settle her down. With her other hand, Avery dug out a treat from her pocket, scents of peanut butter and apples wafting in the dewy air. "Here, have this. A canine cookie baked by the meanie Aunt Laurel herself."

Avery snapped the treat in two and fed half to Rosie. The critter's soft nose and bumpy tongue tickled Avery's palm. As her companion gobbled up the snack, Avery couldn't help thinking, *life is perfect*.

Well, almost.

There was the whole matter that Rosie wasn't a dog, but a skunk. Not to mention Rosie wasn't Avery's pet at all, but rather a wild animal Avery had trapped in the school's garden shed.

"Excuse me? Is that a student in the garden shed? That's strictly forbidden."

The astonished voice belonged to a tall figure lurking outside, visible to Avery between cracks in the shed's wooden planks.

Immediately, Avery recognized the figure. Her stomach dropped.

Headmistress Bunhead.

She thought fast. "We gotta' hide you, Rosie."

Frantically, Avery searched for cover for the skunk. She found a metal bucket and placed it upside down over Rosie. "I know it's dark and scary," Avery whispered, "But it's just until I get rid of Headmistress Bunhead. It won't be long. I promise." She jumped to her feet and smoothed the wrinkles from her fur-covered skirt.

The shed door creaked open to reveal the Headmistress, snarling so her features appeared extra severe. She crossed her arms and stuck her chin in the air. "Miss Avery, you're breaking the rules. Students are prohibited from the caretaker's premises. Care to explain yourself?"

"Ah, I was—" Avery cracked under pressure. "I was looking for the library?"

Headmistress Bunhead eyed Avery suspiciously. "Evidentially, you took a wrong turn. I'd discipline you, but it's the last day of school, so come along now." She clapped. "It's time for math."

Rosie clawed at the metal bucket, the sound like utensils scraping against a plate. Avery fidgeted her hands behind her back, her palms sweaty. She'd have to wait until the bell rang to free the wild animal.

"Yay, math," she offered, half-heartedly, stepping over the bucket. "Oh no!" she cried, tripping on its handle and falling onto her hands and knees.

With a plunk, the bucket fell over to its side, revealing Rosie—angry, spine curved, tail puffy.

The Headmistress squinted, "Is that. . . a dog?"

Rosie bolted.

The blur of black-and-white fur scurried by Headmistress Bunhead. The bony woman grabbed the skunk by the tail and hung her upside down.

"Don't!" shrieked Avery.

It was too late.

Turned out, while Avery could count endless similarities between dogs and skunks—their scampering paws, their bristly fur, their damp little noses—there was a major difference between the two, that up until that point, Avery had conveniently ignored. You see, skunks are infamous for their anal scent glands, and, when the species feels threatened, their anal scent glands produce and secrete a sulfurous chemical so pungent it's detectable to human nostrils up to three and a half miles away.

In other words, when stressed, skunks spray a stinky stench.

An *intensely* stinky stench.

Rosie unleashed her smell in a toxic puff. The garden shed erupted in a piercing, stinging odor. Avery's eyes watered. She could barely see. She choked on the smell, gagging. Pinching her nose, she finished her untimely warning to Headmistress Bunhead, "That's Rosie. She's not a dog. She's a skunk."

CHAPTER 2

Barkleby Biscuits

Avery tramped down the cobblestone sidewalk, shoulders hunched under the weight of her backpack. Her cheeks burnt from embarrassment. Anyone within three and a half miles could smell Rosie's gift.

"What's that horrible stench?"

"Did someone fart?"

Concerned chatter and whispers of disgust came from all directions as Avery trekked by. People gagged and pinched their noses. Dogs on leashes pulled away from their owners, attracted to the girl's stinky school uniform like bees to honey. Snouts twitched in overdrive. Avery wanted to pet the extra-friendly dogs—a smiling hound always melted her troubles away—but their human companions quickly fled to fresh air as she neared with her cloud of toxic fumes. She wished she could disappear, melting into the sidewalk.

Finally, Avery made it to Aunt Laurel's shop, Barkleby Biscuits, a quaint storefront in a narrow, brick building. A red-and-white awning and a gold-painted door marked its entrance. White calligraphy danced on the window, announcing *Cookies for Canines! Peanut Butter Patties! Blueberry Biscuits!*

"That's right, makes sense," Avery muttered.

The chef-owner of Barkleby Biscuits, home to the tastiest canine cookies in all of Chicago, was none other than the dog-despising Aunt Laurel.

Call the news. Launch an investigation. Avery thought to herself. *The baker behind Barkleby Biscuits won't even let her niece have a dog of her own.* Avery could see the headlines now, *A REAL-WORLD TRAVESTY UNCOVERED! DOG-HATING AUNT RUINING HER NIECE'S LIFE!*

As Avery opened the door, bells chimed. Her scent wafted inside like a puff of smoke, overwhelming the pleasant smells of peanut butter, apples, and berries from the baking in the back kitchen. It didn't take long for the customers to clear out, along with their pooches and hounds, purse dogs, and hairless pseudo-rodents alike. Soon, Dogless Orphan Avery was the only one left in the store, basking alone in her horrid stench.

Aunt Laurel bounced a swinging door with her hip, a tray of freshly baked cookies in her oven-mitted hands. She wore an apron over a silk purple camisole, paired with worn black jeans, muddied motorcycle boots, and the rusted locket she never took off. Even when she showered, which was kind of gross in Avery's opinion. Not that Avery could talk. She was, after all, soaked in skunk spray, head-to-toe.

As Aunt Laurel took in the empty shop and putrid smell, Avery sensed a lecture brewing from none other than her least favorite version of her aunt—definitely disappointed Aunt Laurel.

"Before you say anything," Avery began, "this happened because I don't have a dog."

Aunt Laurel sighed in frustration and switched the sign on the door from OPEN to CLOSED. She pulled down the blinds, crossed her arms, and tapped her foot.

Here it comes. Avery cringed. *Serious, strict, and stern Aunt Laurel.*

"Avery Isadora Foster Warwick," Aunt Laurel started in a firm tone, "you need to take responsibility for your actions. You broke the rules. There are consequences."

Avery couldn't help herself. "Since when is it against the rules to give care and shelter to an animal in need?" she answered.

Aunt Laurel gasped. Her eyes widened. "That animal was a wild skunk! And you trapped it in your school's garden shed."

Butters and Toast, Aunt Laurel's black cat and grey cat, slinked under the door from the back kitchen to investigate the raised voices. They slowly stalked Avery, circling the familiar girl with the strange, unfamiliar scent. Toast, the grey cat with green eyes, who was normally quite lazy and motivated only by tuna, sniffed Avery's wool sock and leaped backwards, repulsed. Butters, the hyper and intense black cat with grey eyes, hissed.

Far from the greeting Avery would have gotten from a dog of her own.

"Last thing I need are your opinions right now, Butters and Toast." Avery glared at the devilish felines, who pranced away, tails up. Cats were always *so* judgmental, fitting pets for her aunt. "And, for the record, I didn't trap

Rosie. She wanted to be there. It was nice and warm and safe—"

"You named the skunk Rosie?"

"Yeah, that's what people do with pets. They name them. Rosie was everything I ever wanted. Loyal. A good listener. Funny. She was perfect. Until Headmistress Bunhead butted in and ruined it all."

Aunt Laurel would never understand. It was like Avery and she were opposites in every which way measurable. Never mind families, it was like they were from different planets. And forget aunt and niece, an onlooker wouldn't think they were even related.

Aunt Laurel's hair was bright and wild like wheat shucks in a field, while Avery's was straight and shiny as crow feathers. On Aunt Laurel's rosy cheeks, freckles scattered in the shape of the constellation Orion. Avery was pale as a ghost with no stars to guide her when she sought the company of her reflection. Appearance-wise, the similarity of their eye color—the aunt's a misty grey and the niece's a stormy charcoal—was where the commonalities ended. Their personalities were even further apart.

Avery figured she must take after her parents. She didn't remember anything about them, except what she knew from her only photo of the two which she kept by her bedside. It showed her dad and mom squished together on a swing hanging from a sturdy oak tree, feet dangling over the roots and dirt, their glowing smiles reflected in Avery's own toothless grin from her carrier strapped to her mom's chest.

Avery's parents disappeared before her first birthday. Although she never got to know them, she knew for certain they'd love dogs. Guaranteed. If they were alive, they'd be a happy family which would include at least one dog, but ideally, a Shih Tzu named Caesar, an Australian Shepherd named Boomerang, and a big rescue dog they saved from the pound.

Instead, Avery was stuck with Aunt Laurel and her long list of reasons for not getting a dog.

Aunt Laurel's cheeks flushed, her constellation of freckles glowing like swollen stars. "Your headmistress was sprayed by a skunk because of your actions, because you were hiding "Rosie"—, she gestured air quotes, "—in the school garden shed. Avery Isadora Foster Warwick, they're threatening expulsion. This is serious. You know how lucky you are to have that scholarship."

Suddenly, Avery's backpack weighed five hundred pounds. She shifted its straps. Without the help of a local charity, which funded education for orphans, Avery's tuition at Slug Brook Academy would be unaffordable. Another reminder she didn't belong.

The kids at school lived in sprawling mansions with gigantic yards big enough for whole packs of dogs. One girl, Jessica, had a Labrador in every color: yellow, black, and chocolate. Meanwhile, Avery and Aunt Laurel squeezed together in a one-bedroom apartment on top of Barkleby Biscuits. With two judgmental cats.

Avery looked at her shoes. "I just wanted a pal of my own, like everyone else."

"You have plenty of friends, Ave."

"I have plenty of classmates. Not friends. *Classmates.* And they all have dogs. And country homes and helicopters. The poor little, dogless orphan character doesn't fit in their fairy tale lives."

"We're not poor. The store's doing—" Aunt Laurel hesitated and bit her nail. "The store's doing just fine. And you're forgetting you have pets. Our cats."

Butters jumped on the counter and meowed, arching her back. Toast ignored Avery entirely.

"Butters and Toast? They hate me. We're enemies."

"The three of you used to be such pals." Aunt Laurel scooped Butters into her arms. The black feline melted in her embrace, purring as loud as an engine. "I'd find you cuddled up at night. Butters would guard the tub while you bathed. Toast would wait at the door for you to come home from kindergarten."

"Now all they do is sit on my homework and swat my toes while I'm sleeping."

Aunt Laurel laid Butters in her cat bed and gave her head a rub. Toast hopped up and curled into a ball next to his fur companion, dozing off into a deep sleep. "You know why you can't have a dog."

Avery rolled her eyes. *Here we go again.*

"Come on, you're not actually allergic," said Avery. "You don't so much as sneeze around your customers' dogs."

"My sinuses aren't exactly thriving." Aunt Laurel untied her apron and hung it behind the cash register. With tongs, she packed the leftover canine cookies from the display case into cardboard boxes.

"Ever heard of antihistamines?"

"I'm just not a dog person, Avery."

Avery groaned.

"Then how come you devote your life to making delicious cookies that dogs love? That tracks."

"Your Great-Grandma Elsie's recipe pays the bills. At least, it did." Aunt Laurel struggled with a cardboard take-out box, unable to shut it tight. Frustrated, she crushed its corner flat. "I'll take any help I can get. It's not easy being a single parent who works full-time. Speaking of which—"

She tossed a pair of tongs at Avery and directed her to assist in packing the leftovers from the display case for the local animal shelter. Squirrel-shaped cookies taunted Avery with their icing-drawn expressions. She swore she saw one blink and smirk, but when she rubbed her eyes, the biscuit returned to its stoic, fixed state.

There was nothing magical about Barkleby Biscuits. They were just normal dog treats made by a woman who hated dogs, but for some inexplicable reason, dedicated her life to creating delicious cookies for the enjoyment of canines.

Logical.

"Did Great-Grandma Elsie have a dog?" Avery asked.

"Definitely not." With a rag, Aunt Laurel patted a bead of sweat from her forehead.

"What about a skunk?"

"Of course not." Aunt Laurel tossed the cloth onto the counter by the mint green register, then crossed her arms. "I'm worried about you, Avery. Rules exist for a reason. I didn't raise you to misbehave. You're acting as spoiled as you smell."

"Smell?" Avery lifted her arm and sniffed her pit.

Pee-u.

"It's not me. It's Rosie."

Pitter pattering on the storefront window caught their attention. A friendly boy's face beamed from a crack in the blinds, eyes bright like the lamps of a lighthouse behind round spectacles. His small cheeks were red, as though he had been running. His tawny hair was neatly combed and parted in a straight line.

"Would you look at that?" Aunt Laurel smacked her lips. "It's your friend, Benji."

Then, a smiling man with messy dark hair appeared over Benji's shoulder. It was Joseph, Benji's dad. He waved with one hand, holding onto the leash of their Golden Retriever mix, Graham Cracker with his other. Joseph knocked on the front door and gestured at Aunt Laurel to let them inside.

Avery begged. "You can't let them in, Auntie L. Not when I smell like this."

But it was too late, Aunt Laurel had already unclicked the lock.

CHAPTER 3

Cruel Summer

"Woah." Benji's little face puckered as he entered the store. He swatted the air as if he could fan away the scent. "My olfactory receptors detect a rather pungent odor."

Normally excited to see her best friend, in the moment, Avery wished she could sink into the floor. She wasn't exactly sure what Benji meant, but figured it was along the lines of, "Woah, does it ever smell in here."

Benji's dad, Joseph confirmed this much. He followed behind his son, wearing a wrinkled shirt buttoned incorrectly in a crisscross fashion. Graham Cracker, their Golden Retriever mix, drooled puddles, as though dreaming of a Barkleby Biscuit, or perhaps triggered by Avery's skunk stench.

"I think what Benji Buoy means is, woah, does it ever smell in here," Joseph interpreted.

"Correct, Father," Benji said. He inhaled short breaths through his nostrils. Then he asked, "Is it possible that a Procyon lotor crawled into the ventilation and died?"

"Pro crayon what now?" Aunt Laurel squinted.

"It's the Latin name for raccoon," explained Benji, pushing his glasses up from his pert nose.

Avery couldn't help but to feel impressed. Even though she was in the same grade as Benji, they went to different schools, which was too bad, because Benji was the smartest person she knew. He was always explaining things to adults, which was opposite to how things went for Avery, with adults constantly lecturing her.

But as intelligent as Benji was, Avery did *not* have a crush on him—pinky-promise 100% percent. *Yes*, Benji was a boy. *Yes*, he was Avery's best friend. But he was not Avery's *boy*friend. Avery liked Benji. But she didn't *like* like him. They were just friends. Clear?

"Raccoon?" Aunt Laurel answered, eyebrows raised. "Nope. This smell wasn't the fault of the Night-time Garbage Bandit. This was all Ave."

Benji and Joseph looked squarely at the offender. Avery's pale cheeks flushed pink. She tried to shrug it off. "I got sprayed by Rosie. She's a skunk."

Joseph unclipped Graham Cracker's leash. The Golden Retriever jumped on Avery and licked her face.

"Graham Cracker doesn't seem to mind," Benji observed. "In fact, I wager she prefers you this way, which makes sense because she's drawn to items with particularly putrid smells. Like dirty socks and squirrel droppings."

Avery wasn't sure if she should be offended. Before she could decide, with a furry paw, Graham Cracker swatted Avery's hand down to cover it in licks, slurping up her foul—but to a dog, delectable—scent. Avery softened, giggling. "You know what they say, Benji, a dog will always be your ally."

"Too bad you didn't call," Joseph noted. "I've been tinkering with an idea for a pocket-sized fan that sucks up undesirable odor molecules."

"Or we could just—hang on, one moment," Benji rummaged through his tan fanny pack, reflections of yard spools and spare keys in his lenses. "Aha! Clothes pins!"

Benji affixed a clothespin to his nostrils and smiled proudly, offering his spares with an extended palm.

"A simple and elegant solution." Joseph followed suit, clipping his nostrils shut, while Aunt Laurel and Avery politely declined.

"How can I help you, Joseph?" Aunt Laurel asked, fiddling with her tarnished silver locket.

Joseph squinted at the price list behind the counter and rubbed his eyeglasses with his wrinkled shirt. "Gosh, have the prices gone up again?"

"Unfortunately," sighed Aunt Laurel. "I hate to do it, but I don't have a choice. First, my landlord sold this building to a company I've never heard of, One-Two-Three Loot and Plunder Limited, and they raised my rent tenfold. Then, the farm I get my ingredients from was taken over by a new company, some ABC Vikings Incorporated, and my food prices shot through the roof. You'd think someone's out to get me."

"Luckily, the cookies are so beloved, you can charge what you want for them." Joseph counted his quarters, coming up short. "Can I buy half a cookie for Graham? All my spare change goes to boat parts these days. Living in a floating abode ain't cheap."

Like Avery and Aunt Laurel, Benji, Joseph, and Graham Cracker didn't have the typical family set-up. They lived in a motor trawler, moored in Monroe Harbor on Lake Michigan. And while the boat didn't work, so it couldn't exactly go anywhere, that didn't stop Avery and Benji from pretending they were pirates conquering the seas, as the vessel bobbed in the bay, tied up to a buoy.

Each summer, Benji would travel to Orlando, Florida, to live with his mom, his stepdad, stepsiblings, and as of the summer before fifth grade, a baby. Avery always thought he'd come back with tales of Mickey Mouse and grapefruit picking, but instead, he'd tell her horror stories about how he'd been forced to go skeet shooting or to football camp with his stepbrothers. One autumn, he came back with a broken arm! That, and the fact he flew in an airplane twice a year, showed just how brave Benji was deep down.

"Here. Have these. On the house. We have extra products." Aunt Laurel handed Joseph an entire box, first taking out a cookie for Graham Cracker. She glanced at Avery. "We closed early today on account of Miss Stinky Pants."

"I'm not even wearing pants," Avery pointed out, pulling down on the uncomfortable, wool skirt of her school uniform.

Aunt Laurel tempted Graham Cracker with the cookie, "Alright, Graham Cracker. Ready?"

Aunt Laurel asked the Retriever mix to give her five, and Graham Cracker enthusiastically provided her paw, then quickly gobbled up her reward—a Barkleby Biscuit. Avery suspected that, deep down, Aunt Laurel liked some dogs, *especially* Graham Cracker. She just pretended not to.

"Is there any way I can help out, Laurel?" asked Joseph. "You know I was thinking, with 3D printers these days, I could theoretically build a biscuit cloner. That'd cut down on your production costs."

"No, Joseph, that's all right."

Aunt Laurel never accepted help.

"You sure?" Joseph asked, leaning on the counter.

"I can take care of myself." Aunt Laurel coughed. "Except if you have a gas mask I could borrow. Avery, come on, let's get you in a bathtub of tomato juice."

"Miss Foster?" Benji asked shyly.

"Yes, Benji?" Aunt Laurel replied.

"I was wondering if Avery can come urban scavenging with Graham Cracker and me? Yesterday I found three coins minted in the year of my birth and a rusted key! I'm cataloging my findings and adding them to a new wing in the Museum of Benji." Benji's face lit up. "I hope to find more."

The Museum of Benji was Benji's name for his different sets of collections—from postcards to stamps, rocks to baseball cards, coins to lost keys. Benji stored boxes and binders of cataloged finds in storage cupboards hidden behind couch cushions and under the stairs of his houseboat. Each lost key or coin belonged to part of a bigger collection, and for some reason, that brought Avery comfort and filled her with warmth. She liked scavenging with Benji, rescuing orphaned objects, and finding them a new home, their place in the world. If anything could turn around Avery's day, it was that. That, and time with Graham Cracker, one of her favorite dogs.

But, of course, Aunt Laurel had to ruin everything. Again.

"No, sorry, Benji, Avery's grounded."

"What?" Avery cried. This was news to her. "For how long?"

As though caught off-guard, Aunt Laurel seemed to improvise, "One week." Avery glared and Aunt Laurel shrugged, "Consequences."

"But I'm going to Florida this weekend," Benji frowned. He turned to Avery. "This whole summer, I have to hang out with Tweedle Dee Protein Bar and Tweedle Dumb Football Head. Worse, my stepdad signed me up for Monster Truck Camp! I like saving old things, not seeing them crushed with diesel-powered Goliaths! What will I do without you, Ave?"

"It's okay Benji. You'll survive. Somehow." Avery squeezed his shoulder then clapped her hands together in prayer and begged. "Auntie L, can I please, please, puhlease be grounded next week instead?"

"We're leaving for Great-Grandma Elsie's cabin on Beaver Island tomorrow," Aunt Laurel responded.

"Exactly. I can stay in the city while you're packing up the place."

"Out of the question. You're eleven years old—"

"Eleven-and-a-half."

"You're not staying in the city alone, I will not—"

"You're going away?" Joseph asked, his voice cracking as he tried to conceal his disappointment.

"Yes," exhaled Aunt Laurel. "Just for a few weeks. I have a cabin, well, it was my Grandma Elsie's, but she passed away when I was a teenager. It's been mine ever since, on an island in middle-of-nowhere Lake Michigan. I'm finally going to pack it up and list it for sale."

"Boo," Avery wailed. "Who wants to spend the summer at some shack in the woods?"

"Avery Isadora," Aunt Laurel warned with her tone. "*Manners*."

Avery rolled her eyes. She didn't care to go off to some stinky cabin for the best part of the summer. She'd rather stay in Chicago and scavenge with Benji and Graham Cracker. Judging from Joseph's reaction, he seemed like he didn't want them to go away either.

"Oh." Joseph's face fell. Change jingled in his pockets. "I see. Well. . . I'll have no Benji Buoy this summer, and you'll be gone too. Just Graham and me. Huh. I guess I'll have to focus on. . . work."

"Fix your boat and you can come visit," Aunt Laurel joked.

"Sounds like a plan." Joseph smiled, his posture snapping erect. Something about his voice made Avery think he meant it. She wasn't so sure if Aunt Laurel had caught onto that fact. He continued, confident, "That's what I'll do. And Benji Buoy, you'll come with me. We'll tell your mother I need a crew."

"Father, the polar magnets will shift before that vessel is seaworthy."

"Have some faith in your old man, Benji. Don't underestimate the power of a rational, logical, scientific mind." Joseph returned to rest his elbows on the counter. "Beaver Island you said? Huh, isn't that the island where those

Weirdies used to live? That strange group of pioneers? Yeah, that's right. I saw it in a documentary online. They were said to appear out of thin air and could travel between space and time."

"Really?" Aunt Laurel arched her eyebrows. "Whatever happened to your rational, logical, scientific mind?"

Joseph put his hands in his pockets. "Theoretically, we could exist among other dimensions, undetectable by our five senses. And if that's true, theoretically, a significant amount of energy could open portals to these other dimensions, homes to other beings. *And if that's true,* who's to say they haven't already figured out how to visit us? Theoretically, they could, therefore, thereby, already be here on Earth trying to blend in among us."

"Ah. . . ." Aunt Laurel stood speechless for a moment. Then, she unclipped the clothespin from Joseph's nose. "Hard to take you seriously with this on."

"Woah, does it ever stink in here," Joseph gagged. "Avery, let me know if you need my Stench Destenchifyer, patent pending."

"Alright," Avery muttered.

"Tomato juice," said Aunt directed. "Bathtub. ASAP."

"Tomato juice, bathtub, ASAP," echoed Avery.

CHAPTER 4

Rub-a-Dub-Dub

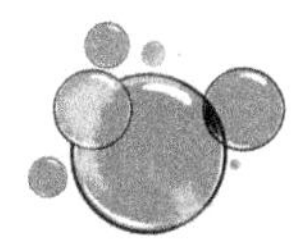

Aunt Laurel dumped a cup of juice over Avery's head. The liquid ran down the stinky girl's face, stinging her eyes.

"I'll never look at tomatoes quite the same."

Avery made a mental note—before befriending a wild animal, ensure it's not a species that uses its anal sweat glands as a defensive weapon. Come to think of it, Avery decided she should avoid animals with venom and quills as well. That ruled out porcupines and Southern short-tailed shrews. Unfortunately, Avery was running out of options for doglike pets which weren't exactly dogs. Annoyed, she shoved the thought to the back of her mind and concentrated on rinsing tomato juice from her hair.

Aunt Laurel stood on her toes to reach for a towel on a rack over the toilet, brushing aside overgrown spider plant ferns, dangling from higher above. She handed Avery the towel. "Dry up."

While Avery wrapped the plush cotton around her torso, dripping splotches of fruit blood onto the bathmat, Butters pushed the bathroom door open with her furry forehead, Toast following closely behind. The door knocked Avery's elbow, squarely on the funny bone. "Ouch," she grimaced, while the cats sniffed at her ankles, whiskers ticklish. "Quit that."

The cats pranced off. Butters hopped onto the narrow ledge of the yellowed bathtub crowded with bottles of homemade shampoo and lotion. Toast took refuge behind Aunt Laurel's eggplant purple slippers and dozed off.

With the jars of lotions, moisturizers, and elixirs, organized on the sink counter, along with the scent of tomatoes absorbed by Avery's skin, the bathroom smelled like a garden of flowers, fruit, and vegetables. It was a welcome change from the perfume Avery wore into the bakery. At least, there was that. Maybe things were looking up.

Hopeful, Avery looked at Aunt Laurel. "Am I still grounded?"

"Definitely," her aunt replied, unmoved. She sat on the closed toilet seat, her bright and wild hair frizzy from steam. "I've had time to think."

Avery groaned. That was never a good sign.

"I'm enforcing strict rules for our time at Beaver Island."

"Fun," Avery said, sarcastically.

"Avery Isadora, it's for your own good. My rules are meant to keep you safe. Beaver Island seems quaint, but it's a wild and dangerous place."

Avery brushed her teeth, spitting out a gob of foam into the sink.

"Yet, you and my mom hung out there as teenagers." She flushed her mouth with water.

"How do you know that?"

"I overheard you tell your boyfriend, Joseph."

"Joseph's not my boyfriend. And, you shouldn't eavesdrop." Aunt Laurel's cheeks flushed, her constellation freckles doused in a pink, gaseous glow. "And, I was naïve back then, thought there wouldn't be trouble, but—" Aunt Laurel stopped mid-sentence. She twirled her tarnished locket chain around her fingers. "Remember that nursery rhyme I taught you?"

"How could I forget?" Avery rolled her eyes.

"Recite it," cued Aunt Laurel.

"Must I?"

"Please."

"Fine." Avery cleared her throat and stood straight, recalling the nursery rhyme her aunt used to sing to her each night before bed. How could she possibly forget? It went:

Watch out for Scorned Sliders,
the dangerous outsiders
They come with the rain
to cause dogs much pain

They travel by umbrella
and this is what they tell ya',
'I can grant what you desire,'
Beware, for they are liars

Scalp covered in worms
Hiss, wiggle, twist, squirm
Warts pucker their skin

from their toes to their chin
Though Scorned Sliders may disguise
you won't be surprised
with nostrils kept alert
for smells as putrid as snert

"Very good," Aunt Laurel commended.

Avery squeezed air from the corners of her mouth, making a distasteful, vibrating honk which mimicked flatulence. Once upon a time, she craved nothing more than her aunt's compliments. Now, Avery couldn't help feeling a bit like a trained monkey, or a dog performing a trick for a Barkleby Biscuit.

"What does 'snert' even mean?"

"It's a very stinky pea soup," Aunt Laurel explained. "You're lucky I don't serve it for dinner like Great-Grandma Elsie used to."

"And Scorned Sliders are imaginary dog-hating people from another dimension? Kind of like that story your boyfriend Joseph told, about those Weirdie pioneers?"

"*Not* my boyfriend," Aunt Laurel corrected, fiddling with her silver locket. "And it's not a true story, of course. Great-Grandma Elsie told your mom and me the nursery rhyme to remind us of the dangers of Beaver Island. She said, 'Never engage with a Scorned Slider. If you see one, run as fast as you can in the opposite direction.'"

"Here, I thought sliders were a tasty option on an appetizer menu."

"It's not a joke, Avery. Where we're going, only caution and prudence will keep you safe. It isn't like the waterfront where you go scavenging with Benji. I don't want you out of my sight. That's rule number one."

"Goodie. Guess we're up for a real bonding experience. Tell me, do I have to pee with the bathroom door open too?"

It wasn't a stretch of the imagination. Aunt Laurel, after all, was presently lecturing her from her throne of a toilet seat.

"You're mistaken to assume you're going to find working plumbing in a cottage built in the 1850s."

"What? Where do I go? The *woods*?"

How could it possibly get worse?

"It's called an outhouse." Aunt Laurel stood up behind Avery, her starry freckles seeming to twinkle in the mirror's reflection. She collected Avery's hair in her hands and spritzed a homemade lavender detangler onto Avery's roots, dragging a comb easily through the knots. Aunt Laurel's products worked like charms. Still, Avery pouted.

"Gross, Laurel."

"That's Aunt Laurel to you, missy," she scolded. Again, she fidgeted with the tarnished silver chain of her necklace. Sometimes, Avery wished the chain would snap off. "Come on, p.j. time."

Inside Avery's bedroom fort, divided from the living room by a folding screen, Aunt Laurel tucked Avery into bed. Avery felt her mom and dad watching over her from the photo on her side table under the windowsill. For a moment, it appeared as though Mom's midnight black hair blew in the wind. Avery rubbed her eyes. The photo was still. She was seeing things. Tired. Even though she couldn't remember her parents, she missed them. There was a piece missing in her heart, a hole that could never be filled.

Except maybe by a dog, that is.

Sleepily, she yawned. "Tell me again what she was like. My mom?"

Aunt Laurel laughed. "She was about as rule-abiding as you."

"Did she like dogs?"

"I'm not getting into this now," Aunt Laurel answered, fluffing a pillow.

"Did she like me?" The question escaped Avery's throat like a sour burp. She hadn't meant to ask it. Yet, it had somehow escaped.

"Your mom," Aunt Laurel paused, as though searching for exactly the right words. "Cared about you more than anything. So did your dad."

Avery choked on the thought. Her heart panged, sorrow twisting into anger and confusion.

"Then, why aren't they still here?" Avery asked, suddenly wide awake, popping up from her sheets. "If they cared about me so much, why did they abandon me?"

"Avery, they didn't abandon you. They went on a trip. It was only supposed to be for a few days. No one ever thought something would happen to the floatplane they boarded."

"Why would they leave me behind? I was just a baby."

"Enough." Aunt Laurel rubbed her temples.

"Why won't you answer?"

"Avery, it's late and we have a long drive to Charlevoix in the morning. We can talk in the jeep."

"Promise?"

"Promise."

"Fine."

"We'll make the best of this summer, Ave." Aunt Laurel tucked the comforter under Avery's chin and then around her body like a cocoon. Avery reluctantly yawned. "That reminds me, I'm going to put our bikes on the jeep's rack. Remember to pack your helmet. It will be fun. I promise."

"Yeah, fun," Avery muttered.

CHAPTER 5

Avoidant Aunt Syndrome

In Avery's opinion, Aunt Laurel had a serious case of Avoidant Aunt Syndrome, an official medical term for nieces like Avery to describe their seriously avoidant aunts. Hence the name: Avoidant Aunt Syndrome.

Symptoms included: changing the subject, biting nails, turning up the radio, and don't forget, the classic, frequenting of fast foods drive-thrus for heaps of hamburgers and fries because speaking with your mouth full is, obviously, forbidden, unbecoming, and against Aunt Laurel's rules.

Go figure, they didn't talk about *anything* in the jeep ride to Charlevoix. Aunt Laurel listened to an audiobook about raising pre-teen girls—which caused Avery's eyes to roll so many times, she felt like she was on an upside-down roller-coaster. Worse, Butters and Toast wouldn't shut up their meowing the entire six-hour drive. The cats screamed and whined, even after Aunt Laurel gave in and let them roam outside of their carriers.

"They're just excited to visit their hometown, I guess," Aunt Laurel excused the annoying creatures.

"Butters and Toast are from Beaver Island?"

Aunt Laurel sipped from a soda, her other hand tightly gripping the steering wheel. "They were strays. Found them in the woods. A neighbor's Spaniel had cornered them in a fox hole."

The mangy felines wailed. Avery plugged her ears. "Should have left them for the dog."

"The island's canines are *not* to be trusted," Aunt Laurel said, punctuating her point with a wave of a French fry. "They may appear harmless, but they will turn on you in an instant."

"Easy fix." Avery shrugged. "Carry around a few strips of bacon and that will make the pooches friendly enough."

"Avery, I'm serious," Aunt Laurel said, so urgently the fry flew out of her hand, landing on Butters's black-furred head. Toast licked at the salt. "Rule number two: no consorting with dogs of any kind on the island. No matter how cute they may seem."

Avery's jaw dropped. "Unfair."

Avery expected this to be The Worst Summer of Her Life.

No Benji.

No Graham Cracker.

And no dogs.

And although Avery had missed the last day of fifth-grade math class on account of the Rosie Incident, she knew the equation pointed to a single solution: No Fun.

A Dreadful, Dogless Summer.

Aunt Laurel and Avery stayed overnight in a hotel by Lake Michigan, then the next morning, they took the first ferry to Beaver Island. And that was when things got weird.

Capitol "W" weird.

Weird.

CHAPTER 6

The Emerald Isle

The lake rippled like bends in a paper fan as the sunrise reigned.

"Calm day for sitting in a jeep in a boat." Aunt Laurel turned on the ignition and rolled slowly onto the vessel's ramp. "Ferries, the turduckens of transportation."

"So long as we don't have to listen to any more audiobooks about raising a pre-teen, today will automatically suck less than yesterday," Avery said from the backseat.

"Watch your language, Avery Isadora," Aunt Laurel scolded.

Butters shrieked a whiny meow from her blanket on the front passenger seat, waking up Toast from his snooze.

"Cancel that," said Avery. "Let's muzzle Butters. Then, it will be a decent day."

The jeep parked like a sardine in a tin, vehicles packed around it on all sides. Avery rolled down her window and stuck out her head, craning her neck for a view. The water reached endlessly beyond the horizon. Beaver Island wasn't technically in the middle of nowhere, though it might as well have been. It sat on the northern tip of Lake Michigan, one of the largest lakes in the world. "So grand it's called a Great Lake," Auntie L had wistfully reminisced.

With a flick of a knob, Aunt Laurel reclined her seat and munched on her pencil while leafing through a book of crossword puzzles. Avery looked out at the water, imagining what it'd be like to go swimming with a dog. Rain pitter-pattered against the jeep's windshield. The lake was no longer calm, the ferry bobbing in the waves. Waves sloshed on the deck.

"I shouldn't have expected a gentle greeting," Aunt Laurel muttered, grabbing hold of a lidless Styrofoam coffee cup she had filled in the hotel lobby. She sopped spilled liquid with napkins from an earlier fast-food order.

After an hour or so of being tossed by the inland sea, the ferry pulled into a horseshoe-shaped bay, the water glinting like green emeralds, and moored to its loading dock. The rain eased to a light sprinkle. As Aunt Laurel drove the jeep onto the island's main drag, there was no longer need for windshield wipers. The mid-day sun melted away the clouds, but not Avery's mood.

Avery pressed her forehead against the windowpane. They passed a gated marina, the masts of sailboats peeking over the yacht club's roof, then a grocer, a whiskey distillery with its shades drawn, and a tavern with a wooden porch. Two girls, around Avery's age, walked down the sidewalk, happy and giggling, each walking a happy dog of her own on a leash. The shorter girl had a small, black dog, fuzzy as a pair of slippers, and the taller girl had a dog that was as sturdy and regal as a greyhound but with a shiny, shaggy amber coat.

No matter where Avery went, everyone had a dog, except her.

"Hey Avery," Aunt Laurel chimed. "If my memory serves correct, there's an ice cream shop up around the corner, and they have the most decadent flavors you could ever dream of. Quadruple chocolate fudge. Whipped cream pineapple heaven. Lemon meringue melody."

"If you're trying to make up for a dogless summer, it won't work," answered Avery, trying to stop her mouth from watering. Her tummy growled in betrayal. "But I'll admit—it's a step in the right direction."

The jeep continued down the main drag around a bend. The storefronts blended together, all pastel window shutters and candy-colored doors, until they crawled up to a lot of burnt wreckage, ashes still smoldering under a charred sign reading: *BEAVER DAM'S GOOD ICE CREAM.* The shop's flesh was burnt to a crisp, all that remained was a skeleton of metal beams and crumbled bricks.

Aunt Laurel gasped at the sight. "What in the world?" She fiddled with her locket while slowing to a roll.

"Let me guess. This is that ice cream shop you were talking about?" Avery grumbled.

"What's left of it, it seems." Aunt Laurel frowned at the wreckage. "Gives a new meaning to a hot fudge sundae, don't it?"

Unamused, Avery slouched in her seat. "Your dad jokes won't make up for the fact I don't have ice cream, Laurel."

"That's Aunt Laurel to you—" A car honked impatiently, interrupting the scolding. Distracted, Aunt Laurel pressed on the gas and continued down the bumpy road. But Avery wouldn't let her misery go unseen.

"No ice cream and no dog. This summer sucks."

"Language," Aunt Laurel warned.

"Fine. This summer is already the *worst*. Dreadful and dogless."

"Not to mention, dramatic," Aunt Laurel mumbled.

As though on cue, a blonde woman in a pink velour tracksuit, her neck, wrists, and ears decorated with glaringly bright diamond jewelry, jogged effortlessly across the road. A man in a formal butler's uniform lagged behind as he pushed a gem-encrusted baby stroller. Avery caught a glimpse of the infant, furry-faced with paw-shaped booties, a snow-white onesie, and whiskered snout. Avery rubbed her eyes. Was she hallucinating a puppy in place of a child? Or was the butler manning a stroller with a small, fluffy Maltese inside?

After the strange procession passed, Aunt Laurel floored on the gas pedal.

"Listen, Avery, you have to understand. I don't want to be here anymore than you do but we're a team and teammates watch out for each other, keep their eyes open, and—"

"Look! Dog! Straight ahead! Stop!"

Suddenly and out-of-nowhere, a tiny terrier, black and tan, spry and scruffy, sprinted across the jeep's path. The minuscule, puppy-sized furball darted across the road, tail up, running too fast for its little legs to keep up. Like a tumbleweed, the terrier somersaulted in front of the vehicle's turning tires.

Aunt Laurel slammed on her brakes and squeezed her eyes shut. Avery screamed. The bumper halted a half-inch from the tiny terrier. The creature crawled to its feet, shook its floppy tan and black triangle ears back in place, a silver tuft of hair on its crown fluffing out like a seeding white dandelion. Off-balance, the pooch scurried a zigzag pattern into a wooded park, where a lighthouse towered over the tree line in the distance.

Avery slapped her palms to the window, her nose squished against the glass, her eyes glued as the puppy's scruffy tail disappeared in the thicket of pine trees and brush. "He's hurt. You hit him."

Avery wanted to run out and help. She hesitated. Aunt Laurel would be furious if she took off her seat belt with the jeep still running.

"I—I didn't. I couldn't have," Aunt Laurel said quietly, as though to herself. "There wasn't so much as a bump. I swear."

Avery wasn't so sure. And if Aunt Laurel had injured the tiny terrier, it was their responsibility to make sure he was OK. He was so cute and little, after all. Avery pried on the door handle. *Locked*. She pulled on the lock pin. *Stuck*. "Auntie L. We have to help."

Traffic from the ferry accumulated behind the jeep. The impatient car to their rear honked again.

"Just, one moment," said Aunt Laurel, frazzled. "Let me pull over."

With her body weight, Avery pushed her shoulder against the jeep door while jiggling its handle and lock.

Click. The door popped open.

"Avery, wait," Aunt Laurel twisted to grab her niece by the end of her tangerine t-shirt, but instead, knocked over the lidless coffee from the cup holder, brown liquid spilling and soaking into the fabric of the passenger seat. Butters jumped on the center console and craned her neck to lick the caffeinated beverage. Avery slid out of the vehicle, onto the road's shoulder.

"Back inside the vehicle. Beaver Island Animal Control!" A uniformed woman in aviator sunglasses ran up the road's ditch as she flashed her badge, her other hand gripping a dart gun holstered in a belt around her hips. The animal patrol officer warned Avery with a stern tone, "This is a dangerous situation, little girly. Suspected case of rabies."

On the officer's left cheek was a patch of bumpy skin in the shape of a crescent moon, the texture like burnt toast. Her nose was thin and hooked, her reddish-brown hair twirled in corkscrews so tight and bouncy they seemed to squirm in the wind under her hat marked with an official-looking crest.

Scalp covered in worms

Hiss, wiggle, twist, squirm

A whiff of foul odor tickled Avery's nostrils. As the officer approached, the smell thickened, reminding Avery of Rosie, but then turning sour.

Like snert.

The nursery rhyme again flashed in Avery's mind.

Though Scorned Sliders may disguise

you won't be surprised

with nostrils kept alert

for smells as putrid as snert

Avery shook the poem from her mind. It made sense for an animal patrol officer to smell foul. She probably dealt with everything from skunk spray to dog doo-doo on a daily basis. Still, the powerful stench unsettled Avery. She could taste it. She gagged, holding the barf in. Could Aunt Laurel smell it too? On the other side of the rolled-up jeep window, the cats swatted at paper napkins as Aunt Laurel tried to sop up the spilled coffee. Her Aunt was clearly distracted.

"Didn't you hear me, girly? Back inside. The terrible terrier is my business alone."

Avery froze, eyes on the officer's utility belt of weapons. Pepper spray. Darts with red fringes. A tranquilizer gun. A whole tool belt of ways to hurt the helpless puppy.

"What are you going to do to him?" Avery asked, horrified.

The officer snarled, "You don't want to get involved in this, little girly."

Avery's knees shook. Her heart thumped in her chest. Here, was this scary-looking, smelly officer, chasing after an innocent, helpless, and possibly injured puppy who just needed help. But the officer didn't seem like the helping type at all. Especially with her hand gripping the tranquilizer gun. Avery wondered if she should follow the officer's orders.

But who else would stand up for the tiny terrier if she didn't?

Avery clamped her hands into fists, digging her

fingernails into her palms as though the pain would bring her courage. "He's just a puppy. He might be hurt. He needs help."

"He's a menace to society. A vicious and heartless creature. He'll chomp off your fingers if you give him a chance." The officer loaded a fringed dart into the shiny tranquilizer gun, then pulled its cock with a violent click. She lowered her sunglasses onto the ledge of her hooked nose. Her grey eyes whirled as viciously as a November gale on Lake Michigan. "So, if you know what's good for you, which I suspect you do, you'll stay away." She bolted across the road, chasing after the terrier's path.

The front passenger door to the jeep swung open. Butters and Toast kneaded at the mess of coffee-stained napkins piled on the seat, and as the officer ran into the wooded park, the wind replaced the stench of snert with smells of pine and lake water.

"Avery, get in." Aunt Laurel commanded. "Avery Isadora, *now.*"

Part of Avery wanted to follow the officer past the park and into the woods. Save the terrier. Yet, something about the folds in Aunt Laurel's forehead and the urgent tone of her voice made Avery realize this wasn't a real option. Reluctantly, Avery ducked into the vehicle.

"What's gotten into you, young lady?" Aunt Laurel geared into drive, squinting as she noticed the officer disappearing into the trees in the mirror's reflection. "Wait. Is that a police officer?"

"Animal patrol," Avery corrected. Her stomach flipped with concern for the puppy. Even though she had listened to her aunt by getting back inside the jeep, she felt like she had made a bad decision. Why did obeying her aunt feel so wrong? Usually, it was breaking the rules that filled Avery with guilt. Not following them. "Auntie L, she's after that dog. She says he has rabies."

"Rabies?" Aunt Laurel grimaced. "That's reason enough to avoid dogs in these parts."

"She had a dart gun."

Aunt Laurel sighed deeply. "Avery, it will just put the dog to sleep for a while. Let the adults do their jobs. I'm sure she has more experience than you."

Avery slumped in the seat and crossed her arms. "Yeah, 'cause I'm not even allowed to get a dog of my own."

Aunt Laurel pushed play on an audiobook on her phone, a soft voice introducing a chapter about taming the wild in prepubescent girls. "Listen, I know you're worried, but the animal patrol officer will find and take care of the dog. That's her job."

Avery realized then that "taking care of the dog" could have more than one meaning. She didn't like the mystery behind that phrase. Not one bit.

"That's what I'm afraid of."

CHAPTER 7

Cliff Cottage

Weeds and wildflowers overflowed onto the cobblestone path to Cliff Cottage, a rundown log cabin shadowed by pine trees and birch, perched on Beaver Island's highest ledge. The cliff's edge was hidden by the woods. Proof of the lake's strength below came in the form of echoes from waves crashing against rocks. Dandelions, dewy from the morning rain, nipped at Avery's ankles.

"Keep mindful of where you walk," Aunt Laurel cautioned. "One second, you're looking for the outhouse, next you're tumbling to your demise. If you're not careful."

"Got it. Relieving myself is an extreme sport."

"Nothing is safe on this island." As Aunt Laurel said this, the rickety top step to the front porch split under her weight. Her boot stomped through the splintered wood, landing in a puddle of mud. "As I was saying." She groaned.

"Welcoming." Avery helped pull her aunt from the wreck. "A dingy cabin with no indoor plumbing on a dangerous island infested with rabid dogs which I'm not even allowed to play with."

Aunt Laurel dusted off her grey jeans, frowning at a ripped knee from the jagged wood. "We're only staying to pack and clean. In and out, I promise, Ave. I don't want to be here any longer than we need." She shivered, fumbling with her locket, as per usual.

The cottage resembled a tired face: the faded wood door like a snoring mouth, the two dirty windows taking the place of sleepy eyes, and the moss growing on the roof's shingles like fuzzy hair. Paint chips unfurled from the features' frames. With shaky hands, Aunt Laurel fussed with her key in the lock, and nudged the door ajar. The cabin inhaled, its exhale interrupted with a coughing fit, dust motes pluming in the air.

"You go in," Aunt Laurel instructed. "I'll get the cats."

Light from the doorway flooded the cabin, joining the rivers of sunlight filtering through moth-eaten curtains. Mismatched furniture and dusty trinkets cluttered a sitting area at the front of the cabin, an old kitchen, and a dining table towards the back. Stiff-posture chairs tucked around a handcrafted table. A cast iron wood stove leered in a corner.

The unfinished floor creaked under Avery's feet. She followed a trail of mess which started at a pilly, orange rug, spread up and over a murky glass table, then led to a mildewy sofa. A board game with dice, fake money, and cards, laid on the rug as though abandoned mid-turn by its players. Weathered magazines, crinkled chip bags, and a long-forgotten snack bowl, along with bottles of nail polish brought Avery to a tattered teal housecoat and mismatched socks scattered over the couch's cushions.

It seemed like the sort of mess Avery's classmates

would leave behind after a sleepover party. If she had ever gotten invited to one, that is. Definitely not the sorts of relics Avery would expect in her Great-Grandma Elsie's cabin.

Entering the cabin, with curious Butters at her ankles and sleepy Toast in her arms, Aunt Laurel noticed the mess and gasped, dropping the grey cat. His paws thumped gracefully against the wood floor, Aunt Laurel jumping at the noise. "Sorry. I wasn't expecting this," she explained, trying to compose herself. "It doesn't make any sense."

Avery picked up one of the magazines, brushing dust from its cover. Though faded, Avery could make out the headlines promising to help the reader choose the perfect pair of low-rise jeans and flatten their stomach in five easy moves. The date read April 2003.

Ancient. Not great-grandma old, but still, from before Avery was born.

She inspected the labels on the nail polish bottles, one metallic purple, the other seafoam blue. "Did a gang of cheerleaders break in for a sleepover?" Avery asked.

She moved to a bowl on the coffee table, finding withered popcorn kernels. She licked one. It was still salty.

"Stop! Don't touch anything." Aunt Laurel tripped over the game board on her way to swipe the dish from Avery.

Her aunt's concern was apparent. Even more than usual. Which was saying a lot.

"Should we call the police?" asked Avery.

"No. Definitely not." Urgently, Aunt Laurel squeezed a pack of hand sanitizer from her jean pocket. "A good clean should do the trick."

Can't be that concerned, thought Avery, rolling her eyes, and dumping her backpack on the sofa before wandering into the kitchen area, host to its own mysterious mess.

A yellowed newspaper sprawled open on the wooden table, accompanied by a mauve mug with a crusty tea bag. Droopy cereal boxes stood on shelves, eaten through at the corners by hungry mice, along with wooden bowls, stone mortars, flasks, and vases of contents indiscernible in the dim light. Avery thought she saw a jar of preserved squirrel heads suspended in vinegar, and another jammed with human ears. Not liking her mind playing tricks on her, she desperately searched for a light switch. "It's got to be around here, somewhere," she mumbled.

"You're expecting electricity when there's no plumbing or running water?" Aunt Laurel scoffed, examining the chewed-through pantry stores with a frown. "Wishful thinking. Your Great-Grandma Elsie built the cabin herself."

"I was just looking for the Wi-Fi password," Avery joked.

She opened a cork-lined icebox, empty but for a soda can warped from having frozen, thawed, then exploded, and a cracked mason jar of shriveled spiders. She flinched and slammed it shut, turning back to the dining table.

On it, the newspaper was open to Sunday's Crosswords section. A pile of chewed pencils lay next to the tea mug. Avery pinched the bag's string in her fingers. CHAMOMILE, blurred ink read on its crusty label.

Auntie L's favorite.

"When was the last time you were here?" asked Avery.

"Apparently, it's been longer than I thought," sighed Aunt Laurel.

"Why's it such a dump?" Avery asked, adding, "No offense."

In comparison to the places Aunt Laurel usually inhabited, the cottage was a disaster. Aunt Laurel ironed bed sheets. Aunt Laurel couldn't relax until her reflection smiled at her in the glass display cases at Barkleby Biscuits.

Who was last at the cabin?

Answers wouldn't come easy. Aunt Laurel ignored Avery. "There's two oil lamps on the wood stove for nighttime, and we have flashlights in the jeep's emergency kit." She smacked her lips. "For now, the blessing of the fourth day will do the trick."

As Aunt Laurel swept open the kitchen curtains, Toast stretched onto his back, basking his pink tummy in the spring sunlight soldiering in through the dirty windows. The grey cat purred and dozed off, green eyes shuttered.

With a garbage tin found in a closet pantry, Aunt Laurel swiftly swept the newspaper and nibbled pencils away. She took the receptacle into the sitting area and collected the magazines. She poured the kernels from the long-forgotten bowl into the trash can too, cleaning with the focus of an emergency physician in heart surgery.

Avery collapsed on the sofa, upholstered with a bluebell patterned fabric. She sunk deep into its cushions. "Woah. This thing could swallow me whole. What is it made of? Quicksand?"

Distracted with tidying, Aunt Laurel sighed. "It's well-loved. Your mother found it at a yard sale when we were teens. We didn't have a car, so we dragged the couch all the way from past Lurk Farms more than two miles. Uphill. On a dirt road. When Wendy set her mind to something. . . ." Aunt Laurel cut herself off. She skittishly changed the subject. "This cabin needs a lot of elbow grease if we want it to sell. It's not exactly inviting, is it?"

"It's messier than my bedroom fort and creepier than a haunted house," Avery said. Butters climbed past her and nested on the arm of the sofa, behind Avery's uncombed, raven hair. Avery could feel whiskers brush against her neck. The black cat purred softly. "Butters apparently doesn't mind. But she's wicked anyway."

"It's old-fashioned, yes," Aunt Laurel admitted. "Still, it was your mom's favorite spot in the world."

"Let me get this straight," Avery said. "You and Mom came *here* for fun?"

"You think I'm strict?" Aunt Laurel laughed, as though letting her guard down for a moment. "You haven't met our mother, Isadora. She was absolutely obsessed with your mom and me blossoming into rule-abiding young women, which meant we had to follow all of her rules all of the time, and there were plenty more than two. She expected nothing less than perfection. This cabin—it was a refuge, really. A place we could get away and be ourselves. A place where we could. . . ." She paused and shook her head. Her tone hardened. "We were young, stupid, and reckless. This island has never been a safe place."

Changing the subject, Aunt Laurel told Avery the bedrooms were upstairs. Avery would take the room with bunk beds, while Aunt Laurel would stay in Great-Grandma

Elsie's main. Then, with a straw broom from an armoire of dried spices, Aunt Laurel busied herself whacking cobwebs from ceiling corners.

Avery sank deeper into the sofa's cushions as though gravity was on double duty. She imagined her mom sitting on the very same sofa in the very same indent. The bluebell sofa fabric warmed against Avery's hands. Strangely, a calming sensation came over her, as though she was a child in her mother's embrace. Her palms tingled. She slipped deeper into a relaxed state.

Then suddenly, a sharp pain stabbed in her neck. Avery shrieked.

Butters had leaped onto Avery's shoulders and dug in her claws. Avery shook the black cat from her back, Butters flying onto the coffee table and sliding across its glass top. The cat landed on the wood floor, raising a plume of dust that took on a twirling shape, forming in mid-air.

Butters hissed. The wisp didn't conform to any normal laws of physics as it spiraled hypnotically, growing in size. The dust billowed into a round cloud and Butters arched her back, black hair standing upright.

"What have you done, Butters?" Avery asked, equally mesmerized and terrified.

With a whoosh, the cloud blew around the corner disappearing up the stairs. Butters kicked over the game board pieces as she scurried in its pursuit.

Aunt Laurel raced into the sitting area, holding the broom like a baseball bat. "What was that?"

Avery lied. The last thing she needed was Aunt Laurel setting down rule three: no chasing after strange dust clouds. She wanted to get to the bottom of matters herself. "Ah, nothing. Butters is going wild after a spider."

"Spider? Where?" Aunt Laurel swung the broom around.

"I think she got it."

Aunt Laurel resumed beating down the cobwebs with renewed vigor. "Be gone arachnids. A new landlord is in town. Consider this your eviction notice."

Avery hastily grabbed her tangerine backpack. "I'm going to unpack." She couldn't lose sight of the strange cloud.

"Oh, Ave?"

"Yeah?"

Aunt Laurel caught her breath.

"Don't touch anything that looks weird."

CHAPTER 8

Beauty Secrets

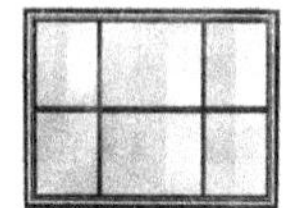

Butters chased the smoky wisp down the upstairs hallway and disappeared into a room. The hallway was dark and reeked of stale air and mildew. Avery followed the cat's slinky tail. She turned the corner, finding herself in the bedroom with the bunk beds, its ceiling sloped with exposed log beams.

The mist expanded into a cloud again at the room's far end, almost as though trying to form a shape. Butters swatted at the apparition, and the vapor evaporated, escaping through a crack in the room's only window.

"What in the world?" Avery ditched her backpack at the door and ran to the glass pane, looking out at the freshwater sea below the cliff's steep edge. The sun glinted like diamonds on the lake's calm surface, with no trace of mist in sight. Avery rubbed her eyes. "Nothing. It was nothing."

Her mind was playing tricks on her. That's all.

Butters hissed, back arched. Avery glared. "Chasing after dust motes now?" A dog would never act so stupid.

Avery took in her new living abode: small and woodsy, kind of like a chipmunk's den in a tree. The cedar logs gave off a faint, forest aroma, or perhaps it was the scent of Cliff Cottage's wild surroundings leaking in from outside through the broken glass.

Butters climbed onto the bed's top bunk and stretched onto her back, over the untucked baby blue sheets. The cat kneaded herself a bed between a scrunched-up teal sleeping bag and a discolored pillow missing its case.

"Sure, take the top bunk, why don't you?" Avery muttered. "Fine. I guess."

The bottom bed, after all, while less exciting, was far more inviting with a plush violet blanket and an assortment of precisely staged purple pillows, as though it belonged in a home decorating catalog. In contrast to the messy top mattress, clearly, two very different individuals had last slept in the bunk beds.

"Purple," Avery said aloud. "Auntie L's favorite color."

No wonder the bottom bunk was so perfect. Did that mean—was the messy top bunk her mom's? Her aunt and mom had come to Cliff Cottage as teenagers, after all. Is that where Avery got her disorganized gene from? Her mom? Is that who had left behind the mess downstairs? Her mom as a teenager? If so, why hadn't she cleaned up? Why hadn't Aunt Laurel? Had something bad happened that caused them to flee before they could tidy? Aunt Laurel was so scared of Beaver Island, so insistent it was a dangerous place.

Avery moved to a chestnut dresser, the bottom drawer partially opened with its contents puking onto the floor.

She riffled through a pile of aquamarine and turquoise tank tops, soft cotton shorts, and mismatched patterned socks.

Huh, I bet I could grow into some of these.

Curious, Avery yanked a reluctant, closed drawer ajar, revealing a stack of neatly folded lilac and lavender blouses. *Purple again, so Auntie L's.* Avery touched the silky tops, then turned to the mess of blue clothes.

Avery picked up a faded cerulean tank top and clasped it under her chin while she ran her hands over its fabric to smooth out its wrinkles. The phrase Lake Michigan: *No Sharks, No Salt, No Worries,* appeared backwards in the vanity's mirror, Avery's reflection obstructed by dust.

These blue clothes must be my mom's old things.

Avery tilted her head. She wondered how much she looked like her mom. They both had dark hair, but is that where the similarities ended? Were their noses the same? Their grey eyes? Their smiles? As much as she'd like to think she could make out resemblances, it was a bit hard to tell from her one photo, her sole memory of her parents. Who did she take after more? She hoped she'd grow up to be as beautiful as her mom, though she thought her father was handsome too. At least from the photo.

The thought reminded Avery of the precious cargo she had packed.

She grabbed her backpack from the doorway, unzipped it with a hurried tug, and dug out a lump of sweaters wrapped around a frame. She tossed the sweaters aside, and, with relief, confirmed there were no scratches or cracks on the photo's glass pane. Her mom wore a sky-blue sundress, Avery strapped to her chest in a baby carrier, while Avery's dad smiled handsomely, his heart-shaped face framed by the collar of his silver shirt. The cuffs of her dad's grey pants were rolled to his ankles. Both of her parents were barefooted, toes dangling over thick roots as they lovingly squished together on a tree swing. Avery hugged the frame to her chest.

"Wish you were here," she whispered.

Avery scanned for the best spot to perch her parents, her eyes landing on the vanity cluttered with vials, perfume bottles, trays of eyeshadows, scrunchies, and tubes of gloss. Avery pushed aside room for the photo. She gave her parents a kiss, pressing her fingers to her lips and then against their image.

"We'd be a happy family. You'd let me get a dog. I'm sure of it."

Butters meowed and clawed at a wood board under the vanity.

"What's your problem now, hyperactive cat? See another ghost?"

Butters had managed to lodge her nails in a floor panel. She meowed again.

"You're stuck?"

Avery crouched down to help loosen Butters's paw from the wood. Freed, the black feline scratched her rescuer's arm. "Ouch! You got some way of showing thanks, furball. What in the world were you doing down there?"

Avery rubbed the red marks on her skin, eyeing the space under the vanity. Curious, she looked closer at the loose floorboard that was resting higher than the others. It took only a wiggle to pop it away, revealing a dusty and dark hidden compartment.

"What do we have here?" she wondered aloud, before sliding her arm into the crevice.

She felt something. Rectangular. Wooden. Pointed edges. She wriggled the object through the pried board. It was a turquoise jewelry box. As she examined it up-close, her hands ignited in fiery prickles until the box was unbearable to hold. Avery dropped the object, which plunked open, photos escaping onto the floor.

Avery gave her hands a shake. "Yowza! Why's that so hot?" She knelt and touched the wooden jewelry box. It was normal. Room temperature. "Weird. . . is this what you were looking for, Butters?"

Avery flipped the box over. On its wooden lid, engraved stars roughly in the shape of Orion seemed to twinkle in the shadowy light.

Like Auntie L's freckles.

Butters brushed her cheek against the box's corner, which Avery took as a yes. Among the mess of photos littered across the floor, one image immediately caught her eye. She smoothed out its creases against her tangerine shorts.

She choked.

Mom.

CHAPTER 9

Foggy Trip Down Memory Lane

Avery's mom, Wendy, glowed like moonshine, even in the faded, water-damaged photo. Captured head titled, Wendy laughed on the front steps of a smiling-faced cabin, her hands on her swollen belly. The mother liked to laugh. She was beautiful. Radiant with the kind of light that shines from a truly brilliant soul. Her stomach was the size of a pumpkin. Was she pregnant with Avery? She must be!

The orphan's lonely heart pounded. Her hands trembled, clammy with a sudden sweat. Her whole life, she viewed the sole photo of her parents as her only porthole into their past. Now, she had a periscope, a lens through which existed a frozen moment of a happier time.

Wait, there's more.

Avery snapped out of her startle to take in the mess of photos scattered around her knees.

Many more.

Her hands tingled again. Magnetically, her fingertips were drawn towards a picture of a man with silver hair fishing from a dock, legs dangling into a lake. Avery squinted. Was it her dad? His back to the camera, she couldn't be sure. Quickly, she reached for the next nearest print.

Her breath stopped.

In this image, the familiar silver-haired man cradled a swaddled infant, his downcast eyes visible enough to reveal their color, green. There was no question. It was Avery's father.

Sparks ignited in Avery's chest. Prickles coursed down her spine. She gathered littered photos into a stack, her fingers itchy with excitement. She began to flip through them urgently, as though the happy snapshots were pages in a book that she couldn't wait to finish so she could read it again and again.

Flip.

Her mom relaxing on the familiar bluebell sofa, her pregnant stomach big as a watermelon under a teal sleeping gown.

Flip.

Her father planting seeds in rich, dark soil.

Flip.

Her parents in front of the smiling-faced cottage, beaming down at a carriage before them. The carriage's orange visor drawn partially over their pale newborn inside.

Avery paused on the photo.

The baby was *her.*

Her family was picture perfect—at least, they had been once upon a time. Her heart ached. She longed to crawl into the still image, just to feel her parents smiling down on her. Her finger popped with a spark of static electricity. She recoiled from the charge.

Then, she noticed something *else* in the photo. She blinked, not believing her eyes. Paws leaned on the carriage. A black snout nuzzled by the baby's creamy cheeks. Puppy dog eyes lovingly gazed at the baby.

It was a dog.

"A beagle?" Avery gasped.

She recognized the breed from his floppy ears, patches of brown and black on his white fur, and a perky, upright tail.

"Did my parents have a dog?" Her voice cracked. "Did *I* have a dog?"

Avery flipped back through the other photos for any evidence. She didn't understand what she was seeing. The beagle was suddenly in all of them! She swore he wasn't before.

The dog looked out over the lake, tail relaxed on the dock, as Avery's father fished.

The beagle's floppy ears drooped protectively over Avery's mom's pregnant stomach as she laid on the bluebell soda in her teal sleeping gown.

Paws dug in the dark, rich soil by her dad's hiking boots, tail sticking up between onion bulbs.

And in the photo of her mom laughing in front of the smiling-faced cabin—this time, Avery spotted a trail of scattered petunia petals and dirt on the walkway to the cottage, then the little white paws, and a black tail with a silver tip, jutting out from an upturned planter pot. It looked as though the pooch had tipped over the flowerpot and curiously dug until his round torso became stuck inside the terrazzo vase.

Avery joined her mother's chuckle. "Our dog was so silly!"

The realization sunk in. "Silly dog. . . . Our silly dog," Avery repeated, the words still sounding so foreign, it was like she was speaking a different language. "What happened to him?" she wondered.

She searched the photo for more clues. The cabin resembled Cliff Cottage, only it was lively and happy, instead of depressed and dreary. The yard was tended, not overgrown. The trees looked similar, the birch and elm familiar.

That's when Avery spotted, in the background of the photo, a figure hidden in the shadows under a wiry elm tree. The stranger's face was disguised by her hooded cloak and black umbrella.

They travel by umbrella.

Suddenly, something in the photo moved. Avery smothered a scream, clasping the photo stack against her chest. She caught her breath, then cautiously, took another look. The figure had stepped out from the shadows of the tree. Avery watched as the umbrella came down to the grass and the stranger pulled down her hood with warty hands revealing a patch of skin waning in the shape of a crescent moon on her cheek and reddish-brown hair that seemed to slither like worms.

"It's the animal patrol officer," Avery gasped.

Suddenly, Avery smelled traces of smoke. The film print charred at its edges, its corners puckering inward as the fire spread into the scene. "No, no, no!" Avery dropped the whole stack of photos, which fluttered out onto the wood floor in a mess.

She stomped the flames with her sneakers, desperate to quell the fire, the soles of her feet hot through the rubber. The flames abated into ash, leaving some photos charred at the edges and the moving photo distorted and puckered.

Avery coughed.

She looked at her hands. Normal. No welts. No burn marks. She was OK. But her head was spinning.

The photo hadn't. . . started to self-destruct? The photo hadn't. . . come to life?

She kneeled to get a closer look at the damage.

The cloaked woman glared from the rubble. The good parts of the photo—her mother and her dog—had burnt away to nothingness. Her mother's face, her mother's laugh, her radiance lost forever. A memory that slipped through Avery's fingers as quickly as dust.

"My mom." Avery's lip quivered. "My dog."

Butters sniffed the soot and meowed, pushing her furry head against Avery's palm. Avery rubbed the cat's head for comfort.

"Whatever's happening here, Butters, something tells me not to trust that animal patrol officer," Avery said.

Butters meowed again.

Avery dusted off her palms and gathered the charred photos back into the jewelry box while setting the ruined picture of the cloaked woman aside. Avery had nearly lost them all as soon as she had found them. It was as though someone didn't want her to learn about her past.

That's when Avery decided. "I'm going to find out what happened to my parents. And my dog." She slammed the jewelry box shut with a thud. "And as for the animal patrol officer, whatever it is that she did to my family, she's not going to get away with it. Not if tell Aunt Laurel."

CHAPTER 10

Cracks in the Rules

"Auntie L, look what happened!" Avery raced downstairs, waving the destroyed film print. "I found a photo of my mom with my dog! And they were in front of a cabin. Maybe Cliff Cottage? It looked different though. *Happier*. But then the *weirdest* thing happened!"

Aunt Laurel abandoned her mop which fell with a bang to the wood floor.

"Let me see that." Aunt Laurel tripped over her bucket of well water. She swiped the warped photo from Avery. Her expression turned concerned. "Who burnt this?" She gave it a sniff and flicked a flake of ash from the film. "Where did you—"

"I had a dog, Auntie L, when I was a baby! A beagle! What happened to him? Where is he now? What was his name? How come you never told me? How come Mom could have a dog but I can't?"

"Please. One question at a time."

"Fine. What happened to my dog and how do I get him back?"

“That’s definitely two questions.”

“Did the animal patrol officer steal him?”

“Who?”

“*Her.*” Avery stepped on her toes to point to the shadowy figure in the photo’s charred remains but couldn’t quite see from her angle.

Aunt Laurel knitted her brow. “It’s a photo of trees and part of cabin? There’s no one in it.”

“Yes, there is.”

Avery hopped up to look. Sure enough, the mysterious woman had disappeared. Vanished without a trace. All the photo showed was the woods in the cabin’s background, branches and trunks stretched and bent from the distortion caused by the flames.

“I swear,” Avery said. “It was the animal patrol officer in the photo, the same woman who was chasing the puppy earlier. Only she was under an umbrella and wearing a hooded cloak.”

Aunt Laurel snapped, “Rule number three, no poking around this cabin.” She tucked the photo into her lavender kitchen apron. “And rule four, no talking to strangers on this island.”

“Are you serious?” Avery groaned. “This might as well be a prison. I promise you, that was a photo of my mom and my beagle. And that officer, she hates dogs. She did something to my dog, and probably had something to do with my parents’ disappearance, and she’s going to do something bad to that poor, innocent, helpless terrier you almost hit. We have to stop her, Laurel.”

“*Aunt* Laurel,” Aunt Laurel rubbed her temples.

"Please settle down, or I'm going to explode. You don't want to be on the local news for having an aunt who burst like a pinata into a million bits, do you?"

"Would it mean I get candy?"

Aunt Laurel shot Avery a look.

"I just want my beagle back," Avery pleaded.

"Your mom didn't have a dog, Avery, okay? We were forbidden. And I don't appreciate you snooping. Now, I'm busy packing and cleaning." Aunt Laurel yanked open a kitchen cupboard full of mugs.

"Forbidden?" Avery asked.

Avery could count at least one million reasons why Aunt Laurel said they couldn't get a dog, but this was the first time she ever heard the word "forbidden". A sour taste came to Avery's mouth.

Thud, thud, thud. Aunt Laurel forcibly unloaded the mugs onto the kitchen counter. "Bring over one of the moving boxes from the front door, will you?"

Avery didn't move an inch. They couldn't just pack up Cliff Cottage and take off without finding out what happened to Avery's family, nor could they leave the helpless terrier behind to fend alone for himself. Avery persisted. "I don't trust that officer, Aunt Laurel. She smelled. Like *snert*. And the picture self-destructed as soon as I noticed her."

Aunt Laurel unintentionally smashed a coffee mug on the counter. "You burnt the photo?" The coffee mug's handle cracked, falling off from the impact.

"No," Avery's hands suddenly itched with a hot tingling sensation. Self-conscious, she clamped them into fists inside her shorts pockets. "It's just. . . it caught fire in my hands. It was the weirdest thing."

Aunt Laurel swallowed air. She urgently reached for Avery's hands. "Let me see your palms."

"What? Why? Wait, no way." Avery took a step back.

"I should have known," Aunt Laurel fretted, pacing. "You're at that age. There's still so much to teach you."

"I listened to enough of your audiobooks about prepubescence that I think I know what you're talking about." Avery shuddered, embarrassed. "And for the record, *eww*."

"It's not that." Aunt Laurel shook her head. "You're starting to manipulate matter. And I haven't taught you any of the rules yet. How can I expect you to become a rule-abiding Lawful Slider if you haven't learned the rules by which you must abide? I meant to keep you safe but. . . now it's too late. Before I know it, you'll be sliding through dimensions, and you don't even know basic safety protocol."

"Wait." Avery scrunched her eyebrows. "A Slider?"

What was Aunt Laurel talking about? Manipulating matter? Sliding through dimensions? Why was she acting so strange? Surely, this was all a distraction meant to get Avery's mind off her beagle and the tiny terrier. Still, Avery's stomach churned uncomfortably, the strange occurrences from the day spinning like laundry in her gut.

The snert smell wafting from the suspicious animal patrol officer.

The ghostly dust spiral forming in Cliff Cottage.

The moving photo spontaneously combusting.

But Sliders were just characters from Great-Grandma Elsie's poem meant to warn the children about the dangers of Beaver Island.

They weren't *real.*

Unless. . . What dangers was the poem meant to caution against? Avery shook the thought.

She decided to call out Aunt Laurel's bluff. "I thought Sliders were just a silly nursery rhyme. You said so yourself that the story's not true."

But then again, Avery's belly cramped with uneasiness.

Aunt Laurel's face went pale, her constellation of freckles shrinking into white dwarves—shrunken remnants of stars. "Avery, there's something important we need to talk about."

Avery stomach spun. Why couldn't normalcy come easily? She had felt it earlier, for a moment, as she looked at the picture-perfect memories from her childhood with her parents and her dog. How had it burnt away so suddenly?

It was okay. Avery took a deep breath. Everything would go back to the picture-perfect normal life once she had a dog.

Because once she had a dog, she would make friends.

She'd finally have her pack.

The tiny terrier deserved a pack too.

Avery would make sure he found it. That the animal patrol officer would never lay her hands on his scruffy fur.

By focusing on that goal, the confusing feelings swirling in Avery's stomach settled.

"No kidding," Avery scoffed. "Important item number one, how can we save the terrier?"

"There are more pressing matters, Avery," Aunt Laurel

said.

"What could possibly be more pressing than rescuing a dog you nearly hit with your jeep, Laurel?"

"*Aunt* Laurel," Aunt Laurel's face flushed with frustration. "*This* is serious, Avery. It's time you learn about Sliders. In fact, it's well overdue."

This again. Avery clenched her burning hands, her chest filling with anger. "You expect me to believe some nursery rhyme is *true*? You treat me like a baby." She stormed to the living area and yanked open the front door. "I just want to save the tiny terrier before he ends up disappearing like my beagle and my parents. And if you won't help me, I'll go looking for him myself."

"Remember rule number one? No leaving my sight."

"Who cares about your rules?"

The door shut violently in Avery's wake.

CHAPTER 11

Meet Sam and Suzy

"I want to turn back. I'm not going any closer."

"Chicken."

Startled by the voices, Avery ducked behind an oak tree near the cabin's log fence overtaken with vines and bramble.

"Seriously, Sam. It's a haunted cabin."

Haunted? They weren't talking about Cliff Cottage. . . were they? Curious, Avery tiptoed towards the voices, scratching her calves on prickly raspberry bushes. She brushed a shrub aside and peered through a crevice between weathered log posts.

The voices belonged to two girls Avery recognized from town earlier, each with a dog of her own. Avery couldn't help but notice that each girl matched her fur companion. The taller girl's hair stuck out from under a muddy baseball cap. Her red locks matched the coat of her regal, large dog, which Avery figured was an Irish Setter. The shorter girl wore her ebony hair in braided pigtails laced with canary bows. Beside her, a tiny, flat-faced mop of black fur scurried. Avery guessed the canine companion was a Pekingese.

"Suzy, grow up. There's no such thing as haunted cabins," said the tall girl with the Irish Setter, as she caught her breath from marching up the hill.

"If there's no such thing as a haunted cabin, then why did you dare me to walk to the haunted cabin? Isn't it just a *cabin* cabin? I mean, really, Sam, it doesn't add up."

Avery accidentally giggled. It was like something sassy she'd say to her aunt. She decided right then that she could be friends with these girls. They looked about her age, and who cared about Aunt Laurel's rule four, no talking to strangers on the island? Avery wasn't a prisoner. Come to think of it, even prisoners, except the very worst ones locked in solitary confinement, could still make friends. Not to mention, she already gathered their names. Sam was the tall one, Suzy the shorter, so they were no longer strangers, technically.

Suzy's Pekingese furball sniffed at the fence like a pig hunting for truffles, as though alert to Avery's scent. The Irish Setter took notice of the black fluffball's raised tail and alert ears, then picked up on the whiffs of the stalker in the air. The canines went wild. *Haaa-Owww! Haa-Ooww! Ah-Oooo! Ah-Ooo*! They howled ferociously at their own pitches, like sirens on an ambulance and firetruck.

"Who's there?" Suzy shook, scared.

No time like the present.

Avery climbed on a stump and popped her head over the fence. "Hi," she waved.

Suzy stumbled half a foot backwards and screamed,

falling onto her backside. Her Pekingese scampered to her side, nudging her snout against Suzy's dainty yellow outfit.

"You okay?" Avery checked, concerned.

Sam keeled over with laughter. Her auburn dog leaped up, placing her paws on Sam's baseball jersey, excited.

"I'm fine." Suzy glared, brushing dirt from her canary skort. "No thanks to my mean friend."

Sam helped Suzy to her feet. "Sorry Suze, but you jumped a mile. It was like you saw something. . . from another dimension."

Before I know it, you'll be sliding through dimensions.

Aunt Laurel's words rang in Avery's ears. Her cheeks drained of color. Her palms began to prickle. She clasped her hands behind her back, self-conscious.

"I'm Sam, by the way," Sam introduced herself to Avery. "I'm from Sudbury, Ontario, in Canada. But I spend summers at my grandma's, here in Michigan. This is Suzy. She's from Detroit. We met on this island when we were little. I'm twelve now and Suzy's ten-and-a-half."

"I know," Avery blushed. "I mean, I overheard your names. By accident. I wasn't spying or anything. And I didn't know where you lived. Or how old you were when you met. I'm not a creepy stalker, I swear. Am I rambling? I think I'm rambling. I'm Avery. I'm eleven-and-a-half." *And I'm certainly not a dimension-travelling Slider or whatever,* she considered adding for extra measure before biting her tongue. Finally.

"Nice to meet you, Avery." Sam's Irish Setter mix pounced at the fence and barked. "Riley. No jumping. Down boy." The dog whined and sat obediently. He panted, his beady eyes fixed on Avery, his floppy, auburn ears like silky, wavy hair, framing his long snout. "Sorry about that. This is my dog, Riley, he's normally very friendly. He's acting so weird."

Auntie L had warned Avery about the dogs of Beaver Island. What if her aunt's story was true? What if Avery was different? Could the local dogs smell that Avery wasn't normal? That she didn't fit in?

Avery awkwardly made excuses not to pet Riley. "I—I love dogs. I'd ask to pet them, but I'm on the wrong side of this rotten fence."

Sam made nothing of it, continuing with introductions. "Suzy's Pekingese is named Pearl. She'd tell you herself, but she's tongue-tied because she's a scaredy-cat."

"I'm not scared," Suzy said in defense. "It's just there's myths about this island. That it's haunted. It's spooky. My brothers read about it online."

"This is what I mean," Sam shrugged. "She's heard too many ghost stories, so this summer, I'm making her live up to her fears. We are going to every supposedly haunted spot on this island, and she'll see once and for all that there's nothing unusual about this place."

A wave of relief washed over Avery. Sam was right. Beaver Island was perfectly normal. And so was Avery. She could fit in with these girls if she just acted ordinary enough and didn't let Aunt Laurel's nursery rhyme about Sliders get in the way. No matter if a mysterious cloaked animal patrol officer with an umbrella creepily came to life in a photo before her very eyes. No matter if that cursed photo somehow spontaneously combusted in her hands.

Avery's palms tingled hotter. She shoved them into the pockets of her tangerine shorts, annoyed.

"Starting with Cliff Cottage."

Avery's stomach lurched.

"Cliff Cottage is haunted?"

The smoky wisp blew through Avery's memory, the one Butters chased from the sofa, up the stairs, then out the bedroom window. Had it been. . . a ghost? A being from another dimension? A Slider? Suddenly, Avery felt a pit open up in her belly.

"It's an abandoned weirdo's cabin," whispered Suzy. "This whole island was once overrun by a colony of weirdos led by a weird man. They called them 'the Weirdies'."

Avery froze. She'd heard that phrase before, 'the Weirdies'. Joseph had said it to Aunt Laurel. Something along the lines of: *"Beaver Island? Isn't that the island where those Weirdies used to live who were said to appear out of thin air and could travel between space and time?"*

Were Sliders and Weirdies one and the same? The same characters featured both in local legends and Great-Grandma Elsie's nursery rhyme?

"Ahem," Sam faux-coughed. "You shouldn't use that word, Suze. The politically correct phrase is 'persons of the congregation of the Fellowship of King Weird'. They were basically just a bunch of eccentric pioneers."

"They ate dogs."

"That's just a legend."

"The men took multiple wives!"

"That's what dudes did in the olden days."

"They cooked dog stew in a cauldron at Stone Circle

and could disappear into thin air and travel by harnessing the power lightning with their umbrellas."

"See what I'm dealing with?" Sam shook her head, exasperated. "Anyhow, Cliff Cottage is one of *many* supposedly-haunted places on our list. There's also Lurk Farms and Stone Circle. Wait, what are you doing here?"

Avery swallowed. If Cliff Cottage was an abandoned Weirdies' cabin, did that mean her Great-Grandma Elsie was a Weirdie? Could that mean what Aunt Laurel had said about Sliders was true? *They travel by umbrella*, the poem said.

What if the everything in the nursery rhyme was real?

Avery brushed away the outlandish thoughts. She certainly didn't want to own up to the fact her family owned the cabin. So, she lied. "Oh, ah, my aunt's a. . . a real estate investor. We're from Chicago. We're selling the cottage." Avery was distracted by a strange smell, like mushy peas, as though snert leaked from her armpits. It wasn't a good sign.

"So, you're here for the summer?" Suzy perked up, smiling.

Self-conscious, Avery crossed her arms tight to muddle the body odor. She continued like everything was absolutely normal. "For a few weeks. Unless my aunt packs the place as quickly as a tornado spinning through Kansas, which is entirely possible."

"I hope you're here for a while," Sam said. "It's so cool to have someone new to hang out with. I'm getting *so* sick of Tomin. He's this rich kid whose summer cottage on the island is a total McMansion. He's super spoiled and only ever wants to play video games. His mom throws the best parties though."

Riley barked in agreement. Pearl, the Pekingese, excitedly yelped, chasing her own tail in circles until she stumbled into a somersault. Suzy stopped the furry tumbleweed's momentum, scooping her Pekingese in her arms.

"Pearl does that anytime 'p-a-r-t-y' is mentioned," Suzy spelled out. "The Fiddlesticks' Fourth of July Freedom Fest is right around the corner, and it's going to be the party," Suzy changed her language for the sake of Pearl, "*Celebration* of the season. Mrs. Fiddlesticks, Tomin's mom, runs the Fiddlesticks Cookies brand. They call her the Cookie Empress—"

"They call her the Sugar Shark."

"They call her cookies *deeeeee*licious. Fiddlesticks Cookies makes chocolate chip *spoodles*, crushed toffee *netzles*, mint chip *oogles*, and *dodo nuts*. All of it. Last year, she had a giant chocolate chip *spoodle* in the backyard that you could climb on and eat. It was awesome."

"It was so awesome," Sam added.

"That sounds fun," smiled Avery. "When is it? Maybe I could go with you?"

"Sure!" Sam replied, enthusiastically. "You have a dog, right?"

Avery frowned. "No, I have a black cat, Butters, and a grey cat, Toast. Butters is wild and Toast is lazy. They're both kind of annoying."

"Oh, that's too bad," Sam said, scratching her leg. "The invite this year says you need a dog to attend. It's some canine cookie launch thingy. But don't feel bad. It doesn't sound fun anyhow."

"Yeah, I'm not even looking forward to it," Suzy cooed, looking down at her yellow rubber boots.

"We can hang out some other time though," Sam suggested, "Hey, have you been to Stone Circle?"

Avery shook her head. "Isn't that the place where pioneers made dog stew? According to Suzy's brothers?"

"First, that's just a rumor. Second, it's way cooler than that," said Sam. "It's Beaver Island's very own Stonehenge. It dates back over one thousand years."

"And it's haunted, deep in the woods, and we should stay far, far away," cautioned Suzy.

"On the contrary, we should go near, near, close," urged Sam.

"Sounds fun," Avery forced a smile. Truthfully, she still stung from her exclusion from what sounded like the best party of the season. She never could quite fit in. So long as she was an orphan. So long as she didn't have a dog like every other normal family in America. She bit the inside of her lip to keep the tears from welling in her eyes and put on a strong face. She asked with a croak, "Um, then, what else is cool to do around here?"

Sam thought. "Well, I like playing catch with Riley in the park, swimming in the lake, and fishing for bass."

Suzy enthusiastically interrupted, eyes lighting up like flashing billboards. "Downtown has the cutest tourist shops. There's a souvenir store with pretty postcards, a candy cart with *the* yummiest taffy, and a clothing boutique with adorable hats. And a lighthouse. Oh, and there was Beaver Dam's Good Ice Cream, but it burnt down last night."

"Now we're stuck with frozen yogurt from the grocery

store." Sam faux gagged. "It was a freak accident apparently."

"It was Weirdies," warned Suzy.

Sam's eyes wandered. "What's with all the 'no dogs allowed' signs on your fence? Did the last owner hate dogs?"

"Ah, must have," Avery stammered, nervously.

"Avery." Aunt Laurel's voice boomed from the parked jeep in the driveway. She waved while taking down a bicycle from the vehicle's rack. Then, she put her hand over her eyes like a visor. "Who are you talking to? Are those dogs?"

"You should go," Avery said urgently to Sam and Suzy. "My aunt, the real estate investor, has allergies. I'll see you soon."

With that, Avery leaped from the stump and ran to the porch leaving Sam and Suzy perplexed.

Leave it to Auntie L to ruin everything.

"You weren't consorting with strangers or dogs, were you?" Aunt Laurel tapped her toes and scowled. She sniffed. "I can tell you were breaking my rules by the way you smell. You're at that age."

Avery's cheeks reddened. "Goodness forbid I have any friends. After all, it'd be terrible if I actually had a social life. The end of the world, really!"

Avery slammed the front porch door.

Aunt Laurel sighed. "Pre-teens."

CHAPTER 12

The Suckage of Not Having a Dog

Avery braced herself for a lecture. She pouted in the rocking chair while Aunt Laurel sat, all cross-legged and judgmental, on the bluebell sofa. The cabin sparkled and shined, fresh with lemon scent. It wasn't a good sign. Aunt Laurel cleaned whenever something was on her mind.

Brow furrowed in thought, as though a lecture was brewing behind the creases of her forehead, Aunt Laurel dunked a tea bag in the mug with the broken handle, since repaired with duct tape. She exhaled, meeting Avery's eyes. "I wanted to apologize, Ave. For exploding earlier. I lost my cool. I'm sorry."

That was unexpected.

"You're sorry?" Avery stuttered, thrown off. She took a moment to register whether Aunt Laurel's apology changed anything. It didn't. Avery was still angry. She turned her gaze to her tangerine sneakers. "Whatever. It doesn't matter. I'll never make friends on this island anyway." She ignored the steeping mug which Aunt Laurel had prepared for her, steaming from a coaster on the streak-free glass coffee table. Didn't Aunt Laurel know chamomile tea was for old people? Avery liked ginger beer and colas.

"We're only here for a short time."

"Doesn't mean we should be hermits."

Aunt Laurel took a moment, staring at her tea. She tried again. "I admit, I'm overprotective. You're nearly a young adult, Avery."

"Then treat me like one."

"Okay."

"Wait. What?" Avery's eyebrows lifted, her surly glare softening into an expression of surprise.

"You're right, Ave. I have to stop babying you. Even if that means you'll make mistakes on occasion."

"Really?" Avery brightened, a sparkle returning to her charcoal grey pupils. Her shoulders relaxed. The chamomile tea suddenly didn't seem so wretched. Avery leaned forward in the rocking chair to accept the warm mug from the coffee table and give it a try.

"Yes." Aunt Laurel nodded. "Consider it a change of strategy."

"What's the catch?" Avery sniffed the tea before committing to a sip. It reminded her of Headmistress Bunhead's cloying hairspray. Still, she slurped up a mouthful of the hot liquid. It tasted like medicine as it went down her throat.

"Cliff Cottage reminds me what it was like to be a kid," Aunt Laurel reminisced, as she took in the cabin. An audible sigh escaped her constricted throat. "Your mom and I were under so much pressure to follow the rules so that we'd blossom into Lawful Sliders. This was our place to escape."

"Come again?" Avery wasn't sure if she had heard Aunt Laurel right. Lawful Sliders? She was still going on about that silly nursery rhyme. Had Aunt Laurel accidentally inhaled cleaning detergent fumes? Consumed a moldy piece of cheese from the ice box? Had she gone mad?

Not that Avery was able to judge her aunt's sanity. The image of the cloaked animal patrol officer—pulling down her umbrella with warty hands, revealing slithering hair and a crescent moon birthmark—flickered in Avery's mind. People in photographs didn't move. Photographs didn't catch on fire for no reason.

Maybe she'd gone mad too?

The rocking chair creaked as Avery swayed back and forth gently. She took another sip of the hot, medicinal-tasting tea, as though it may flush away her uncomfortable thoughts.

Aunt Laurel bit her lip. Her fingertips lingered on the tarnished locket dangling from her silver chain. Resistantly, she resumed her story with a sigh, "Your grandma, Isadora, wasn't exactly pleased when she found out your mom and I were spending time here on Beaver Island, contrary to her rules."

"My Grandma Isadora?" The mention of her grandma again jarred Avery. While other grandparents smothered their grandchildren with birthday cards and Christmas gifts, phone calls and freshly baked cookies, Avery's Grandma Isadora seemingly wanted nothing to do with their family. "As in, the grandmother I got my middle name from? The one who lives aboard and has never cared to meet her granddaughter?" She swallowed more tea. It now reminded her of something a grumpy grandmother might serve with stale biscuits and bitter candies. The taste went sour in her mouth.

"Interdimensional travel isn't easy on joints." Aunt Laurel twirled the locket, twisting the necklace chain as she longingly looked towards the front door. "Our home dimension is light years away."

"What?" Avery choked on her beverage. She accidentally spit out a mouthful of chamomile as she jerked forward in the rocking chair, wiping her face with the sleeve of her tangerine t-shirt. "I thought Grandma Isadora lived in Finland. You're saying she's never visited us because she lives in *another dimension, light years away*?"

It occurred to her that Aunt Laurel was off her rocker, even though Avery was the one in the rocking chair.

"Don't use your t-shirt, Avery. Here, let me help." Aunt Laurel crouched beside her niece, setting the teacup aside on the coaster, dabbing Avery's chin with a lavender cloth. The material felt scratchy. It smelled like dish soap. Aunt Laurel continued, "The truth is, your grandma, Isadora, avoids this place as much as possible. Rightfully so. She worked hard to distance our family from our Weirdie past."

Weirdie past? The strange pioneers who ate dog stew at Stone Circle and lived in haunted cabins. . . like Cliff Cottage? The same group the nursery rhyme called Sliders?

Avery's shoulders tensed. Her nervous system kicked into alert. She felt on edge. Horrible. Thrumming with a shaky energy.

"What are you talking about?" Avery lightly swatted

the lavender cloth away from her face.

Aunt Laurel took a deep breath. "The story I told you, passed down from Great-Grandma Elsie, it's not a nursery rhyme."

Aunt Laurel titled her chin towards the wooden floor and wrung the lavender cloth nervously. Something was bothering her, terribly. Her grey eyes found Avery's again. Sadness lingered deep in her pupils.

"We come from a long line of Sliders—*Lawful* Sliders," she qualified, eyes wide. "We're not the Scorned kind the poem warns about. Well, so long as we follow the rules. There have been exceptions in our bloodline, unfortunately." She timidly gathered the lavender cloth into a ball in her fist. "We're from another dimension. But we're still God's children. It's just, God made us different. Just as doves fly, dolphins breathe underwater, and giraffes stretch tall with their necks, we have some different abilities than humans."

Avery's body froze, though her brain spun dizzily with questions, too overwhelmed to stop and focus on verbalizing them. She felt like she might faint.

Sensing Avery's imbalance, Aunt Laurel draped the lavender cloth over her shoulder and reached for Avery's hands, taking them into her own. She turned her niece's palms up, examining the lines that branched out on Avery's hands. Or was she looking for some proof of arson, evidence that Avery set fire to the mysterious photo? She traced a wrinkle in Avery's skin.

"We have *enhanced* abilities, shall we say," she explained.

Enhanced abilities?

Avery felt a pit form in her gut.

Her entire life, she had never felt normal. She didn't fit in at school, or with other kids—except for her best friend, Benji. But she chalked that up to the fact she didn't have a dog or a regular mom and dad around. Since arriving at Beaver Island, her otherness had geared into overdrive. Within the span of a few hours, she had gone from a dogless orphan to a dogless orphan living in a haunted cabin who burnt up supernatural photos with her hands, possibly because she was some sort of interdimensional Slider being with "enhanced" abilities.

This was horrible news.

If her differences went beyond the fact that she didn't have a dog, how would getting a dog solve anything? If Aunt Laurel was telling the truth, Avery would never be normal. She would never belong, even if she had a fur friend of her own.

Aunt Laurel was lying.

That was the only rational explanation.

Or was it?

CHAPTER 13

Upside Down

I'm a human." Avery snapped her arms to her torso, crossing them at her chest. She slid as far back in the rocking chair as she could go, distancing herself from Aunt Laurel. The chair swayed back and forth from the movement. "A *normal* human."

"Half-human, technically," Aunt Laurel explained. "Your father was human, after all."

"And my mom?" Avery asked, terrified by Aunt Laurel's implication.

"A Slider. Like me," Aunt Laurel said, kneeling before Avery, steadying the rocking chair by its wooden arms. "And it's not a bad thing, once you learn how to harness your abilities. So long as you follow the rules."

Avery felt trapped in an Aunt Laurel cage. A desperation bubbled inside her chest. She burst.

"I didn't burn that photo, Auntie L! Nothing weird is going on. It was static electricity, that's all," Avery reasoned, startled by the sense she was making amidst the chaos of her aunt's revelations. Static electricity seemed like the perfect explanation. She went on, "You know how when you rub a balloon against your head, and it makes your hair stick up straight? Well, the same thing happened with the photo."

"Avery, I know this isn't easy for you. It's an awkward time, blossoming into your Slider self. But soon, you'll be able to create energy with your emotions. You'll learn how to manipulate matter, which will allow you to do all sorts of wonderous things. Shapeshifting. Transforming one thing into another. Sliding through space and time!"

No, none of this is real! Avery shouted in her mind.

Tears collected in her eyes. She shut her eyelids to keep them inside. All she could see was the photo of the cloaked animal patrol officer bursting into flames.

She swallowed and pushed out the only response she could manage, "You're joking right?"

"Not at all," Aunt Laurel said, her expression serious. "And it's my responsibility to teach you the rules you must follow so that you bloom into a Lawful Slider, rather than a Scorned one. Number one, first and foremost," she stood up and raised a finger, pacing as she spoke, her eggplant purple slippers flopping on the wood floor, "we are forbidden from manipulating animate matter. You can repair a teacup or a coffee mug, for example, but you can't use your abilities to transform a skunk into a dog."

"That sucks." Avery hid her discomfort with sarcasm, slouching in the rocking chair.

"I'm serious, Avery," Aunt Laurel stressed. "Break too many rules, and you'll transform into a Scorned Slider. Worm hair, warts, snert smell, and all."

Worm hair, warts, snert smell.

Was Aunt Laurel saying the animal patrol officer was a Scorned Slider?

A terrible worry rattled Avery.

What did the nursery rhyme say about Scorned Sliders?

They come with the rain
to cause dogs much pain

To. . . cause. . . dogs. . . much . . . pain!

"What's the matter, Avery?" Aunt Laurel asked.

"Nothing," Avery shook her head in denial.

Her head spun. So did her stomach. She raised an eyebrow at her aunt. "What kind of tea are you drinking exactly?"

"You think I've gone bonkers, don't you?" Aunt Laurel's face fell, distraught.

"People can't manipulate matter." Avery nervously scratched her neck. Her fingers tingled on contact with her skin, sparking a curious thought. *If* Sliders were real, and *if* they had "enhanced abilities", and *if* Avery was a Slider and therefore also had "enhanced abilities", maybe she could use them to save the terrier? To find out what happened to her beagle and her parents? She set that aside. She was letting her aunt's wackiness get to her. Still, she wanted more information. "Manipulating matter sounds like a super-power."

"Anyone can manipulate matter," Aunt Laurel's face renewed with brightness, charged by her niece's smidgen of interest. "It's simple physics, Avery. People, plants, and animals are constantly transforming one thing into another."

Aunt Laurel went to a windowsill and pushed back a moth-eaten curtain. Afternoon sunshine danced on her freckled cheeks as she looked out to the birch and pine. "Tree leaves take sunshine and turn it into food."

She whipped around and pointed at the cast iron stove in the corner of the cabin's kitchen. "Melt the impurities from ore to make iron. Mix tin and copper together and make bronze."

She jogged towards the counter and grabbed a wooden bowl. "A baker starts with eggs, sugar, milk, and flour, then, *voilà*!" She mimed stirring ingredients together. "With a whisk and some heat, it all transforms into a delicious pancake."

"Oh," Avery's shoulders fell. The way Aunt Laurel was describing matter manipulation, it didn't seem that special at all. No matter how much enthusiasm the teacher put into her lecture. "Then what's the big deal?"

"Sliders' abilities follow that same concept." Aunt Laurel dropped the bowl back onto the counter and excitedly slid into the sitting area on the tips of her eggplant purple slippers. "You see, our universe is intelligent in design. Everything is matter, all matter is intelligent information." She gestured around the space, twirling.

"So?" Avery shrugged.

Aunt Laurel cleared her throat and took a different approach from the perch of the glass coffee table. "God granted all living beings the ability to alter the world around us. Sliders aren't unique that we can affect the universe, it's just that we can do it more intently and purposefully than average folk." She smiled. "You'll learn. At our strongest, we can harness energy to transform our surroundings and even make portals in space and time. It takes a lot out of us and it's a skill that must be used responsibly and according to the rules. Otherwise," Aunt Laurel took a deep breath and smacked her hands to her lap, "*Consequences*. Snert smell, warts, and wormy hair included."

Avery curled her legs up in the rocking chair. She wasn't sure what to make of all of this. Still, the tingle in her palms burnt hotter. She ignored the sensation, stuffing them under her clammy legs.

"So, let me get this straight," Avery said, skeptical, but trying to sort out all she'd learned. Sliders could alter matter and something about making portals? But they weren't allowed to change *live* matter. She parroted her understanding, "I can bake pancakes and fix teacups, but I can't turn a wild animal into the dog of my dreams because if I do, I'll sprout worms from my scalp, grow warts, and exert the smell of pea soup from my armpits?"

Or worse, she might accidentally set fire to something with her palms.

Aunt Laurel's expression turned concerned. Stern, even. She clasped her locket.

"It's a side effect of not following the rules. It will rot you from the inside out."

"Ah, ok. Whatever you say."

"You're not taking this seriously." Aunt Laurel twirled the locket chain. "It's alright. You'll come around. What's important is that I raise you to become a Lawful Slider who follows the rules. Maybe, admittedly, that would be easier if there were *less* rules to follow at home so we can focus on what matters. No pun intended." She stood up and snapped her hands to her hips.

Less rules? First, Sliders. Now, *less* rules. Was Avery hearing things right?

"What does that mean?" she asked, equal parts wary and startled.

Aunt Laurel looked to the front door, then back to Avery. Her chest inflated and then deflated with a big breath. "Consider yourself off-leash. Like I said, I need to start treating you like the young Slider you're blossoming into. And that means less babying."

"Really?"

Avery's heart skipped a beat. Was Aunt Laurel seriously granting her freedom? Maybe things were looking up? If Avery could get her aunt off her back, maybe she'd have a good summer after all. She could rescue the terrier and maybe even make some friends.

"Yes," Aunt Laurel said with some hesitation. She walked to a bookcase where she dusted off an old recipe book. "You can start by biking into town to fetch groceries. How about I bake us Pavlova, then we play Scrabble?"

"If this is about having a good summer, those are things you like doing, not me."

"What would turn your frown upside down then?" Aunt Laurel flipped through the recipe book for ideas. "I dare you to dream up a more fun night than word games and light, fluffy meringue decorated with fresh fruit."

"A night with a dog."

"You're relentless." Aunt Laurel went to her fringed purse and dug out a twenty-dollar bill. She handed the money to Avery. "We'll start Slider lessons first thing tomorrow. For now, go enjoy the island. Come back with butter and eggs, the fresher, the better. And, ah, baking soda if they have any. It's about time I make you a homemade deodorant." Aunt Laurel pinched her nose.

"Auntie L!" Avery blushed bright red.

"You'll start noticing changes to your body as you get closer to coming into your Slider abilities."

Avery felt mortified. Her palms prickled. She shoved them into her pockets. "Can we not talk about this?"

"All right. Later," Aunt Laurel relented. She returned to the recipe book and stopped in the middle, flagging a page. "Ave, if you like, grab lemons. I'll bake you a lemon meringue."

Avery licked her lips. "Now, we're talking."

Toast meowed from his resting place on a kitchen chair, hungry and sleepy as usual.

"That was your dad's favorite too, you know. Get a move on before the storm blows in. Your bike's on the porch."

Finally, a 'Get Out of This Awkward Conversation' card. Avery was eager to leave the cabin and go for a bike ride. It would give her some time to organize her thoughts. Still, a chill fluttered down her spine with the thought of the animal patrol officer. Determined to play it cool with Aunt Laurel and not raise any bells or alarms for concern, Avery brushed off her fear with a joke.

"You're not worried a Scorned Slider may abduct me? Or worse, that a poodle may wag its tail in my direction?"

"You can take care of yourself. I need to have faith in that."

Avery smiled. Maybe Aunt Laurel was serious about this newfound trust thing. Even if it was brought on by moldy cheese or cleaning detergent fumes.

Avery turned the doorknob.

"Oh, and Avery," Aunt Laurel called. "Make sure to wear a helmet."

CHAPTER 14

Ghizwhisch—You Can Call Me Mrs. Fiddlesticks—Fiddlesticks

Avery tied an orange bandana around her forehead to keep loose hair from her eyes, snapped on her helmet covered in dog stickers, and mounted her bicycle. She glided down a winding dirt road, so steep butterflies flitted in her stomach. The sensation reminded her of plunging over a waterfall on a log ride. Fitting, as with all the strangeness of the day Avery felt as though the Earth had opened beneath her tangerine sneakers. She was tumbling like Alice down the rabbit hole. Her heart thudded.

Avery didn't believe Aunt Laurel's story, did she? Her practical mind said no, but the *weirdness* of the day so far pointed to the plain fact that Avery wasn't like other kids, that she didn't belong. Could she really be a Slider? A Weirdie?

Cedar and birch trees blurred into green, white, and brown swirls as Avery whizzed by the thick woods before rolling past a gilded gate, the name SUGAR SHACK emblazoned on a plaque affixed to a brick pillar. The driveway beyond the gate was gold. Further in, a fountain spewed pink, bubbly liquid. It was dwarfed by a colossal mansion of quartz brick and white columns set at the end of the gold drive. Avery suspected this was the venue for the Party of the Year, the Cookie Empress's humble summer McMansion.

A cold breeze raised goosebumps on Avery's skin. She continued to peddle, despite the wind's objection. She passed a barn with an untended corn field and an abandoned Colonial. Maybe, it was the haunted Lurk Farms Sam had spoken of earlier. Maybe it was haunted by Scorned Sliders? A broken rocking chair swayed eerily on the homestead's decaying porch, sending a chill down Avery's spine. She shook her thoughts away. She cycled faster. The weather was changing, the tree leaves rustling, the sky darkening.

She turned down a road lined with symmetrical cottages with white picket fences and pastel lawn chairs. White sheets billowed ghostlike on a clothesline. A medium-sized, shaggy black-and-white dog growled as Avery biked past a lawn of pink flamingos and creepy gnomes. The canine lunged forward, testing the limits of its leash, baring its teeth. Could these dogs sense something different about Avery? The thought troubled her.

Suddenly, a bubblegum pink Cadillac sped past Avery with such force her bike vibrated. "Woah," Avery sounded, tightening her grip on her handlebars, and stopping to regain her balance. The driver slammed on the brakes and reversed as fast as she had accelerated, tires kicking up a plume of sand and dust. The Cadillac halted beside Avery.

The tinted windows rolled down to reveal a middle-aged blonde woman with a pink-lipstick-enhanced smile and hungry eyes. Her pink tank top read, FUR MOTHER, SUGAR LOVER, the chandelier diamond earrings stole the faintest glints of sunshine slicing through the sky crowded with angry storm clouds.

"Excuse me, little ragamuffin, where's your raincoat?" The lady's eyes scanned Avery from muddy sneakers to stickered helmet.

A white Maltese dog, small and fluffy as a teddy bear, yapped as though chastising Avery, from a luxurious silk pillow propped on the leather passenger seat. *Another unfriendly pooch.* Though it was hard to take the canine seriously when the pup was dressed in a tutu and decorated with pink bows in her hair, her collar covered in diamonds.

"You'll get soaked," the woman added, snidely.

"It's not raining yet." Avery shrugged.

The pampered ballerina growled.

"It's about to pour." The woman narrowed her eyes and leaned towards Avery. "Are you a runaway? Where are your parents?"

"Who knows? They disappeared," Avery answered, dead-pan.

The woman's eyes widened, but not out of concern. No, it was more like a predator locking on its prey. Before she could swoop off with the orphan in her talons, Avery continued, "I live with my aunt. She's selling Cliff Cottage."

"You're the Foster girl's ward, aren't you? Laurel Foster is your aunt, isn't that right? The owner of Barkleby Biscuits in Chicago?" she asked, excitement coloring her voice.

Avery nodded, surprised. "Yeah, how'd you know?"

Set on her own agenda, she ignored Avery's question. "Forgive my manners, I'm Ghizwhisch Fiddlesticks. You can call me Mrs. Fiddlesticks."

The Sugar Shark, thought Avery, remembering her conversation with Sam and Suzy. *The Cookie Empress.* This was the woman who owned Sugar Shack, the humble summer McMansion. The woman behind the dog-required party of the year.

Mrs. Fiddlesticks extended her hand delicately out the window for Avery to shake, her gemstone rings glittering like shiny lures. Avery took the bait. Mrs. Fiddlesticks's grip was surprisingly firm, draining the strength from Avery's palm. "This is my beloved baby, Princess." Mrs. Fiddlesticks nodded towards the pampered pooch on its silk pillow.

Princess snarled.

"I'm Avery." Avery winced, extracting her hand from the talon grip.

"Well, Avery, you'll have to stop by Sugar Shack one of these days for a play date with my son, Tomin. He's twelve." She gestured to the back seat. Avery craned her neck to see a lanky boy, his knees bent at sharp angles. Princess's passenger seat was pushed as far back as it could go, leaving too little space for Tomin's long legs. The boy punched senselessly at the air, a giant helmet over his eyes, ears, and scalp. "Tomin." Mrs. Fiddlesticks swatted her son's head.

He petulantly took off the virtual reality headset, revealing a staticky mess of haystack-colored hair and blue eyes. "Ow, Mom. What the? I was playing Dinosaur Hunters X. You made me lose."

"No, dear, you get your losing streak from your dad's side of the family," she said in a sweet-song voice. "Now, say 'hi' to your new friend, Avery."

"Yuck, no, I hate girls," he spat the words in disgust.

Mrs. Fiddlesticks shook her head. "Now Avery, let me ask you, what type of dog do you have?"

Avery bit the inside of her lip. "I don't have a dog."

"Well, that sure is odd," Mrs. Fiddlesticks replied. "You'd think Laurel Foster, proprietor of the most-famously delicious dog treats in the Midwest would have a dog. That is an interesting piece of information. Too bad. I would have invited you both to a little shindig I'm having on Saturday to announce some big news. It'll be a blast. I hired a circus and a fair's worth of cotton candy machines, but you need a dog for a spot on the guest list. That way, not only do I generate publicity for my new canine cookie brand, but I can write the costs of the entire party off on my taxes. Brilliant, right?"

"Ah, sure." Avery supposed that was true, never having had to worry about taxes.

"Well, it's really too bad you don't have a dog, Avery. Really, it truly is. I like playing with my prey before I go in for the kill."

"Ah. . . what?" Avery scrunched her nose in confusion.

"Nothing, Avery. Just one of my little sayings." Mrs. Fiddlesticks took her foot off the brake. "Watch out for the weather. When it rains on Beaver Island, it storms."

With that, Mrs. Fiddlesticks drove away, tires spitting gravel from the dirt road, and as she did, the sky leaked. Avery stood next to her bike, wishing more than ever that she had a dog, but realizing Beaver Island was a very strange place.

A Weird place.

The kind of place where a silly nursery rhyme might reveal itself true.

CHAPTER 15

The Nightmare of Her Dreams

As Avery cycled closer to town, the weather worsened. Wind howled from the dark lungs of the pitch-black sky. She pedaled onto a beach boardwalk and squeezed her brake. For a moment, she watched in awe as the storm rolled in across mighty Lake Michigan's horizon. Waves crashed over a break-wall. *Roar*. The tossing waters smacked against the concrete barrier and then fled, rushing back to the freshwater sea. Sharp rain pellets stung Avery's cheeks. She blinked. Down the break-wall, a lighthouse burst with fuchsia rays—*on, off, on, off, on, off*. The illumination dispersed by the fog created a surreal, other-worldly glow.

Avery looked out to the horizon, thinking for a moment about her parents and how they disappeared in a float plane while flying across Lake Michigan—apparently. Was there more to the story? Goose bumps prickled on her arms. She rubbed them to try to warm up. What *really* happened to her parents? To her beagle? Would the terrier meet the same fate?

Zap!

Lightning struck a birch tree hanging over the pier's pathway. Sparks flew. The bolt seared a deep wound in the tree branch. Avery threw herself out of the way, just as the chopped limb collapsed onto her bicycle. "That was close," she gulped. Thunder crackled.

A baby bird cried in the nearby bushes. Or was it something larger, a mouse, or even a bunny? Either way, the calls for help stirred Avery. She riffled through the brambles, prickles stinging her bare shins and arms until she found the source of the whimpers: a familiar, scruffy puppy with tan and black fur, a silver tuft of hair on his crown and darker fur around his button eyes.

Avery knew exactly who it was, yet she couldn't believe her eyes. It was the tiny terrier! The one the animal patrol officer was after. The little guy who Aunt Laurel almost hit. He laid curled in a fetal position, licking his hind leg. Avery rubbed her eyes. It couldn't be. But there he was, there was no denying it. Avery had found him. It was the same dog that apparently had rabies.

Avery let that thought sink in for a moment. This was a stray dog, possibly with rabies, the virus that turned cute little fur animals into deadly zombie beasts.

Avery cast aside her concern. He didn't seem vicious, he was hurt. The fur on the terrier's hind leg was matted with a pinkish substance, brighter and lighter than blood, but his skin looked shredded beneath as though he'd been clawed or sliced. He needed her.

"You're hurt?"

The little guy howled. His round, doll-like eyes

desperately pleading for help.

"It's okay. I'll take care of you." She threw off her helmet and untied the orange bandana from her hair. "This won't hurt," she assured the terrier. "Well, any more than it already does." She leaned down and noticed a piece of fruit in the glob in his fur. Was it strawberry sauce on his leg? The kind you would pour on an ice cream sundae? The terrier whimpered and Avery quickly wrapped the bandana tightly against his wounds. The pooch gently licked her fingers with gratitude. So far, this was the nicest dog Avery had met on Beaver Island.

"I'm going to get you help."

Avery carefully cradled the runt in her arms, noticing a gold collar with a heart-shaped tag, slick with rain. So, he wasn't a stray. And he didn't seem rabid. Then, why was that animal patrol officer after him?

Avery read the tag's engraving: MY TEDDY, it said on one side. On the flip side, PROPERTY OF HARMONY CORPS.

"Teddy? Is that your name?" Avery asked.

The puppy yelped in a way that sounded like a yes.

"Harmony's your owner then?" Avery deduced.

Zap! Bang! Lightning struck again, followed by a roaring thunder.

Zap! Bang! The sky erupted. Teddy stiffened, his expression etched with terror, the silver tuft of hair puffed upright. He leaped from Avery's arms and staggered towards the lighthouse with jerky lurches as fast as he could manage.

"Wait. It's not safe." Avery chased after the terrier, her

sneakers slipping on the wet concrete.

Roar!

A colossal wave slammed against the break-wall, nearly knocking Avery off the stony pier. The water subsided into the lake just as quickly. Avery, soaking from hair to sneakers, sprinted after the dog.

"Teddy, where are you?" She pushed wet hair from her brow. She couldn't see the puppy anywhere. Did the wave sweep him into the water?

The wooden door of the lighthouse flew open, smacking against the stones of the cylinder silo. The silhouette of a small terrier flickered in the doorframe.

"Teddy!" Avery shouted.

The dog hobbled inside.

Zap! Bang! A bolt of lightning ignited directly against the lighthouse's cupola. The horizon erupted in blinding light. The lighthouse's massive LED lamp exploded, shattered glass raining down by Avery's sneakers. She shielded her eyes. Shards glistened on the concrete.

Just as suddenly as the light show started, pure darkness took over. A shrill cackle of laughter rang in Avery's ears.

She wasn't alone.

Watch out for Scorned Sliders,
dangerous outsiders.
They come with the rain
to cause dogs much pain.

Avery wiped her eyes. A figure in a billowing onyx

cloak, an umbrella propped above her head, had materialized in the lighthouse doorway.

They travel by umbrella
and this is what they tell ya',
'I can grant what you desire,'
Beware, for they are liars.

With her back to Avery, hands puckered with warts, the figure lowered the parasol, revealing a scalp covered with worms. Slithering worms. Like the ones Avery would find in the park after a rain shower.

Scalp covered in worms,
Hiss, wiggle, twist, squirm.
Warts pucker their skin
from their toes to their chin.

A sulfuric smell suffocated Avery. She gagged. It was the same sour smell that came with the animal patrol officer earlier in the parking lot. The familiar rhyme pounded in Avery's head.

Though Scorned Sliders may disguise
you won't be surprised
with nostrils kept alert
for smells as putrid as snert.

There was no denying it this time.

The figure rotated her neck in Avery's direction. Her

head of worms squirmed as they preened for skin flakes.

Avery froze, horrified.

Under the creature's right eye was a patch of bumpy skin in the shape of an upside-down crescent moon.

The animal patrol officer.

Only, she was in her true form as a Scorned Slider!

The nursery rhyme was true.

Scorned Sliders were real.

Sliders were real.

"I'm a Slider." The words fell out of Avery's mouth before she could admit to their meaning.

Avery's charcoal grey eyes fastened like magnets with the Scorned Slider's coal-dark stare.

"Didn't I tell you to stay out of this, little girly?" She smirked and opened the umbrella towards Avery, its ferrule tip pointed at the girl's heart. The umbrella canopy was patterned with a black-and-white spiral which, as it twirled, led deeper and deeper, into an infinite abyss.

A sense of calm enveloped Avery. A voice cooed in her head. *You didn't see me here. You're imagining things. Tired. Go home. You don't want to be weird. Go home. Be a normal girl. Go home.*

Lost in the umbrella's swirling pattern, Avery nodded. The voice was right. It was all Avery wanted—to fit in. She just wanted a dog like everyone else, a normal family like everyone else, and a bunch of friends at school so she wasn't forced to trap a skunk just so she could have someone to talk to. The last thing she wanted was for people to think she was weird.

Avery looked at her tangerine sneakers, soaked wet.

She would go back to Cliff Cottage.

She turned on her heel and began walking away down the break-wall through the sloshing rain.

Why am I out by the lighthouse in a rainstorm, again? Avery wondered. *I must be confused. I'm going to end up as weird as a Weirdie if I'm not careful.*

Then, a dog's howl snapped her out of her hypnotism.

Teddy!

She remembered.

That's why I'm here. To save my new fur friend!

In the lighthouse doorway, the Scorned Slider brought the umbrella over her head and when she closed it, her appearance had changed. The black cape and withering worms were gone. She wore a baseball cap, aviator sunglasses, a collared uniform, and a holster of fringed darts and sprays. In fact, her umbrella had been replaced by a catch pole.

The Scorned Slider had transformed into her disguise as the animal patrol officer.

Aunt Laurel's nursery rhyme was true.

Told as a real warning of the dangers of the Scorned Sliders of Beaver Island. And there before Avery's eyes was one of them, with a sole purpose to harm dogs, to cause innocent pooches "much pain".

And this Scorned Slider was after Teddy.

Avery clencher her fists with determination.

She'd have to get through Avery first.

CHAPTER 16

Thunderstruck

Avery dashed into the lighthouse. Above her, the Scorned Slider's boots clanked against the metal steps of the spiral staircase. Emergency lights gave off a sinister, red glow. For a moment, Avery hesitated. Looking up the concrete silo, the countless steps to the eerie, red-lit EXIT sign resembled the markings atop a conch shell, wide circles coiling tighter and tighter until they were reduced into a single point far in the distance. The crash of a metal door echoed down to Avery's ears. The Scorned Slider had chased Teddy out of the lighthouse and onto its balcony. A dead end. High, far from the ground.

Avery had to help.

She climbed the stairs, calves cramping as she doubled her speed. Soaked, she couldn't distinguish sweat from rain. Finally, she made it to the heavy door at the top of the staircase. Through the door's reinforced windowpane, Avery could see the catwalk balcony circling the lighthouse's busted lamp. A shadowy figure loomed over a shaking dog.

Never engage with a Scorned Slider. If you see one, run as fast as you can in the opposite direction.

Great-Grandma Elsie's warning, as told to her by Aunt Laurel, popped into Avery's mind. Avery sensed there would be no turning back if she opened the door. But if she turned around now, what would happen to Teddy?

Avery was the tiny, innocent terrier's only hope.

As she twisted the rusted knob, the wind commandeered the door, and it smashed violently against the lighthouse's silo. Rain splattered on the wood deck circling the shattered lantern pane and broken lamp, the storm at the peak of its temper tantrum. The air reeked like boiling pea soup.

Teddy trembled, backing away from the disguised Scorned Slider, until his tail brushed against the rope guardrail, a mere symbol of a barrier between the balcony and the seventy-foot fall to the concrete pier. There was nowhere for him to go, no more space to reverse. He was cornered. He growled, baring his teeth.

"You can't escape. Not this time," the Scorned Slider cackled, as she advanced towards the little dog. "I got you now." She swung her catch pole.

Teddy barked. The catch pole slipped around his neck and the officer tightened its grip. The tiny terrier struggled.

Avery called out, "Leave him alone."

The Scorned Slider snarled, face twisting with annoyance and frustration, "I thought you wanted to be a normal girl." *A normal girl. . . a normal girl. . . a normal. . . .* The phrase rattled in Avery's mind.

Desire to fit in flowed over her in a rising tide. Her whole being ached with the desire to leave the lighthouse, go back to Cliff Cottage, and pretend everything was okay.

But there was something she wanted more. Something that kept her from falling under the Scorned Slider's hypnotism again. And that was the dog.

"I care about helping Teddy more," Avery answered, bravely.

The Scorned Slider, distracted, didn't notice Teddy had loosened himself from the catchpole's grip until the terrier sunk his teeth into her ankle. She howled and hopped on one foot, her disguise flickering on and off from animal patrol to Scorned Slider, from uniform to cloak. The catchpole clanked on the wood platform, transforming back into an umbrella.

"Run, Teddy!" Avery hollered.

Avery and Teddy sprinted down the stairs almost as though they were in flight. Once outside the lighthouse, Avery caught up with the terrier. He was wobbling like a drunken sailor. He took four staggering steps towards Avery and fainted.

"Teddy!"

Footsteps echoed from inside the lighthouse. Avery scooped Teddy into her arms. The orange bandana wrapped around his wounds was no soaked with rain and what looked like blood. The clang of footsteps grew louder. The Scorned Slider was on her way.

"I'll get you, girly! And your little dog too!"

Avery raced down the break-wall to the beach boardwalk. She kicked the birch branch from her bike, lifted its frame upright, and carefully secured Teddy in her handlebar basket.

"Hang in there," she whispered to Teddy, whose tiny body was ragdoll limp.

Avery threw all her might into pedaling, faster than she thought possible. She refused to look back, even as the putrid smell of pea soup lingered in her nostrils and she felt a cloak flapping close to her neck.

Teddy's eyelids drooped. "Stay awake, Teddy. Please. Stay alive."

Tears formed in Avery's eyes. A headlight appeared in the fog. As the vehicle honked, Avery made out its make and color through the heavy mist.

It was an eggplant purple jeep and in the driver's seat, illuminated by the glow of the radio, was Auntie L.

CHAPTER 17

Can I Keep Him?

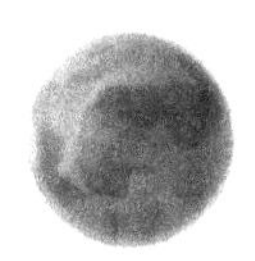

The waxing moon poured its bright light into the bunk bedroom at Cliff Cottage. Avery pushed the silver tuft of hair from Teddy's button eyes, the terrier curled up on the end of the bottom bunk. With his floppy tan and black triangle ears and fluffy face, he resembled a stuffed animal. Yet, his breath warmed Avery's fingers as his torso ballooned and deflated ever-so-slightly while he snored.

Aunt Laurel's tincture had worked wonders. When Avery brought Teddy inside, her aunt had tended to his injuries with the concentration she normally reserved for cleaning or baking Barkleby Biscuits. She washed the strawberry sauce glob from his fur, sanitized his cuts, then treated his wounds with a mixture of yarrow and aloe. Almost instantly, Teddy's skin seemed to mend. And now, he nestled by Avery. It was a miracle.

Or was it something more?

Had Aunt Laurel used enhanced Slider abilities to heal the terrier? Manipulated matter? It was against Slider rules to manipulate animate matter, but had Aunt Laurel done something to boost the healing power of her plant concoction?

With the tiny terrier curled by her side, Avery wondered, who was Harmony, his owner? Was she looking for him, or was Teddy an orphan like Avery? In a strange way, Avery's dreams were coming true. Next to her, she had a dog just like she always wanted.

Yet, in the same moment, she was living in a strange nightmare.

Sliders are real, the thought burned in her mind.

Scorned Sliders are real. And why was a Scorned Slider after Teddy?

Avery wasn't the only one with questions.

"So, Avery Isadora," Aunt Laurel crossed her arms, as she leaned against the doorframe, eyeing Avery and the stowaway. From Aunt Laurel's tone of voice, Avery figured Super Healing Aunt Laurel was gone, replaced with a suspicious version of her aunt. "You want to tell me how you ended up with a dog? On your first foray of freedom?"

"He's Teddy," Avery whispered, not wanting to wake the terrier from his slumber, but also nervous that someone else might hear. Could the Scorned Slider be lurking in the night sky? Was she still burrowed somewhere in Avery's brain like a parasitic worm? "He's the terrier the animal patrol officer's looking for," Avery explained.

"The rabid canine?"

"He doesn't have rabies. The officer was lying. She's evil. Bad. She's—" Teddy fluttered his eyes open. Avery smoothed his fur, and the puppy yawned, then fell back into slumber. Avery lowered her voice again, "Look at him. He's the sweetest thing you've ever seen."

"And how did you find yourself with Teddy in your bike basket, exactly?" Aunt Laurel asked.

Avery's stomach twisted. Giving away the tiniest fraction of the truth would make Aunt Laurel freak out. Guaranteed. Forget keeping Teddy, they'd be on the first ferry back to Chicago. *If you see a Scorned Slider, run!* Of course, Avery had done the complete opposite. She could hear her aunt's inevitable lecture, *"Consequences."* And those consequences would definitely include a Dreadful, Dogless Summer. Grounded for months, if not years. And that of course. . . that left no one to protect Teddy from the Scorned Slider.

Or figure out what happened to her beagle.

Her parents.

So, to save Teddy and pursue the truth, Avery kind of, sort of, decided not to say *exactly*, or *entirely*, what happened.

"I found him by a bramble bush," she said. "He was alone and hurt and crying for help. What else could I do, Auntie L? I had to help. I was all he had."

"That's the full story?"

"Ah, basically."

"You're telling me absolutely everything?"

A bead of sweat formed on Avery's brow. "Yes."

Aunt Laurel scrunched her nose. "Doesn't smell like it. I can tell when you're lying these days, Avery Isadora. You must be getting close to coming into your Slider abilities. If there was ever a time for obedience and truth-telling, it's now."

"I've told you what happened. *Exactly* what happened."

Avery pressed her armpits to the side of her torso, tight, as though trying to lock in any snert stench. She hated lying to Aunt Laurel, but how else could she keep Teddy safe from the Scorned Slider? Keeping Teddy for the night would be enough of a stretch for Aunt Laurel. It'd be a different story if she knew she was harboring a Scorned Slider's target.

With a burp-like snore, Teddy woke himself up, shaking his silver tuft. Avery took his scruffy head and floppy ears into her hands, nuzzling her forehead next to his.

"Isn't that right, Teddy? And Auntie L's going to let me keep you forever and ever and we'll finally be a happy family." He licked her nose with his bumpy tongue. It tickled, and Avery giggled, caught up in her joy, her heart swollen so large she could burst.

"And now, we can go to the party of the year," Avery smiled. "It's on the Fourth of July, and everyone cool's going, but you need a dog to get in. Now we have one."

Aunt Laurel's face tensed. "That doesn't sound like the kind of party we should go to."

"Why not?" Avery asked in knee jerk reaction.

"There's something else I need to tell you, Avery." Aunt Laurel's gaze sheepishly went down to her eggplant purple slippers. "The real reason we can't have a dog."

Forbidden from having a dog, the phrase Aunt Laurel used earlier rang in Avery's mind.

"This should be entertaining." Avery crossed her arms, readying herself for another wave of craziness.

Aunt Laurel covered Teddy's tan and black triangle ears with her palms. She whispered to Avery, "Sliders and dogs are sworn enemies. They've been at war for centuries."

Avery laughed. "That's the worst excuse you've ever given for why we can't have a dog."

Obviously, Scorned Sliders didn't like dogs, for whatever illogical reason, but not *all* Sliders hated dogs. Avery was proof of that!

"It's not an excuse. Sliders *can't* love dogs. It's impossible. That's an ability God reserved for human beings."

"But I *love* dogs!"

As Aunt Laurel bit her lip in thought, Teddy attacked her hands with kisses. Aunt Laurel pulled them away, wiping away the dog's salvia on her jeans and crossing her arms. "Could be the human in you. From your father's side of the family. Affection towards canines is just not in our Slider DNA."

Avery scrunched her face. "You do remember you own a canine cookie shop, right, Auntie L? You spend most of your time baking for the enemy?"

"I'm completely aware," Aunt Laurel answered. "It's a way to lure the neighborhood dogs to me, so I can keep my eyes on them."

Teddy ruffed. It gave Avery an idea. She decided to play along. She could use Aunt Laurel's nonsense to get what she wanted.

"Then, this party is the perfect opportunity to spy on the dogs of Beaver Island! It's for the launch of a dog biscuit line. *All* the island's dogs will be there."

"Dog biscuits? It's not a party at Ghizwhisch Fiddlesticks's summer mansion, is it?"

Avery recalled the strange, diamond-clad woman driving the pink Cadillac and how she had known of Aunt Laurel and her canine cookie shop. "You know each other?"

"She tried to buy Barkleby Biscuits a few years back."

"And you said no?"

"Of course, I said no. Barkleby Biscuits is my whole life, besides you, that is." Aunt Laurel tempered her comment. "I heard Ghizwhisch was trying to break into the canine cookie market but not having much success. Geez, they make everything: Chocolate chip *spoodles*, crushed toffee *netzles*, mint chip *oogles*, *dodo nuts*. Name a famous cookie, she created it. Rumor is there's a lazy river in her backyard made of chocolate milk."

Avery's grey eyes glinted. The problem of convincing Aunt Laurel to let her attend the party seemed a lot more solvable than the issue of being a Weirdie Slider person. "So, I'm basically missing an event at Willy Wonka's Chocolate Factory?"

"What part of, 'dogs are our sworn enemies' don't you understand?"

Avery's face fell. A discomfort itched up her spine. Teddy's ears flicked back, alert.

THUDD.

The noise came from the beauty vanity. Teddy barked at a shadow. Avery flinched.

"Who's there?" Aunt Laurel asked, clutching her tarnished locket.

Avery's eyes turned to the silhouette of a cat arched on the vanity.

The noise had been Butters.

Horrified, Avery noticed the photo of her parents had toppled onto the wooden floor.

"Butters! No!" Nearly tripping on the ends of her orange and cream flannel pjs, Avery ran to the fallen frame. She crouched to the floor and frowned at the cracks in its glass pane. "It's broken. Way to go, clumsy cat. Thanks."

Butters lurked away, black tail up, as Avery traced her finger over the cracks, tears burning the backs of her eyes.

Even in the dim light of the moon, her mother shone radiantly, as though bursting with loving energy. Avery longed to slip through time and join her mom and dad, happily swinging from the tree swing. She imagined curling up with her mom, Dad, and Teddy and their beagle in front of a fireplace. She thought of them all at the beach, tossing branches for their dogs to fetch in the lake. They'd be a happy family, a truly, happy family.

Avery wondered about her mom sliding between dimensions. Could people disappear in those places too? Had she really vanished in a float plane, or was there more to the story?

Before Avery realized it, Teddy was nibbling on the photo frame. "Hey," she gasped, "Teddy thinks it's a stick." She tugged it away from his teeth. He was certainly as good as new—playful and energetic.

Aunt Laurel rubbed her hand on Avery's back, as she took the frame from her niece, returning it to its spot on the vanity. "Come on, kiddos. Back to bed. We'll buy some glue to fix this frame and a new glass plane in town tomorrow." As Aunt Laurel squeezed Avery's shoulders, directing her to the bunk beds, the locket spilled from her blouse. Its cold silver brushed Avery's ear. "Right after we visit animal patrol."

"No!" Avery shouted, the air knocked out from her. Teddy yelped, pouncing on Avery's calves. Animal patrol? The Scorned Slider was pretending she was animal patrol. What if going to the pound would lead her straight to Cliff Cottage, directly to Teddy? "You can't."

Then, noticing the gold collar under Teddy's scruffy fur, she had an idea. "I mean, you certainly don't need to. He's not a stray. He has an owner." She pushed back the fur on his neck and cupped his ID tag with her palm. "See? It says his owner is Harmony Corps. We can find her on our own. I'll check the phone book. I'll make lost dog posters! Post on the internet!"

"Harmony Corps, you said?" Aunt Laurel asked, slowly, as though with a twinge of recognition.

Did she know who Harmony was? Was she an islander Aunt Laurel knew from her teenage years at Cliff Cottage?

"That's what it says on Teddy's tag," Avery said, considering this might mean Teddy would be reunited with his owner, leaving her dogless, yet again. But that was a better option than Teddy falling into the hands of the Scorned Slider. Whatever it took to keep him safe. She pleaded, "Please, please, puh-lease, Auntie L. I'll do whatever it takes to find Harmony."

Aunt Laurel lowered her eyes to her eggplant purple slippers. She tangled the chain of her silver locket around her fingers. "One night. That's all I'll agree to."

Teddy groaned, flattening his chin on the lower bunk's

mattress, as though defeated, or maybe just exhausted.

"With that attitude, I can see why you get along with Avery," said Aunt Laurel to the puppy. "Good night, you two."

"Night," echoed Avery, sad and miserable.

Avery promised herself not to sleep a wink. She'd think of a way to stop Aunt Laurel. To save Teddy from the Scorned Slider. Even if that meant finding Harmony. She promised she wouldn't sleep even as her eyelids grew heavier. . . and heavier. . . and even as. . . .

She fell asleep.

CHAPTER 18

Knock, Knock, Ring, Ring

The next morning, Avery knelt in the sitting area of Cliff Cottage, surrounded by packed boxes labeled FAMILY SECRETS, REPRESSED MEMORIES, AND HIDDEN SKELETONS. "Teddy, where are you?" She peeked under the glass coffee table to find the tiny terrier gnawing on something fuzzy and purple. Like a lavender stuffed animal or—

Avery's eyes widened.

"Auntie L's eggplant purple slippers!"

Avery tried to tug the slippers from Teddy's grip. Teddy pulled back, his tail wagging. The fabric slipped from Avery's hands and Teddy somersaulted backwards, toppling over a stack of boxes. The sound of glass shattering echoed in the small room.

"What was that noise?" Aunt Laurel emerged from the kitchen with her cheeks flushed. She wore an apron over a lilac, ankle-length jumpsuit, her sandy blonde hair tied back in a ponytail, a mauve rag draped over her shoulder. Her expression darkened as she took in the collapsed wreckage of her packing efforts, then Teddy's paws on her chewed slipper, his tail swishing on the wood floor.

"He just wants to play." Avery attempted to excuse the dog's naughty behavior.

"My slippers aren't a toy." Aunt Laurel bent down to take the destroyed mess of purple fuzz from Teddy's paws. "Bad puppy." The tiny terrier covered Aunt Laurel's cheeks and hands with puppy kisses. "Enough, down boy." Aunt Laurel couldn't help but giggle.

"I think that means he likes you?" Avery offered.

"I think it means he can taste what I was baking." Aunt Laurel dusted her hands on her apron, and Teddy happily howled, sitting on her sock feet.

"See, he's useful," said Avery. "He could be a taste tester for Barkleby Biscuits. Join the family business."

She could tell Teddy was already starting to rub off on Aunt Laurel. It wouldn't be long until he was part of their pack. Then, if they didn't find Harmony, Teddy would be Avery's forever. A wave of relief washed over her. There was no way Aunt Laurel would bring Teddy to the pound.

There was no way Sliders were enemies of dogkind. At least, not *all* Sliders.

"Not so fast," Aunt Laurel cautioned. "I called animal patrol, Avery."

Avery's stomach flipped. Teddy whimpered and hid under the glass coffee table.

"What? Why would you do that?"

Avery ran to the window, and pushed the curtains aside, peering out. Animal patrol meant the Scorned Slider and that meant Aunt Laurel might have led the wormy-haired dog hater straight to Cliff Cottage. They were like sitting ducks. Worse, a sitting 11-and-a-half-year-old and her new best fur friend.

"Avery, Teddy isn't ours," Aunt Laurel lectured. "He belongs to someone else."

Avery stared outside, half-listening. Her stomach twisted in knots. There was a horrible feeling someone was watching her from the forest. Tree branches twisted and swayed like spiny fingers. A shadow flickered.

"Avery, did you hear what I said?" Aunt Laurel asked, Avery barely heard the words over her racing heartbeat. "They had no record of Teddy. So, I guess, it's up to you and me to find Harmony."

KNOCK, KNOCK, KNOCK.

Avery didn't have time to absorb Aunt Laurel's comments. Someone was thudding on the door. She noticed a repugnant smell lingering in the air. But was it cat farts or snert?

KNOCK! KNOCK! KNOCK!

Whoever it was, really wanted in.

"Huh, speaking of which, maybe that's someone for Teddy now?" Aunt Laurel adjusted her ponytail and went to the door. Teddy growled from under the table. He dashed by Aunt Laurel's ankles and barked protectively at the door. About to put her hand on the doorknob, Avery lunged in front of Aunt Laurel, blocking her way.

"What's gotten into the two of you?" Aunt Laurel said.

"It's. . . It's just that," Avery couldn't think of an excuse in time, so Aunt Laurel gently nudged her aside and turned the knob. The door swung open.

Standing on the porch was not what Avery expected.

It wasn't the Scorned Slider at all, but rather a strange man dressed formally in a butler's tuxedo and shiny patent shoes as though he was more suited for a ballroom than the dilapidated porch of Cliff Cottage deep in the pine and oak forest.

"Ah. . . Hello?" Aunt Laurel greeted, apprehensively.

"Salutations, Ms. Laurel Foster."

With white gloves, the gentleman displayed a silver platter with a domed cover, as though a five-star food delivery server was about to reveal a steaming lobster Thermidor.

"Who are you?" Aunt Laurel crossed her arms, suspicion written clearly on her features.

"It matters not. I come but as a loyal servant of Mrs. Fiddlesticks, the royal Cookie Empress of whom my family has served since the invention of the chocolate chip *spoodle*, generations ago. If it comforts you to know an individual salutation by which to greet me, you may use my first name along with my professional title, Marcus the Butler."

"Ah. All right Marcus."

"The *Butler*. Marcus *the Butler*," he corrected. "For without my station in life as a servant of Mrs. Fiddlesticks's humble cookie empire, I would lack purpose altogether."

Avery leaped to her feet and squished herself in the doorway next to Aunt Laurel. Teddy pushed in front of her, a personal bodyguard, his hind paw stepping on Avery's socked foot.

"Okay, um, so what are you doing here, exactly?" asked Aunt Laurel, winding the chain of her locket around her fingers.

"Do not fret, I shall be prompt and to the point. I deliver an official invitation on behalf of Mrs. Fiddlesticks herself, to attend Fiddlesticks' Freedom Fest Fourth of July Party sponsored by Fiddlesticks Cookies."

Marcus the Butler lifted the dome to reveal a single, golden envelope on the silver platter. Aunt Laurel reluctantly plucked the invitation from the tray.

Avery's eyes lit up. "You came to invite us to the party of the year?"

Marcus the Butler smugly took in the young girl: hair-uncombed, tangerine shorts covered in dog hair, socks mismatching shades of orange. "So, it seems."

Avery smiled. This was way better than an animal patrol officer showing up at the door. Avery's worries melted away. The Scorned Slider hadn't been there at animal patrol when Aunt Laurel called. Nor at the front door of Cliff Cottage. And Avery sort-of, kind-of had a dog of her own, and she would finally fit in, regardless of whether she was from another dimension or not. She shook away thoughts about her differences. Things were looking up. She couldn't wait to tell Sam and Suzy that she could join them at the party.

With a sour look on his face, Marcus the Butler continued, "Now that you find yourself in possession of a canine, you are eligible and indeed, naturally, compelled to attend. No matter how much you may lack in class or taste."

"I see word travels fast," Aunt Laurel eyed Marcus the Butler.

"Indeed. Like the breeze. May I inform Mrs. Fiddlesticks of your affirmative RSVP?"

"We'll think about it."

"What?" Avery cried.

Marcus the Butler, flustered, patted his sweating forehead with his pocket square. "That's not an option."

"I decide my options," said Aunt Laurel, "and I've decided, I'll get back to you."

As Aunt Laurel shut the cabin door in Marcus the Butler's face, he quickly slid the silver platter into the frame, holding the door open a small crack.

"But, what shall I tell Mrs. Fiddlesticks?" his voice quivered with concern.

"That I'll check my schedule."

Aunt Laurel nudged the platter away and with relief, found herself inside the privacy of the cabin once more.

"Why didn't you say 'yes'?" Avery whined. "It's not like you have a roaring social life, Laurel."

"That's Aunt Laurel, young lady." Aunt Laurel rested on the bluebell print couch. She put her lilac purple sock feet onto a box labeled PAINFUL MEMORIES.

Avery couldn't understand her aunt sometimes. It was like she was a hermit. Who wouldn't want to go to a dog-mandatory party? Even if there was a Scorned Slider with worm hair running around disguised as an animal patrol officer, chasing after cute terriers like Teddy.

Wait a minute, Avery stopped on a thought. Why was the Scorned Slider after Teddy? Why him and not the other dogs of Beaver Island? Avery shivered. She didn't want to think about that. All she cared about was going to the party where she could show off her new dog. If only she could convince Aunt Laurel.

"Why can't we go? Afraid you might double-book plans with an exhilarating night of crosswords and chamomile?" Avery asked in frustration.

Aunt Laurel rubbed her neck. "We have Slider lessons to get to, remember? Besides, Teddy's not in good enough health to go to a big party with a bunch of dogs. I'll consider taking you to the July Fourth Farmer's Market instead."

"Teddy's fit as a fiddle," Avery said. "Watch this. Teddy, roll over."

Teddy's ears flicked forwards and back. He leaped to his feet and easily rolled his body. He stuck out his tongue and panted.

Avery beamed proudly. "Isn't he the smartest dog you've ever met?"

"Finding this dog his real home is our top priority. After getting this place packed. We don't have time for Freedom Fest."

Teddy moaned and laid on his stomach, chin flat on the floor.

"But, what if Harmony's at the party?"

"Ah, I see what you're trying to do, young lady."

"We could ask around about her. Bring Teddy. See if anyone recognizes him. Doesn't that make so much sense? You really can't say 'no' now, Auntie L."

Aunt Laurel opened her mouth to speak. *BUZZZ BUZZZZ BUZZZZ.* Her phone buzzed like an annoying mosquito. She groaned. "If that's Marcus the Butler, I tell you, I will have him added to my do not disturb list."

"He's certainly persistent," noted Avery.

"Remind you of anyone?" Aunt Laurel raised her eyebrows. She noticed the Caller I.D.: *UNKNOWN*. Aunt Laurel touched her screen to accept the call. "Hello? . . .What? . . . I can't hear you, you're breaking up—" She pressed the phone closer to her head and plugged her other ear. She jumped to her feet in search of better reception. "You're what? Are you—? Oh no. Okay, I'll be there as soon as I can."

Aunt Laurel went pale as a ghost, her Orion constellation freckles shriveling into dead white dwarves. Hurriedly, she fetched her keys from an ornamental bowl on the window ledge and her fringed purse from a coat hanger, tripping over a stack of boxes.

"What's going on?" Avery asked. "Where are you going?"

"We gotta go," Aunt Laurel urged. "That was Joseph. He's with Benji and Graham Cracker in the harbor. Their boat is sinking!"

CHAPTER 19

Joe, Joe, Row Your Boat

Joseph, red-faced and sweating, rowed an aluminum dinghy towards shore away from his motor trawler. His heaving breath fogged his crooked eyeglasses as he sliced wooden oars through the emerald-green lake, his motor trawler home about one hundred feet behind him threatening to sink into the bay's depths. The vessel's stern teetered above the water line, showing off its name, ICARUS, and port, MONROE HARBOR CHICAGO, like a billboard advertising Joseph's incompetence as a captain.

On the wooden bench of the dinghy's bow, slumped Benji in a bright orange life jacket, amongst piles of clothes, pots, pans, and tools rescued from the sinking ship. Graham Cracker excitedly hopped onto the bow, snout pointed forward.

"Look!" Avery called from the beach, pointing out to the water, as Teddy nipped at her tangerine-sneakered heels. "It's Benji, and Joseph, and Graham Cracker! They're in a rowboat!" She cupped her hands around her mouth and shouted out over the bay, "Benji, Joseph, Graham Cracker!

Over here! Look, I have a dog of my own!"

"He's not our dog," Aunt Laurel qualified.

"His name is Teddy!"

"Teddy the Temporary," Aunt Laurel added.

Teddy splashed in the water, excitedly chasing waves. "He's the most terrific terrier in the world. I can't wait for you to get to know him."

The bottom of the dingy scratched the pebbly lake bottom, as it grounded ashore. Joseph jumped from the small boat into the water, soaking his hiking boots. Benji carefully crawled out onto the beach and Graham Cracker immediately joined Teddy in wave hopping fun.

Amongst the splashes, Joseph bellowed, "Watch the H20! I've got a world-changing invention aboard."

Sprawled over the haphazardly packed belongings, over and under clothing and ship stores, limp like a dead octopus, was the Dog Lingo 42. The machine's head was a turquoise-and-white Macintosh monitor from the olden days, connected to a lawn mower engine by a rubber tube. Its limbs were winding cables that led to a microphone, a keyboard, and a vintage gramophone.

The invention seemed curious, but Avery really couldn't be bothered. She was too eager for Benji and Graham Cracker to become best friends with her new dog, Teddy.

Well, sort-of, kind-of, her dog. But definitely a dog, at least. Teddy, while not technically Avery's, was definitely not a skunk. At least, they had that going for them.

"Benji, it's so cool that you're here!" Avery exclaimed, bouncing up and down. "You arrived just in time really, because you get to meet Teddy, and we're invited to the party of the year, Fiddlesticks' Fourth of July Freedom Fest, which is a party you can *only* go to if you bring a dog, and, well, like Aunt Laurel said, Teddy's not really mine, but that's a minor detail really, because he can still do all the fun things with us that Graham Cracker does, like fetch and scavenging. I bet we can even teach Teddy all the tricks that Graham Cracker knows," her verbal tirade faltered.

Benji's face grew redder and redder until he burst into tears, his eyeglass lenses fogging.

"What's wrong Benji?" Avery thought he'd be more excited to meet her adorable, brave, cuddly, doe-eyed puppy.

"My collections." Benji's lip quivered as he looked out to his floating home, which was no longer floating, but instead sinking into the bay. Benji's clothes and belongings floated to the surface of the lake around the submerged vessel, the pilothouse and cabins completely underwater. "The Entire Museum of Benji, *gone*. My blue paper clips, my collection of coins minted in the year of my birth, my postcards from Hawaii featuring Hula dancers with close-lipped smiles." Benji's white socks floated in the current, then a pair of his polka-dotted underwear, "My *delicates*." He covered his eyes, embarrassed.

"I'm so sorry Benji," Avery wracked her brain to figure out how she could best cheer up her friend. "We could go scavenging on this island for new treasures. I bet it's brimming with cool stuff. Just look at the stuffed manatee in the reeds."

"Mr. Manatee?" Benji's expression twisted with dread

as he realized his favorite stuffie, Mr. Manatee, was floating into a marsh of reeds. A seagull cawed and pecked at the sea cow's eyes. "My beloved Mr. Manatee!" Benji wailed.

Nearby, Aunt Laurel helped Joseph pull the dinghy further up to shore. "So, what happened, Joseph?"

"Ah, yeah, right." Joseph blushed as he slicked his floppy hair from his eyes with a sweaty palm. "Remember when you said I should visit if I got the trawler running?"

"Ah, yeah?" Aunt Laurel scratched under her necklace chain.

Benji moaned, water dripping from Mr. Manatee's fin as he held the stuffie upside down. "And remember when I said pigs would fly before the vessel was seaworthy?"

"Well, she got us to Beaver Island and I didn't see any boars flapping their wings," Joseph boasted. "Good ol' ship waited politely until we nearly made it to our destination before springing a leak. Even let me get my world-changing invention to safety in time."

Aunt Laurel looked strangely at the tubes and wires and machinery. "This thing?"

"That," Joseph said, eyes beaming like lamps in a lighthouse behind his fogged eyeglasses. "Is the Dog Lingo 42. Hurry now, let's all lend a hand bringing her to a safe, dry place."

"The dog *what-o*?" Avery asked, peering at the robotic creature spread like a limp squid in the wooden boat.

"My dad's latest invention," Benji groaned.

"The Dog Lingo 42," Joseph boasted. "It's my breakthrough. My masterpiece. My Mona Lisa. My Laurel Fost—" He froze and blushed. Tongue-tied he went on, "Ah, I mean, it's like Laurel's canine cookies, yeah that's it. Sheer perfection. Benji Buoy, lend your pop a hand. Then we'll turn our ingenuity and attention to rescuing our vessel, Icarus, and the Museum of Benji."

With all human hands on deck, on the count of five, they lifted the Dog Lingo 42 from the aluminum dinghy. Their fingers ached from the weight of the machine as they inched towards Aunt Laurel's jeep. "So, what does it do exactly, Joseph?" Avery asked.

"Great, great question, Avery," Joseph exclaimed, between labored breaths. "You likely won't believe me until you see, or rather *hear* it, for yourself."

"It's a musical instrument?"

"Oh, goodness, no. It's much more important than any concert trinket. In fact, it's a device that will promote a greater understanding of the human species' relationship with beasts more than ever before."

"Wait, this doesn't have to do with skunk stench?" Avery asked.

"That was the Stench Destenchifier. Patent Pending. This is the Dog Lingo 42. It translates dog speak into English, accurately, every time. At least forty percent of the time."

"*Cool!*" Avery's eyes lit up, imagining the possibilities. "We can talk to Teddy and Graham Cracker. I wonder what they think of us. I bet Teddy will say he wants to stay with me forever and ever. We should ask him."

Aunt Laurel tensed. "It, ah, it works, you say?"

"Oh yes," Joseph beamed. "On my alpha testing, the Dog Lingo 42 was able to understand that Graham Cracker's barks meant, 'I want food.' Isn't that unbelievable?"

"Wow. We figured out our ravenous Retriever was hungry. A miracle, indeed," Benji said, sarcastically, his face hidden behind the computer monitor he carried. "Can we hurry please?"

Joseph continued, "Imagine how this will change our relationships with dogkind. We can finally understand what dogs have been trying to tell us for thousands of years! I can't wait to show you, Laurel. We can test it on your new dog, and all the other dogs on Beaver Island."

"Yeah, ah, that's an idea," Aunt Laurel muttered.

"I bet they have a lot to say," Joseph said. "In a way, dogs know all our secrets. They are very perceptive. They reveal our true selves. You can't hide anything from a dog."

Aunt Laurel's arm shook, and she nearly dropped her corner of the lawn mower engine she carried with Joseph.

"Careful now," cautioned Joseph. "This is my life's work. Nothing can happen to it, or else—"

Graham Cracker and Teddy sprinted out of the lake and shook their fur, soaking Joseph, the humans, and most worrisome, the Dog Lingo 42.

"Or else, I don't know what I'll do," Joseph groaned, water dripping from his forehead.

"Oops," said Avery.

"Let's lay it down to dry." Aunt Laurel opened the door to the jeep's trunk.

Joseph fretted. "I don't think things can get any worse."

A giant burp sounded from the lake and with one gulp, Joseph's houseboat, Icarus, descended below the water's surface, the entire motor trawler disappearing in the bay. The floating home would no longer be suitable for anything other than fish or a sight for underwater divers exploring the bay's depths.

"Uh oh," Avery voiced, watching the vessel suck into the bay.

Joseph smacked his forehead. "Why did I say that?" He tossed off his flannel shirt, stripped down to his tank top, and ran into the lake, waist deep. "ICARUS!"

"My things!" Benji cried. "The Museum of Benji was not intended for fish!"

Benji ran behind Joseph towards the water line, Avery following close by to help—not realizing Aunt Laurel had been left alone with the Dog Lingo 42, a desperate glint in her eyes.

CHAPTER 20

True Friends

"Five silver safety pins, two pink erasers, one green pencil, and two-and-a-half Barkleby Biscuits." Benji sullenly laid the contents of his fanny pack on the plush violet blanket, as he perched on the lower bunk bed in Cliff Cottage. He turned his fanny pack inside out, cookie crumbs scattering onto Avery's bunk bed. "That's all that's left of the Museum of Benji."

A wet nose snuck out from under the covers, then, *snatch*! Teddy scarfed the canine cookies into his pocket-sized mouth.

"Zero Barkleby Biscuits." Benji sighed.

"I'm so sorry, Benji," Avery said. She hated to see Benji in such a rut. Especially when he should be focused on having fun with Avery and her new awesome, brilliant, courageous dog, Teddy. "This is why we *have* to go to the Fiddlesticks' Fourth of July Freedom Fest," she urged. A party would definitely cheer Benji up. If he was concerned about losing his dog biscuits, well, there'd be cookies and dogs *everywhere* there.

Avery went on, "Rumor is, Sugar Shack is like Willy Wonka's chocolate factory. There's floaties made of jellybeans. A lazy river of chocolate milk. A waterslide of licorice that leads into a pool full of ice cream sundaes. At least, that's what Sam and Suzy told me. They're my new friends, and they'll absolutely flip out when they see I have a dog of my own. If only Aunt Laurel would let us go."

"New friends?" Benji asked, Avery barely registering the twinge of jealousy in his voice.

"Oh, they are so cool," bragged Avery. "Sam's Canadian and has an Irish Setter named Riley, and Suzy's from Detroit and has a Pekingese named Pearl. They say Freedom Fest is the party of the year."

"I don't want to go," Benji pouted. "Not without my Three-Hundred and Sixty-five Jokes for Any Occasion calendar, or my New Years' Eve noisemakers, or my jolly yellow bow ties, or my—"

"It's going to be okay, Benji," Avery said, trying to cheer up her best friend. "We'll go to the party and show off our dogs and you'll forget all about your stuff once you're having fun."

But Benji's frown didn't move. Avery tried harder.

"Then we can go scavenging in the woods with Teddy and Graham Cracker and catch toads and swim in the lake and pick blueberries!"

"But Avery, my museum wing of deflated Congratulations balloons is gone. My pencil box of cake candles—sunken. My stack of birthday cards sent from my mom in Florida—submerged." Benji choked on a tear.

Avery's heart panged. "Birthday cards?"

"Yes," Benji sniffled. "All the cards my mom mailed since she split with my dad. Probably nothing more than fish toilet paper now."

That's when Avery realized, these weren't just things Benji had lost. The Museum of Benji was chock-full of memories. Reminders of his mom's love. Memories that he once had a picture-perfect family, complete with a mom, a dad, and even a dog. Just like Avery.

But it didn't last long. Benji's mom and dad broke up, and now he had two homes in two different parts of the country. Just like Avery's picture-perfect family hadn't lasted long either, vanishing before she was one year old. Maybe that was all picture-perfect families were, Avery thought—something that didn't exist in the real world but only in illusions.

The thought made Avery pause. Then a sudden inspiration struck her. "Hey, wanna see pics of my mom and dad? And the dog I had as a baby?"

"You had a dog before?"

"I think so," Avery said.

Avery pried the Orion-starred jewelry box from its hiding spot in the vanity and unclicked its top. She brought the stack of photos to the bunk bed and nudged herself beside Benji. They flipped through the scorched-edged, faded pictures.

"This dog looks a lot like a beagle," Benji said, squinting at the mystery dog in a photo, sneaking bacon from a plate.

"I know. Right?"

Across the room, Teddy hopped on a ball of yarn that

Butters had been gently pawing. Butters swatted at Teddy, though he, thinking the cat was trying to play, bounced up and down and chased Butters out of the room, paws echoing as the pair raced downstairs.

Avery laughed. "I wonder if my beagle was as energetic as Teddy?"

"What happened to your old dog?"

Avery scoffed. "Like Aunt Laurel would ever tell me. But I think it has something to do with a lady I thought I saw in this photo of my mom—" Avery uncrumpled the burnt photo, which she had retrieved from a kitchen drawer.

Benji furrowed his brow, looking closely. "I didn't know your parents lived here."

"They didn't," Avery corrected. "Wait. What do you mean?"

"This cabin in the photo. It's Cliff Cottage."

"No, it's not." Avery pressed her nose close to the film.

Although the image was partially burnt away, the background still showed a cabin beaming like a proud grandma, its window eyes bright and its mouth door gaping with cheery surprise. Cliff Cottage was cranky and tired, and that wasn't where the differences ended. The yard in the photo bloomed with bluebells and sprouted with vegetables. The shingles were free from moss. The windows sparkled and the fresh paint glistened, as though catching the sunshine, even in the faded, distorted image. Besides, apparently, no one had been to Cliff Cottage since Aunt Laurel and Avery's mom were teenagers. That was the only explanation for the sleepover mess left behind.

"Yes, it is," Benji said, matter of factly. "Someone gave the cabin a bit of elbow grease before the photo was taken, but it's the same." He flipped to another photo, holding it up to the window of the bedroom. "This one too. It was taken in this very same room."

"What? Let me see that," Avery swiped the photo from Benji.

Baby Avery smiled from her crib, under carrot-colored curtains. Like the room they were sitting in, the photo showed a sloped ceiling with exposed log beams. The lone window in the image matched the lone window in front of Avery, with—Avery nearly crossed her eyes—yes, it had to be—the very same view. She stood up and looked out to the woods, to the waves crashing against the rocks below the cliff's drop.

"Cliff Cottage was my home?" Avery mumbled. "But why wouldn't Aunt Laurel tell me that?"

It didn't make any sense. The bunk bedroom in Cliff Cottage looked like it had been left a mess by two teenagers. Why did the photo show a crib in the same room? It was as though the time Avery had spent there as a baby had disappeared. Like the room had traveled back in time, erasing Avery's past.

Sliders could manipulate matter.

Could they twist time?

A sudden pain buzzed in Avery's ear. "Ow!" She covered her ears with her palms, but the sound grew louder and louder, roaring like an engine. It sounded as though a car was pulling up to Cliff Cottage, but also like that car drove straight into Avery's mind. The noises increased in volume, sounding in Avery's skull. Then, a door slammed, boots on pebbles cracked, so loud, it was like someone walking into her eardrum. A sour scent. *Snert.*

She could smell her.

Avery panicked. She tried to move but her limbs were frozen. Benji stood still as a statue too, eyes unblinking.

Avery could sense her.

The Scorned Slider at the door.

Taking out her umbrella. . . .

Spinning it in a circle. . . .

You want to be normal. . . .You don't want anyone to think you are weird, that you are a Weirdie. . . . You will give me the dog. . . .

Avery wanted to shout, but she couldn't. She wanted to run, but her body wouldn't respond. Then, footsteps echoed in her mind. An engine rumbled and peeled away, tires squealing. She fell to the floor.

"Teddy," she shouted, looking up at Benji. Her friend blinked, appearing confused as he came out of his frozen trance. "She came for Teddy. Where is he?"

CHAPTER 21

Who Let the Dog Out?

Teddy? Teddy, you in there?" Avery cried as she crawled inside a kitchen cupboard. A spider web dangled near her head, tickling her ear. She brushed it aside, annoyed. Silhouettes of wooden bowls and mason jars towered in her vision. She began tossing items behind her, digging herself further inside the dark storage.

The last time Avery had seen the terrier, he chased Butters out of the bedroom. And now, he was gone. Avery had sensed the Scorned Slider's presence—she couldn't explain it, but it was as though she had been frozen in time, unable to move as the wormy-haired cloaked woman's footsteps and voice and engine rumbles danced in her brain, and now Teddy was missing. Avery hoped he'd found a good hiding spot when he sensed the Scorned Slider coming.

Maybe *too* good of a hiding spot.

She held her breath that any second, his silver tuft of fluff would sprout from a tower of cast iron pans. She longed to feel Teddy's cold, damp nose pressed on her palm as he scarfed down Barkleby Biscuits. Or his paws scraping against her knees as he jumped for a ball. Or the sound of his snoring at the foot of her bed. She hadn't even had the chance to sneak him bacon yet!

He had to be hiding, somewhere.

"Avery, settle down," Aunt Laurel said. "You're—" she dodged as Avery tossed a spoon over her shoulder which hit the Dog Lingo 42's computer monitor with a clatter. "You're making a gigantic mess."

"Who cares? We need to find Teddy!" Avery shouted back, her voice echoing in the cupboard. She scuttled out, facing her aunt, head-on, grey eyes stirring like storm clouds. "He's in danger." She ran to the window, looking out to the dusty driveway. "You sure no one came to the door?"

"Yes, why do you keep asking that?"

"Someone with an umbrella perhaps?"

She wasn't going to rule out that Aunt Laurel had been hypnotized. What if her aunt had handed over the terrier and forgotten? Avery chewed on her nails.

Sliders were real. That was a fact. And if Avery really was a descendant from a long line of Sliders, she must have some of their weird abilities too. She wished she knew how to use them so she could find Teddy. But she didn't know the first thing about any of it. All she had done so far was burn up a photo, apparently.

Aunt Laurel had answers.

Avery needed her knowledge—her powers.

Now.

"What's going on, Avery? Is there something you're not telling me?"

"I need to know. If Sliders are real, and we're Sliders, you must have special powers. You can manipulate matter, right? Can you do something to save Teddy? To find him?"

"Avery," Aunt Laurel's jaw tensed. She gripped her locket in a tight fist and looked towards the closed front door. Benji and Joseph were with Graham Cracker looking for the lost terrier outside. Aunt Laurel quieted, studying the doorknob as she spoke. "We shouldn't talk about—" she lowered her voice to a whisper—"*matter manipulation.* Not when company is around. The worst that could happen is for Joseph and Benji to find out we're not normal."

"Are you serious?" Avery's face turned beet red. She was fed up. Didn't Aunt Laurel realize Teddy was in grave danger? "Why are you suddenly obsessed with what Joseph thinks?"

"I'm—I'm not," Aunt Laurel defended. She crouched down to Avery's eye level. "I just don't want him to think I'm weird. I just want to be normal."

It was the same desire Avery had felt at the lighthouse after she had lost her senses staring at the Scorned Slider's umbrella.

"You are hypnotized. *She* was here. Snap out of it."

"Who was here?"

Avery was desperate. If Aunt Laurel was hypnotized by the Scorned Slider, who knows what she might have done! Had she handed Teddy directly into the warty hands of his enemy? The enemy who wanted to harm him?

Enough was enough, already.

"I know Sliders are real," Avery admitted. "I know you're a Slider. You said we can create energy, transform matter, and make portals in space and time. So, do something!"

"Avery, could you keep your voice down?"

"What's the point of being a Slider if you can't even help out? You know what I think? That you're refusing to do anything because you're scared Joseph won't think you're normal."

"No, that's not it." Aunt Laurel fiddled nervously with her locket.

"Because you're ashamed of who you are?"

"No—"

"Because you're afraid?"

"Because the Goodness Council forbade me!" Aunt Laurel snapped.

Avery froze and stared with wide eyes.

"Wait, what?"

She was not expecting that.

Aunt Laurel covered her face in her hands. She went to the bluebell sofa and slumped down on a cushion. She averted her eyes, her face ashen, lips trembling. As Avery approached, she heard her aunt sniffling. Was she holding back tears? Avery had never seen this Aunt Laurel before: sad, sullen Aunt Laurel, hurt and humiliated Aunt Laurel. Carefully, Avery sat beside her aunt. "What's the Goodness Council?"

"I'm ashamed, all right? I don't like talking about it," Aunt Laurel confessed. "The Goodness Council resides in our home dimension. They oversee Sliders, make sure we follow the rules, and judge Sliders as Lawful or Scorned. They took away my ability to manipulate matter. They banished me to Earth. It was either that or face the fate of a Scorned Slider, warts, snert smell, worm hair, and all."

"But. . . you always follow the rules. You're so perfect."

"No, I'm not," Aunt Laurel swallowed. "I didn't mean to hurt you, Avery. I don't want you to follow my path, understand? You deserve the chance to prove yourself lawful to the Goodness Council."

Avery didn't care about some silly council who sat around determining who was good and bad.

"I don't want to be a Slider at all, I just want to make sure Teddy is safe," said Avery.

"This is what I was afraid of. That my decisions would ruin everything. That I'm a bad influence."

What had Aunt Laurel done that was so bad that the Goodness Council took away her Slider abilities and banished her to Earth? From Avery's point of view, her aunt was *perfect:* rule-abiding, disciplined, and hard-working. Whatever it was, it was tearing Aunt Laurel apart, Avery could see that much.

"What did you do?" she asked. "Let me guess, you trapped a skunk in your school's garden shed?"

"No." Aunt Laurel choked on a laugh. "I came back to Cliff Cottage. Against my mother, Isadora's, rule," Aunt Laurel said, her face falling, as she clutched her locket. "Your Great-Grandma Elsie was a Weirdie, a Slider who settled on Beaver Island hundreds of years ago. They followed King Weird, a banished member of the Slider Royal Family. All they wanted was a home of their own. But the island locals didn't take kindly to them. One night, they attacked King

Weird and chased our kind off the land with pitchforks and torches. They used their dogs to hunt down those who hid. With nowhere to go, the Weirdies had to beg for the forgiveness of the Goodness Council in order to return to the Slider Realm.

"My mother, Isadora was determined to distance our family from our Weirdie past. She worked fastidiously at her goal, doing whatever it took to climb the ladder and win back the Goodness Council's approval, so we'd be held in high esteem once more. That meant distancing ourselves from Beaver Island. When Isadora discovered that your mother and I were spending our time here, at Cliff Cottage, she freaked out. She created a rule forbidding us from ever stepping foot here ever again. A rule that if we broke, we'd face the ultimate price."

"But you came back?" Avery asked.

"Yes," admitted Aunt Laurel, shamefully, sadness glinting in her eyes. Her face was indented as if she was biting the inside of her cheeks to keep from crying. "Sometimes, doing what's right makes it impossible to follow the rules."

"And, my mom came back too, didn't she? Is that why she lost her power? Is that why she couldn't save herself? Make her way back to me?"

"No—" Aunt Laurel looked down and away. Her voice trembled. "Why would you ask that?"

"I lived here, didn't I? When I was a baby, before my parents disappeared? That means my mom came back too. That she broke Grandma Isadora's rule."

Then, the door creaked open.

"Avery, Avery!" Benji called. The night sky twinkled

behind him in the door frame, the beam from his flashlight flickering in Avery's vision. "We found paw prints. They lead to the woods."

"Brilliant!" Avery's stomach flipped. Teddy hadn't hidden. Aunt Laurel hadn't handed him over to the Scorned Slider. Teddy had run away. Smart guy. Somehow, he escaped.

A twinge in Avery's gut told her she needed to find him. Fast. Before anyone else did. Even if it was against Slider rules. Even if it did mean breaking those rules would make her smell like snert, spurt worm hair, and grow warts. Hating dogs was a ridiculous rule in the first place. Why was it a rule? She didn't care. She ran to a drawer and fished out a flashlight. "Let's follow his trail!"

"Nah uh." Aunt Laurel placed her hand on Avery's shoulder. "Not so fast," she said. She plucked the flashlight from Avery's grip. "Benji, toss your dad your light. It's dark and I won't have either of you kids falling off the cliff's edge on a wrong turn. This is a job for the adults. Benji and Avery, you go upstairs. Joseph, Graham Cracker, let's go dog searching."

"But," said Avery.

"We'll find him. I promise."

CHAPTER 22

LOST DOG TEDDY

- Scruffy tiny terrier with a silver tuft on his crown •
- Definitly not a skunk •
- Likes: Chewing on slippers •
- Dislikes: Lightning, thunder, and animal control
- If you know where he is, call 555-6897 ASAP
- Whatever you do, do NOT bring him to the pound

CHAPTER 23

Today We Celebrate Our Independence Day

"Give one to everyone you see," commanded Avery. Buckled in the back seat of the jeep, Avery separated a stack of Lost Teddy posters in her lap. All night long, she tented herself under the sheets of the lower bunk with a flashlight, working her pencil crayons down to stubs, her knuckles raw with blisters. She'd find Teddy before the Scorned Slider did. She had to.

She handed half of the posters to Benji, over Graham Cracker's shiny mane as the Golden Retriever mix sat in the middle seat.

"Everyone? Even babies?" asked Benji, riffling through the pages. "What about the visually impaired? How about tourists who don't read English?"

"Everyone," Avery said with urgency. There wasn't time to split hairs. "The longer Teddy is missing, all alone—" What would happen if the Scorned Slider found him? Worse, what if she already had him? And why did she want him so badly, over all the other dogs of Beaver Island? Avery shuddered.

"We can probably limit it to one poster per family," said Aunt Laurel as she drove lakeside into town. "Save some trees?"

"This isn't the time for forest conservation," snapped Avery. "It's not like a birch tree can play fetch. It's not as though an elm can cuddle you during a thunderstorm." Annoyed, Avery flashed a poster and pointed to her pencil-crayon drawing of a scruffy terrier. The resemblance to Teddy was. . . questionable, at best. "Do you know how many tries it took to get Teddy's silver tuft just right?" Eraser marks streaked the page.

"From this angle, he kind of looks like a skunk," noted Benji.

"A skunk? What? No." Avery examined the image sideways. She sort-of, kind-of, saw what Benji did in the drawing. She panicked, desperate. "How will we ever find Teddy if this looks like a Lost Rosie poster?"

"Avery, I promise we'll try our best to find Teddy," Aunt Laurel said, wistfully.

"You and Joseph only searched the woods for a hundred and eighty-two minutes. I know because I counted. That's hardly trying your best. I would have stayed up all night searching."

"You *did* stay up all night." Benji yawned. "Making posters. The scratching of your colored pencils kept me awake."

"That's why we're going to the Farmers Market today," Aunt Laurel reminded them. "It's always packed on the Fourth of July. At least, it was back when I was a teenager. There'll be lots of people you can hand out your Lost Dog fliers to. It's already looking crowded."

Joseph sighed, his expression forlorn. "Great. I'm really looking forward to meeting new people," he said without meaning it. "Hello, I'm Joseph, the captain who sank his motor home trawler in the bay, also known as the failed inventor with yet another failed invention under my belt."

Earlier, after drying out the Dog Lingo 42 on the dining table at Cliff Cottage, Joseph had hopefully turned it on. He cranked the machine's handle until it powered up, only for it to explode in a puff of smoke, sounding, "*Poop, poop, poop*," on repeat.

"Are those acrobats?" Benji slapped his palms against the jeep's windows. "At a farmers market?"

"What in the world?" Aunt Laurel said. "This seems a bit much."

As the jeep rolled closer to the marina, the Farmers Market appeared more like a bustling circus fair than a country square. Starry streamers decorated red, white, and blue tents. The grounds swarmed with villagers, tourists, and their dogs, along with caterers and entertainers of all shapes, sizes, and abilities. Clowns juggled sparklers. Poodles in American-flagged top hats walked on their hind legs. Performers in shiny leotards balanced upside down in painful contortions.

Out on the sidewalk, an Irish Setter pranced regally in front of two girls. It was Sam and Suzy. Sam wore a baseball jersey, her amber hair springing out from under a ballcap. Suzy carried Pearl in her arms, the Pekingese's midnight black fur clinging to Suzy's daisy-patterned floral frock.

"Riley! Sam! Suzy! Pearl!" Avery called out, through the closed window. She tried to roll down the glass, but it wouldn't budge.

Child locks. Typical.

"Auntie L, those are my friends." If anyone would take Teddy's disappearance seriously, it would be Sam and Suzy. They loved their dogs. They would understand and help. Avery was sure of it.

Graham Cracker barked at the sight of the pooches.

"Pipe down please," Aunt Laurel hushed him, her eyes narrowed in concentration. "Finding a parking spot requires Einstein levels of concentration today. I've never seen the marina park so crowded."

"But they can help us find Teddy! They know this island better than either of us. Let me out." She pressed on the door desperately.

"Patience, Avery Isadora. We're a team, okay?"

Avery crossed her arms and slouched, the edge of her seat belt slicing into her neck, as Aunt Laurel circled the fairgrounds at a painful, turtle's pace.

"Hardly."

CHAPTER 24

Party in the U.S.A.

Servers in silk vests, emblazoned with American flags, offered baked goods and flutes of milk in a chaotic ballet at the archway to the Farmers Market. Bouquets of exotic flowers lined the market grounds. Looking closer, they weren't lotuses and orchids at all, but rather macaroons and cotton candy arranged to look like plant life.

But the sugary sweets couldn't distract Avery from her mission. She craned her neck, taking in the sea of people, kids, and their dogs—big and small, shaggy and well-groomed, but none with Teddy's distinctive silver tuft.

And it seemed she was the only one of their so-called "team" with any focus at all.

"Ninety-seven, ninety-eight, ninety-nine—I've never seen so many cookies in my life." Benji counted, enchanted by the baked goods sculptures.

"I didn't realize they farmed biscuits on Beaver Island," Joseph said, grumpily.

"Neither did I." Aunt Laurel suspiciously eyed a banner over the park gate.

The banner read:

BEAVER ISLAND'S FOURTH OF JULY
FARMERS MARKET
SPONSORED BY FIDDLESTICKS COOKIES

"Huh, go figure. Ghizwhisch Fiddlesticks has her hands in all the cookie jars around these parts," Aunt Laurel said, as they entered the market grounds.

Fountains overpoured strawberry and raspberry blue sodas, while cart attendants helped children roll cotton candy onto cardboard cones. Flamingos pranced around picnic tables decorated with elaborate cookie bouquet centerpieces. An orchestra by the gazebo played a jazz tune Avery recognized from a Fiddlesticks Cookies commercial. Waiters flitted about.

"May I offer a *spoodle*?"

"Mint teztle eetzels?"

"Glass of dairy milk? Or do you prefer cashew? Almond? Soy? I also have oat. Macadamia? Pickle? Pony?"

Avery placed a flier on the waiter's tray. "Have you seen this dog around? A tiny terrier with a scruffy silver tuft on his head?"

"Goodness, no," the server gasped, wide-eyed. "I'd remember a dog that looked so much like a skunk. What happened? Is he a genetic mutation or a rare crossbreed?"

"Never mind," mumbled Avery. "My aunt's cell phone is on the poster if you see anything."

Benji grabbed handfuls of cookies from the waiters' trays and displays, stuffing as many as he could fit into his mouth while squishing those that couldn't make it into his fanny pack for later. Graham Cracker happily gobbled up crumbs like a personal vacuum cleaner hovering near Benji's Veloce shoes.

"Where are the carrots?" Joseph strained his neck for a view above the crowd. "Aren't Farmers Markets supposed to have radishes? Celery? You know, *vegetables*?"

"Dooggle oogle?" a perky waitress with perfect teeth offered. Benji eagerly reached for a biscuit. The waitress tsked and swatted Benji's fingers away. "For the *dog*," she chastised, in disbelief. She lowered the tray of biscuits to Graham Crackers' eye level. The cookies were shaped like fire hydrants and squirrels. Graham Cracker sniffed at the cookies and turned away, uninterested. "It's from the Fiddlesticks Canine Cookie product line. Still very much in experimentation and development."

"They look just like Barkleby Biscuits," Benji noted.

"Let me see those." Aunt Laurel moved by Benji.

Avery called out, annoyed, "Enough snacking, more searching for Teddy!"

Benji whipped around, crumbs flying from his mouth. "Sorry, Ave, I only get oats and raisins at home. These cookies are genius. Sweet. Sugary. They should award Mrs. Fiddlesticks a Nobel Peace Prize for inventing these glorious delights."

"A cookie is not an invention," Joseph scoffed. "Baking is hardly impressive. It merely requires following a set of rules to produce a predictable result. Excellent baking is, at best, indicative of a mediocre mind."

"Ah, thanks, Joseph?" Aunt Laurel said, unsure if she should be offended. "You do know I'm a baker, right?"

"Oh, I don't mean you, Laurel." Joseph blushed. He stuffed his hands into his wrinkled cargo shorts. "I only meant this Mrs. Fiddlesticks, well—" He looked around at the fairgrounds glittering with more sparkle than a jewelry store. "It seems like appearance and success are all that's important to her. There's more to life. Like adventure."

"Ahem, attention *si vouz plait*." A voice boomed over the speakers. Marcus the Butler appeared on a gazebo stage in the park's center.

Avery and the gang walked closer.

Marcus the Butler tapped his white glove against a microphone, the sound deep and throbbing like a dinosaur's stomps. "Attention! Attention! *Vite, vite*!" A crowd formed.

In a garden chair behind the podium, Mrs. Fiddlesticks's son, Tomin, sat slumped in oversized basketball shorts, an argyle sweater vest, and a sullen expression. In contrast, Mrs. Fiddlesticks beamed from the chair beside her son, her posture upright, glittery pink sneakers crossed at the ankles, as she stroked her white, fluffy Maltese, Princess's mane. Princess snarled, poor thing dressed like the Statue of Liberty.

"Ladies and gentlemen, boys and girls, dams and studs, it is time," Marcus the Butler announced. "Time to bask in the greatness of those who made today possible. And no, I speak not of our Founding Fathers, who birthed our great country, the United States of America, but of a different kind of founder, the Cookie Empress herself. The founder of the world's largest snack food brand, the corporate sponsor of the Fourth of July Farmers Market, and the only person to have ever baked a cookie on Mount Everest, the

Marianna Trench, *and* the Moon—"

"Ah, yeah, she's not adventurous at all, is she?" Avery muttered.

Joseph huffed, "How is that even possible? The atmospheric pressure alone would make it impossible for someone to bake a cookie that far below, or above, sea level."

Marcus the Butler clapped his white gloves together, "Put your hands together for Mrs. Fiddlesticks."

The crowd erupted in applause, as Mrs. Fiddlesticks gently placed Princess on a silk cushion, then took control of the gazebo stage. Her gemmed bangles jingled as she gave a royal wave, her hair styled in bouncy waves cascading down her shoulders. She wore a tank top that read, MOM LIFE IS RUFF, pink sweatpants, and a fortune's worth of diamonds.

"Thank you, oh you're too kind, settle, please, please," she insisted with faux humility. "I'm not an icon or a legend as your applause would suggest. I'm merely a super successful businesswoman with a knack for total domination. And yes, I've been to the deepest depths of the ocean, the highest summits of the Earth, and even beyond our planet to outer space. And it's true, I speak ten languages, and hold seventeen world records demonstrating my natural talent for virtually anything I try, but most importantly," she paused for drama and looked over her shoulder to where Princess sat by her son. "I'm a mom."

A reaction of "awws" came from the audience. Someone behind Avery whispered, "A mom first. Wow, she is so down to Earth." Someone else replied, "She obviously knows what matters most in life."

Mrs. Fiddlesticks's cheeks flushed pink. "I know what you're all thinking. With a figure like that? She's a mother?" She put her hands on her hips, showing off her slim waist. "But it's true, my baby is the center of my universe. Everyone, I'd love for you to meet—"

Tomin propped his spine a bit straighter in his chair and waved. He nearly stood onto his feet, when—

"Princess! My glorious Maltese!"

Princess hopped from her throne and scurried over to the podium, gracefully leaping into Mrs. Fiddlesticks's arms.

Tomin glared, slinking further down in his seat looking as if he'd rather be anywhere else.

Mrs. Fiddlesticks pressed her nose to Princess's snout. The dog snarled and tried to bite her face, but the woman hugged the fur ball close to her chest. "Naturally, I want to provide the best for my darling angel fairy poo, Princess. But then, I discovered, tragically, there simply aren't any nutritious, yet delicious, dog treats on the market that I, as a mother—" She seemed to hone in straight on Aunt Laurel and Avery in the audience. "—a *real* mother, feel comfortable feeding to my baby."

Aunt Laurel's jaw dropped. "As if."

"That's why, tonight at Fiddlesticks' Freedom Fest, I'm launching a new line of dog treats. A brand-new recipe with the Princess Seal of Approval. These ones are five-stars compared to what your dogs may have sampled today. That's right, tonight at my party, your pooches can be the first ever to taste the new-and-improved, Michelin-quality Fiddlesticks for Fur Friends Cookies."

Everyone in the crowd cheered. Well, everyone but Aunt Laurel, Avery, Benji, and Joseph. Aunt Laurel fiddled with her locket.

Mrs. Fiddlesticks, high from applause, shouted like a dictator, "Nothing will stop me until I reach total domination! Crush all my competitors! Loot and plunder their shops like a Viking!"

"Loot and plunder?" Aunt Laurel stammered. "Viking? Why does this all sound so familiar?"

"Perhaps you read about the seafaring Norsemen in an encyclopedia?" Benji suggested.

"No, that's not it," Aunt Laurel shook her head.

"Every dog from Beaver Island will be at Freedom Fest tonight. I've made sure of it. And when I set my mind to something, it happens. There won't be a single pooch on this patch of land that's not sampling my canine cookies." Mrs. Fiddlesticks seethed, like a power-hungry machine. "See you tonight at the biggest dog party this island will ever boogie down at."

Every dog on the island?

Avery realized that would, technically, include Teddy too.

CHAPTER 25

Face-Off

We have to go to Freedom Fest." Avery pulled on the arm of the mauve hoodie tied around Aunt Laurel's waist, as her aunt pushed through the crowd in a rush, handing out fliers.

A toddler mistook the handout for a cookie and stuffed it in her mouth. A pack of tourists in lederhosen, speaking German, looked curiously at one of the fliers.

Far ahead, a middle-aged woman in a visor hardly looked at the poster from Benji, tossing it aside to shower Graham Cracker with affection and pepper Joseph with questions. ("Are you married?" "What's it like being a single dad these days?" "Would you like my sister's phone number?") As the crowd flowed, Avery lost sight of them completely.

"Please, please, puhlease, Auntie L," Avery begged. "*Every* dog will be at that party."

"No way," Aunt Laurel snapped, passing a half-stack of posters to a senior citizen with a walking cane and thick reading glasses. "We're getting rid of these, then we're going back home."

"What?" Avery couldn't believe her ears. "But you promised we'd try our best to find Teddy. We can't just go back to Cliff Cottage when we run out of fliers."

"I'm not talking about Cliff Cottage." Aunt Laurel unlatched the straps of her fringed purse and stuffed the posters inside, grabbing her cell phone. She scrolled onto the webpage for the ferry schedule. "I gotta go back to Chicago. Figure out a way to turn Barkleby Biscuits around. If Mrs. Fiddlesticks is seriously launching a dog cookie brand, I'm in no shape to compete. With my rent, and ingredient prices so high, I'll be knocked out of business."

"Her canine cookies can't match yours. Graham Cracker wouldn't even try one. And she'll eat anything."

"You heard her. She's debuting a new recipe tonight. They got the Princess Seal of Approval."

"Princess has horrible taste. You should see the outfits she wears."

"That dog's probably been spoon-fed caviar her whole life. If Ghizwhisch Fiddlesticks has impressed Princess, she's onto something. We need to go home. Save our shop."

"Teddy needs saving too."

"There's other people for that."

"Who? Animal patrol?" Fear stirred in Avery's chest thinking of the Scorned Slider. What could she possibly want with the tiny terrier?

"Avery Isadora," Aunt Laurel hissed. "Even if we did go to Freedom Fest, what do you expect? That Teddy's just going to show up alone in a bowtie with a housewarming plant?"

She had a good point. But even still, how could Teddy miss the party of the year?

"Mrs. Fiddlesticks said every dog from Beaver Island will be there. That includes Teddy."

"She didn't mean it literally," said Aunt Laurel. "It's puffery. Gibberish. You can't take what she says as truthful. They call her the Sugar Shark for a reason."

"It's because I stalk my prey," cooed Mrs. Fiddlesticks, appearing from behind a cookie stand, stroking Princess's mane.

The Maltese growled at Avery, foam seething from her bared fangs.

"Ghizwhisch," Aunt Laurel replied, pulling her purse strap close to her body. She nervously looked around. "This is quite the production. All for some dog treats?"

"*Mrs. Fiddlesticks*," she snarled. "I mean, please, call me Mrs. Fiddlesticks."

"All right, Mrs. Fiddlesticks."

"It's a pleasure to finally meet you in person, Laurel," said Mrs. Fiddlesticks. "You know what I say, seeing an enemy up close allows the giant to realize they were fighting a mere ant."

"No, I haven't heard that one," muttered Aunt Laurel.

"Page eighty-three of my book, *How to Totally Dominate Everything*." Mrs. Fiddlesticks scanned the aunt and niece, confusion flitting across her features. "Where's your dog? The pathetic, orphaned terrier?"

The pity in Mrs. Fiddlesticks's tone irritated Avery. "He's not pathetic, thank you very much, and there's certainly nothing wrong with being an orphan. I should know."

Aunt Laurel shot a look at her niece. Avery mouthed "What?" not sure of what she'd done wrong exactly.

"He's not ours," confessed Aunt Laurel. "My niece, Avery, found the dog, by the lighthouse. He was hurt and stayed with us while he recovered. But he ran away."

"If you've heard anything—" Avery interrupted, offering Mrs. Fiddlesticks a flier.

Mrs. Fiddlesticks turned up her nose, ignoring Avery. She stroked Princess's head with her diamond-clad fingers, as she pondered, though neither her eyebrows nor forehead furrowed an inch. "Hmmm, so you don't have a dog after all? Wouldn't you agree it's a bit strange, weird, even, that Laurel Foster, creator of Barkleby Biscuits, doesn't have a dog of her own?"

"That's what I've been saying my whole life," Avery agreed.

Aunt Laurel elbowed her niece. "Ever heard of allergies, Ghizwhisch?"

"*Mrs. Fiddlesticks,*" she corrected, sternly. "I'm just supposing aloud, Laurel, that perhaps your canine cookie shop is failing because you don't actually like dogs."

"My shop is doing just fine," Aunt Laurel lied.

"Oh, is that so?" Mrs. Fiddlesticks sidelined her gaze for a moment to Avery. The hair on Avery's neck prickled, standing up straight. "That's odd, because a little birdie on a bicycle said you're selling your grandmother's cabin. She was one of those weirdo outsiders, wasn't she? A *Weirdie*?"

Aunt Laurel clenched her jaw.

"My family is none of your concern."

Mrs. Fiddlesticks pouted, tickling her Maltese's nose. "Oh, Princess poo, to see Laurel Foster parting with a family heirloom, Cliff Cottage. Shucks. It breaks my heart."

"I didn't ask for your sympathy," said Aunt Laurel.

"My apologies," Mrs. Fiddlesticks backed down. "I merely wanted to help. You know, I'd be willing to take Barkleby Biscuits off your hands—for a price that reflects its struggling position in the market, that is."

"I'll consider it. When pigs fly."

"Says the lady with Weirdie blood," taunted Mrs. Fiddlesticks. "Just consider this first—" She snapped her fingers. Nothing happened. She clicked louder, stomping her feet, frustrated. "I said, *just consider this first*."

Marcus the Butler seamlessly flew out of nowhere, crumbs on his chin, napkin tucked into his lapel. He pinched a slim slip of paper in his white-gloved fingers. "My apologies, Madame, I thought it was appropriate timing for a lunch break, as these preceding seventy-two hours, I have not had a chance to consume nary a stick of celery—"

Without so much as acknowledging Marcus the Butler's presence, Mrs. Fiddlesticks snatched the slip from him and flipped it to Aunt Laurel.

"What's this?" Aunt Laurel asked.

Avery stood on her tiptoes to look over Aunt Laurel's shoulder. It was a check. That much was obvious, but she couldn't make sense of all the zeros written behind the number one.

"Woah, it's at least one thousand—no. One hundred, no. One million?" Avery counted. "For you, Aunt Laurel!"

"Your niece is a smart girl," Mrs. Fiddlesticks smirked.

"Considering she's an orphan."

Avery's cheeks and palms tingled hot. "Considering *what?*"

"It's you," said Aunt Laurel, eyes frozen on the check she scrunched tightly in her grip.

"No, those aren't U's, darling. They're zeros. Lots of them." Mrs. Fiddlesticks winked.

"No, it's *you!*" Aunt Laurel shouted, attracting the attention of curious onlookers. A crowd formed around the quarreling women, families whispering and pointing, teenagers recording with their phones. Storm clouds formed in Aunt Laurel's grey pupils. "This check is drawn on the account of 'One-Two-Three Loot and Plunder Limited, a parent company of ABC Vikings Incorporated'. Those are the companies that bought out my landlord and the farm I buy my ingredients from. You're behind my increased costs. You're trying to drive me out of business. You're the one sabotaging my shop because you don't want me as competition!"

A devilish smile took over Mrs. Fiddlesticks's expression. "Guilty." She basked in her evil aura. "Ask yourself though, does it really matter if the price is right?"

Aunt Laurel crunched the check into a ball. "You act like some kitchen hot shot, but when was the last time you turned on an oven? Mixed your own batter? Separated an egg white?"

"What are you getting at, darling? Is that a 'yes' to my very generous offer? Because I don't have all day. Time is money, after all. Let's not forget that very big check I wrote you."

"I'm just supposing aloud that perhaps you're threatened by me because you can't bake anymore."

"No one's a better baker than I." Mrs. Fiddlesticks's eyes glinted, as though Aunt Laurel triggered a chemical explosion in her gut. "I challenge you to a bake-off. Tonight, at Fiddlesticks' Freedom Fest. We each whip up one-hundred dog treats at the party to prevent any cheating on your part. Whoever's cookies get gobbled up first by the fur guests in attendance, wins."

"Why would I play your silly games, Ghizwhisch?"

"Because, if you win, I'll solve all your problems. I'll not only give you the deed to your shop, but I'll throw in the farm you get the ingredients from. And let's add Cliff Cottage to the mix. I'll buy the cabin and pass you the keys. No strings attached."

"And if you win?"

"*When* I win, you turn over Barkleby Biscuits and the keys to Cliff Cottage."

"Wait, no," Avery protested. "Cliff Cottage was my home—"

Aunt Laurel could never say yes. Mrs. Fiddlesticks was asking for their entire lives as a wager, essentially. There was no way tough cookie, cookie chef Aunt Laurel, cautious, careful Aunt Laurel, responsible and reasoned Aunt Laurel, could agree to this ridiculous bet.

"Deal," said Aunt Laurel.

Avery's hands pulsed with a surge of disbelief. She stared open-mouthed at her aunt.

"Oh, and I forgot to mention," Mrs. Fiddlesticks said. "I never lose, Laurel. That's a promise."

CHAPTER 26

Walking On, Walking On, Broken Promises

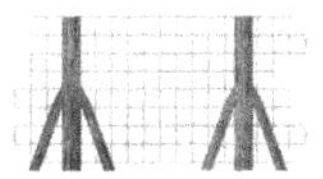

"Auntie L, you're not thinking this through." Avery tried to reason with Aunt Laurel, but her aunt was acting so headstrong, so stubborn, so. . . much like Avery? "You're acting recklessly. Like a child. Like *me.*"

Aunt Laurel halted. She crouched to meet her niece at eye level, her hands on Avery's shoulders. "Avery, my recipe is unbeatable."

"That's awfully confident of you."

Yes, dogs adored Barkleby Biscuits, but how could Aunt Laurel act so sure of herself? And how had she so easily forgotten about her promise to find Teddy?

"It has nothing to do with my confidence." Aunt Laurel's grey eyes pierced into Avery's. She lowered her voice. "You know my recipe was passed down from your Great-Grandma Elsie. What you don't know is that she stole it. From the Dog Dimension."

"There's a dimension for dogs?"

Avery pictured herself in a palace packed with puppies, playing, and ponying around. "Can I go there? Can

I live there? Where is it?"

"There's no time for questions, Avery," Aunt Laurel hushed her. "We need to buy ingredients and practice a batch at this altitude. This is the only way to get Ghizwhisch Fiddlesticks off my back."

"Are you forgetting about my missing dog?"

Ignoring Avery, Aunt Laurel dug in her fringed purse for paper and a pencil. Using her thigh as a makeshift writing table, she scrawled a list and handed it to Avery. "These are the ingredients I need. The fresher, the better."

Avery flipped the page over. It was one of her lost dog fliers. "What about Teddy?"

"Avery, there's no time," urged Aunt Laurel. "Not right now. We can look later."

"You promised."

"Think of it this way. You get your way. We're going to Fiddlesticks' Freedom Fest. Maybe Teddy will show up."

"What do you expect? That Teddy's just going to show up alone in a bowtie with a housewarming plant?" Avery echoed her aunt's question from earlier. She really had swapped places with Aunt Laurel who was acting like an out-of-control pre-teen.

"Fine, I'll go get the ingredients." Aunt Laurel grabbed the list back from her uncooperative niece. "You find Joseph and Benji. Let's meet back at the jeep in ten minutes."

"But—"

"Avery, I need your help. Please."

"Fine."

"Promise?"

"Promise."

What was a promise worth anyhow? Nothing to Aunt Laurel, apparently.

Avery could break promises too.

She squished through the crowd of red, white, and blue. She climbed on a picnic table, scanning the horizon for Benji, Joseph, and Graham Cracker—wondering if Teddy was out there somewhere, too. That's when the scent curled into her nostrils.

Snert.

Avery whipped around. Across the lawn, leering from behind a fenced-off petting zoo, was a woman in an ankle-length black dress, the brim of her floppy, dark sunhat grazing a crescent-moon birthmark on her cheek. Her reddish hair squirming by her shoulders.

"The Scorned Slider," Avery gasped.

The woman disappeared into the swarm of colorful tourists, families, and caterers.

"Oh no, you're not getting away that easy."

Avery jumped from the picnic table and ran towards the pen of goats. The woman had disappeared without a trace. Avery sniffed the air, though she couldn't detect any snert over the smells of manure and hay from the petting zoo. A goat shrieked. Startled, Avery spun on her heel to spot a woman in head-to-toe black walking past the chicken coops.

Avery sprinted through the goat pen to catch up, muddying her tangerine sneakers. "You," she cried. "Where's Teddy?"

The woman turned around. "Who's Teddy? Is that your bear's name? Have you lost your Teddy bear, young girl?" It wasn't the Scorned Slider at all. It was an old woman with bulbous eyes and wrinkled skin. She burped and it reeked. "Oh, excuse me, my granddaughter served pea soup for lunch."

CHAPTER 27

Everyone's Hanging Out Without Avery

"Avery. Over here!"

From a patch of grass, Benji waved a bean bag in the air. Graham Cracker leaped after the toy. They didn't appear concerned about finding Teddy. In fact, it very much appeared they were more concerned with their game of cornhole. And they weren't alone.

Standing at a mound, Sam took the stance of a baseball player. She tilted her ball cap, then spun her arm like a windmill, lobbing a bean bag towards a slab of wood with a hole cut in the middle. It would have been the perfect shot, if not for her Irish Setter, Riley, intercepting the throw mid-air. "Dang it," she said, kicking a dandelion.

Riley showed off his loot with a grin, until Suzy's Pekingese, Pearl, scurried underneath the large dog's torso and snagged it away with her little jaws hidden behind her flat snout. Suzy skipped after her dog. "Pearl! It's my turn. Give that back!"

Pearl scampered to Avery's feet and dropped the bean bag by her muddy, tangerine sneakers, tail wagging. Avery bent over and rubbed the Pekingese's fluffy, midnight black mane. "Good snag. Now have you seen Teddy? My terrier with a silver tuft of hair?"

"Avery!" Suzy greeted, surprised. "Where did you come from?"

"Hi, Ave," Sam waved.

"I see you all started a game," Avery noted, unable to hide her annoyance. Her hands prickled. Why wasn't Benji looking for Teddy? "Without me."

"You can take my turn," Benji offered. "I go after Suze."

Suze? Avery cringed, irritated that Benji and Suzy were already on a nickname basis. Apparently, Benji had given up on looking for Teddy. Just like Auntie L. Was Avery the only one who cared?

"What happened to handing out fliers, Benji?" Avery adjusted the straps of her backpack.

"You two know each other?" Suzy asked.

"Yes," answered Benji. "Avery is my friend from Chicago."

"*Best* friend," corrected Avery. "Or so I thought."

"You're so lucky, Avery," Suzy gushed. "Benji has *the* cutest dog ever. Isn't that right Graham Cracker?"

Graham Cracker rolled over onto her back, belly up. Suzy curled over the Golden Retriever mix and rubbed the dog's stomach.

"Graham Cracker's such a cool dog," Sam twisted her baseball cap backwards on her head of red hair. She bent down to join Suzy in petting Graham Cracker's belly. Benji's dog howled with excitement. "What a good girl. How did you come up with her name, Benji?"

"My mom wanted to call her something cute, like Biscuit or Honey," explained Benji. "But my dad wanted to name her after a famous inventor like Alexander Graham Bell. They settled on Graham Cracker. Neither of them was very happy about it."

Suzy melted. "She sure is a cutie."

"She has lots of energy and she's very friendly," noted Sam. "You did a great job training her."

Avery's palms tingled and grew hotter. She clenched her fists in her pockets. If only she had Teddy, then her new friends would see how brave, smart, and amazing *her* dog was. They could all talk about how she had done such a great job saving Teddy from the woods in the thunderstorm. Even if she left out the details about the Scorned Slider, it still made for a good story. Why were Graham Cracker and Benji getting so much attention? There were important things to do. Teddy's *life* was at stake! Avery's palms throbbed with pent-up energy.

"We should all play toss," Sam suggested. "Or even better, sardines."

"We're too busy for games," Avery snapped.

"What's sardines?" asked Benji.

"It's backwards hide-and-seek," chimed Suzy.

"One person hides then everyone else goes looking for them," Sam explained. "The catch is, if you find the person, you don't say anything at all. Instead, you sneakily squish into their hiding place with them as quietly as you can. By the end, one person is left looking while everyone else is hiding together, packed in a small space like sardines."

"That sounds so fun." Benji beamed. "I love searching for things."

"Then help me search for Teddy," Avery insisted. "And we have to meet Aunt Laurel at the jeep in less than ten minutes. She's in a frenzy because she bet away our livelihood in a bake-off with Mrs. Fiddlesticks."

"That seems rash," noted Benji.

"You think?" said Avery, like duh. "If she loses, Mrs. Fiddlesticks gets Cliff Cottage *and* Barkleby Biscuits. She could lose her shop and my childhood home."

"I thought you said your aunt's a real estate investor?" asked Suzy, suspicious.

"She's not," said Benji, plainly. "She's a dog treat chef. The best."

"Huh?" Sam lifted her eyebrows. "Wait, Suzy's right. I remember you said your aunt's a real estate investor. And that she's allergic to dogs."

"Miss Laurel doesn't have allergies," said Benji. "She certainly never sneezes around Graham Cracker or her customers' dogs."

"You lied to us, Avery?" Suzy accused, clearly hurt. "It's not nice to lie to new friends."

"Maybe she had a good reason?" shrugged Sam.

"I'm not." Avery's cheek reddened. "I mean I didn't." Her hands flared with heat, so hot, that she could no longer keep them in her shorts pockets. She clasped her hands behind her back.

What had Aunt Laurel said about Sliders creating energy? Why did this have to be happening now?

No one cared what Avery was going through. Her

whole world was crashing down around her, and she didn't even have anyone to talk to. At least, anyone she could talk to truthfully and honestly. What could she say to her friends, after all, that she was a Weirdie? Possibly an enemy of dogkind? That she was worried she had lost the only dog she could remember ever having to a Scorned Slider? Avery's words burst out, "I mean, I did. I mean, I'm not sure what I mean. But I'm not a liar. I even have my own dog."

"Really? A dog of your own?" Sam's eyes widened. "What kind?"

Avery's hands calmed. Finally, it was her chance to prove she fit. "A terrier named Teddy with a scruffy, silver tuft on his crown. I found him by the lighthouse."

"You found him?" repeated Sam, voice raising into a question. "So, he's not really your dog?"

"Well, I guess not. Not technically, but he was mine for a little. Technically, he belongs to a lady named Harmony, whoever she is, and we were looking for her but then Teddy ran away."

"So, you don't have a dog?" asked Suzy.

"Well, not right now. But I'll find him and—"

"Hmmm, Avery," said Sam. "I don't know. Maybe he ran back to his owner? Maybe you were actually his kidnapper, did you ever think of that?"

"No."

"Maybe a Weirdie got him." Suzy gasped, scared.

"Suze, you're just spooked since you heard Garry, the mechanic, spotted a Weirdie at Lurk Farms," scoffed Sam.

"You shouldn't talk around about that," Suzy warned. "It's bad luck. You'll end up cursed by Weirdies' evil magic."

"Real magic is science," said Benji. "Did you know scientists are making an invisibility cloak? Or that with gene-editing technology it's possible to create chimeras, which means a cross between animals, all in a lab, like a Pegasus or a minotaur?"

"Really? What about a cross between a cat, a dog, and a horse?" Suzy imagined.

"Sure!" exclaimed Benji.

Avery's shoulder tensed. "Weirdie sightings? At Lurk Farms? What do you mean?"

Maybe it would give Avery a clue. Maybe it would help her find Teddy.

"Relax Avery, no one's really seen Weirdies around," said Sam.

"So, no one happened to see a woman with warts and worm hair walking around with an umbrella?" Avery asked, disappointed to lose her only lead.

"Hey, how did you know?"

"What?"

"That Garry says he saw a Weirdie with worm hair, and that she had an umbrella? I didn't mention those details," said Sam.

"Lucky guess?" Avery lied.

"Well, you can't take Garry's word for much," said Sam. "My grandma says he's a conspiracy nut. And that he likes his whiskey."

Avery soaked in this information. The Scorned Slider had been at Lurk Farms. She had been after Teddy. What if she had him? What if she was holding him hostage at Lurk Farms?

Suddenly, Avery had an idea. If no one would take her quest to find Teddy seriously, she'd trick her friends into helping her. "We should go to Lurk Farms," she suggested, overly eager. "Play sardines. Wouldn't it be the perfect spot?" She remembered biking past it the day she found Teddy, all the hiding places in the tall grass and abandoned buildings. The rocking chair had seemed to sway on its own. A chill went down Avery's spine. But she wouldn't let fear get in the way of finding the terrier.

"Count me out." Suzy shivered.

"Let's go scavenge seashells or pinecones," Benji said. "I could start rebuilding the Museum of Benji."

"I like that idea." Suzy lit up. "Let's start at the beach. So long as we can stay out of the dirt."

"The whole beach is dirt, Suzy," said Sam. "That's the definition of a beach."

"Come on," urged Avery. "I thought you were facing your fears this summer, Suzy. Isn't Lurk Farms one of the supposedly haunted places on this island? What better time than now?"

A shadow cast over Avery. She felt a warm breath on her neck. She tensed. She didn't like the storm brewing in her gut, or the prickles tingling in her palms. She could feel someone lurking over her. And it wasn't anyone she wanted to see.

CHAPTER 28

Tomin's Invitation

"And I declare a winner. The ugliest girl award goes to," a nasally pitched voice announced. It was Tomin. In his hand, he gripped a blue ribbon which he taped onto the back of Avery's t-shirt. "Avery! The girl is so ugly, she's gotta' kidnap a dog to have someone to play with. Heck, she doesn't even have parents because she's too ugly for them."

Avery ripped the ribbon from her back and smacked it on Tomin's shoulder. "Take it back."

"Where's your pathetic orphan dog?" he taunted. "Did he run away from you because you're an ugly orphan?"

"No one cares about your opinion, Tomin," Avery said.

She tucked her raven hair behind her ears.

Tomin took in Avery, from dirty tangerine sneakers to her messy wisps of flyways. "I speak facts, not opinions."

"Don't talk to my best friend like that," said Benji.

Graham Cracker barked.

"And who are you?" Tomin puffed his chest up, shoving Benji. "A pauper? Need I remind you, I'm the Cookie Prince around these parts."

"Tomin, isn't there a video game you should be playing?" asked Sam, annoyed. "Little kids on Twitch you should be bullying?"

Tomin frowned. "I'm grounded, Sam, thank you very much. No virtual reality, online games, or streaming for a week. All because I said my mom's dog cookie business is stupid. I mean, what's so special about dogs anyway? All Princess does is lick herself. Anyone could do that. The Fiddlesticks Cookie Empire should sponsor a video game tournament. Now, that'd be my chance. I could finally show my mom I'm a winner."

Marcus the Butler appeared from behind a hedge of macaroon cookies shaped like a shark. He interrupted with a polite cough. "Excuse me, Master Tomin, pardon the intrusion. Your driver awaits in the limousine."

Tomin smirked. He glanced at the obscenely large wristwatch, loose around his scrawny arm. "I guess it's that time. Well, my ride's here, see you losers at my party tonight." He raised his eyebrows at Avery. "Except you Avery."

"What? I'm coming to the party. I have an invite."

"You got invited when you had a dog. Word is he ran away from you cause you're super ug'." Tomin took a crumpled flier from the pocket of his basketball shorts and tossed it at Avery's face. She didn't flinch.

"Whatever. I'm going anyway. My aunt is in a bake-off with your mom."

"The rule is you can't come to the party unless you have a dog," said Tomin. "You can't just break rules when they don't suit you."

Avery's hands tingled. She eyed Tomin's wristwatch and wondered if she could make it heat up, light it aflame, like the photograph of her mom and their beagle in front of Cliff Cottage. She tried concentrating on the prickling sensation. She urged her palms to warm. But nothing happened. Then, she thought of another idea, inspired by none other than her promise-breaking Aunt Laurel and Tomin's ambitious mother.

"How about a bet then?" Avery tempted.

After all, the Fiddlesticks family seemed unable to turn down competition.

"A bet? Like what?"

"We take that limo of yours to go play sardines at Lurk Farms. Keep score. If you win, I stay away from your party. If I win, I go to the party, and you never speak to us again."

"Sure, why not," Tomin yawned. "Not like I'm allowed to play video games to entertain myself."

"Heck yes!" Sam pumped her fist in the air. Riley leaped with excitement. "This day just got interesting."

"I'm not going," Suzy stomped, Pearl hidden by her ankles. "No way."

"You gotta', Suze," urged Sam. "Sardines only works with enough players."

Suzy crossed her arms. "Fine. I'll go if Benji does."

Benji looked at Avery. "Didn't you say we were supposed to meet Miss Laurel in the parking lot?"

"Forget about Aunt Laurel. I'm done with her orders and rules."

CHAPTER 29

Bait and Switch

Last one to the farmhouse is a rotten Weirdie," Tomin taunted, his lanky body half out the door as the limousine rolled to a stop on the dirt road by Lurk Farm.

A cloud of dust puffed into the posh vehicle, sprinkling the leather seats and Avery's cheeks with soil. Through the dust cloud, the silhouettes of a colonial farmhouse, silo, and barn loomed in the distance, hazy haunted mirages.

Riley's paws squished Avery's sneakers. The Irish Setter leaped onto the road and charged into the sunny field, chasing after a squirrel. Graham Cracker lumbered afterward, finding a sniff-worthy bag of potato chips littered in the ditch.

"Hey, wait up!" Avery hollered, wiping her face with her sleeve. She hopped onto the shoulder of the gravel road. Graham Cracker circled under her legs. A sour smell blew by with an unexpected chill. She shivered as she sniffed the air. Was it snert?

"Cool. Right?" Sam ducked out of the limo. She looked

out to the graveyard of dead grass. "The Weirdies left a lot of strange things behind. I once found a cauldron in the corn stalks."

"Really?" Benji lit up, his interest piqued. "One time, I found a Monopoly game board in the dumpster of a pizza parlor. But both the thimble and the iron pieces were missing. What's the point of even playing, if you can't pass Go while pretending to smooth creases out of a shirt or stitch a pant cuff?"

"Don't touch anything," Suzy warned, eyeing a can of soda and a headless toy soldier tossed in the ditch. Pearl yapped at Suzy's ankles, begging her with baby doll eyes to be picked up. Suzy scooped her flat-faced fluff ball into her arms. "You never know what could be cursed."

Avery took in the horizon. The property went on for miles, puckered by the decrepit farmhouse, silo, and barn, and bordered by thick forest and dirt road. The remains of decayed crops hid rusted equipment and rotting carriages. There was a lot of ground to cover. Where would she even start?

Then, in the field far ahead by the farmhouse, the grass rustled, but in a way that wasn't natural, almost as though it was being plowed by a small animal in a rush to get somewhere or escape something. Avery rubbed her eyes—itchy from the dust. The rustling stopped. Had it all been her imagination? There was no way. She couldn't lose the trail.

"Come on, Tomin's way ahead!" Avery called over her shoulder to her friends. She jogged towards the farmhouse, her tangerine sneakers crunching against the flattened yellowed grass.

The farmhouse was made of faded, white-painted wood. On its crooked porch, Tomin slumped in a broken rocking chair, smacking cookie-flavored bubble gum. As he pushed the seat back and forth, it creaked and moaned. Behind him, a shattered window let light into the abandoned home. Suddenly, a shadow moved by the window behind him, inside the building.

"Tomin!" Avery shrieked.

"That's my name, don't wear it out," Tomin teased, oblivious.

Avery sprinted up the porch stairs. She peered past the broken glass of the window into the farmhouse's empty sitting room. A worn chair hibernated in the corner by a fireplace stuffed with sticks and hay. Cobwebs cast a sticky net over the space, as though undisturbed for years. Not a single footprint marked the layer of dust covering the splintered floor.

"I. . . I thought I saw someone," Avery muttered.

Had the shadow been a trick of lighting or Avery's mind? Or was it something more sinister?

She squished a mosquito against her skin. Where was Teddy? She worried and picked at the itch left by the insect.

"What a dump, right?" Tomin scoffed, scaring Avery as he snuck up behind her. "If I were a king, I'd have better digs than this pile of crud."

"Not everyone can live in a Sugar Shack, Tomin." Sam huffed as she climbed the stairs. Riley barked at a crawl space, having cornered a frightened squirrel.

"A king lived here?" Benji asked, walking to the farmhouse with Graham Cracker, and Suzy, who was nestling Pearl like an infant.

"Yep. King Weird, the leader of the Weirdies," Sam said. "Along with all of his wives. Rumor is, he had forty-four."

"Gross. Girls are dumb," spat Tomin.

Suzy stroked Pearl's head. "Not true."

"Suzy wants to marry King Weird," Tomin teased.

"Na uh." Suzy stuck out her tongue.

"Got your hat." Sam grabbed Tomin's ball cap and ran off.

Tomin chased after her, yelling, "Hey, give that back."

Avery ignored the childish bickering and focused on her mission—finding Teddy.

"Hey, Sam?" Avery called. "Did Garry happen to mention where he saw the Weirdie with worm hair and the umbrella?"

"He said she left the barn over there." Sam paused from fleeing Tomin to point to a faded barn by the tree line. "Put her umbrella up even though it wasn't raining, and then, she flew right into the woods." She zipped her hand over to the forest beyond the overgrown field.

"Probably heading to Stone Circle," Tomin snatched his hat from Sam and placed it over his greasy, blonde hair. "The ancient stone henge where Weirdies made dog stew."

"That's the most haunted place on this island." Suzy's voice shook as she cuddled Pearl tighter. "I hate it here. Let's go back to the Farmers Market."

Benji dug into his fanny pack. "You can have one of my safety pins, Suzy." He offered a shiny pin. "It may make you feel safer. It is, after all, called a safety pin."

"Are you going to chicken out, Suze?" Tomin balked, flapping his arms like poultry.

"No! It's just, I don't even really like sardines." She placed Pearl at the heels of her strappy sandals and affixed the safety pin to her summer frock, right over her heart. "I never win. I'm small but my allergies always let people find me. My sneezing gives me away."

"I have allergies, too," Benji sympathized.

"Really?" Suzy beamed. "What kind? I'm pollen, tree nuts, gluten, and dairy."

"I'm pollen, dander, kiwi, and mites. Do you like stamps?"

"I like stickers."

Avery grumbled. She had more important matters at hand than swapping lists of common interests and autoimmune reactions. For starters, searching the barn. If Garry had seen the Scorned Slider leaving the barn, maybe Teddy had been there too. Impatiently, she urged, "Can we get the game going already?"

"Yeah, what the orphan said," Tomin echoed. "Some of us have better things to do."

"I thought you were grounded from playing video games?" Sam rolled her eyes.

"Watching paint dry is better than hanging out with you chickens."

"We're not chickens," Suzy protested.

"All right, 'fraidy cats." Tomin clawed his hands in the air like a feline.

"Let's go over the rules quickly," said Sam. She held a

fistful of sticks, all appearing the same length. "Whoever pulls the shortest stick is the sardine and hides first. The sardine can hide anywhere within the boundaries: the road to the south, the forest to the north, and the broken gates to the east and west. For the rest of us, we'll count to one hundred then head off to search. No teaming up. Understood?"

"Fine, whatever." Tomin grabbed a stick from Sam. It was as long as his hand.

Avery's stick was shorter, but once they all compared, Benji had drawn the shortest stick.

"I guess you're hiding first, Benji," said Avery, noticing her friend's frown.

"Me? Do I have to?"

"You can bring Graham Cracker," assured Avery.

"What if I step on a nail and get lockjaw? What if a ladybug lands on my wrist and it pees on my hand? What if I get lost in a sinkhole?"

"Alright, maybe I should hide first," Avery grumbled.

"No way," Tomin interrupted. "He picked the shortest stick. Rules are rules. We count to one hundred while the scared pauper hides."

"You'll do great, Benji." Avery squeezed his shoulder. "It's just like scavenging in Chicago. Only, you're scavenging for a place where you can hide quietly."

"Okay," Benji said, reluctantly, staring at his shoes.

"Besides you have a safety pin." Suzy smiled, pointing to her pin over her heart. "So, you'll always be safe."

"Now, eyes closed," barked Tomin. "Even the dogs."

Riley laid on his belly and placed his paws over his

eyes, while Pearl mushed her face in the dirt.

"Ninety-nine, ninety-eight, ninety-seven—"

Benji's and Graham Cracker's footsteps crunched further in the distance. Avery's hands tingled. She wondered where Teddy might be.

"No peeking allowed," Tomin insisted. "Keep your eyes completely shut and don't cheat. Don't even think about cheating."

"Ninety-six, ninety-five, ninety-four—"

"Cover your pupils. Pull down your eyelid blinds. Keep counting and—" Tomin's voice drifted further and further away as the girls counted.

Riley barked, and Pearl joined in. Something was wrong.

Then, the sound of an engine thundered. Wheels squealed away. Avery opened her eyes. A storm cloud of dust puffed from the road.

"Sam, Suzy, stop counting!" Avery cried.

The limousine. It was driving down the dirt road, exhaust puffing. Tomin rolled down a window and stuck his tongue out. "So long suckers!"

"Tomin's left without us!"

CHAPTER 30

Lost and Found

The limousine peeled down the dirt road, leaving the three girls and two dogs in a cloud of dust.

"That conniving butthead." Sam kicked at a pebble. "I bet that was his plan all along."

"It's hours to walk back." Suzy frowned at her choice of footwear. "Blisters guaranteed."

Sam stuffed her hands in the pocket of her jean shorts. "Well, we better call out Benji and get a move on."

Avery's heart skipped. Move on? No. They couldn't. Not now. Not when Teddy was still out there, all alone. Her hands tingled again—the hot, scratchy sensation beginning in the middle of her palms, then intensifying towards her fingers and the ends of her fingertips. She curled her hands into fists.

"We can still play sardines," Avery urged. "Who needs stinking Tomin, right? He doesn't have to ruin our fun."

"We needed his ride," Suzy moaned. "If we wanted to make it to Freedom Fest before dark."

Sam rallied. "Let's find Benji and start walking to Sugar Shack ASAP. Maybe we'll make it in time for fireworks."

"Come out, come out, wherever you are!" bellowed Suzy.

"Game's over!" shouted Sam.

As they searched for Benji, they came to a spot where the field opened on the faded barn with a skeletal frame of crooked planks and wood slabs, contorted like an old man with a hunchback. A rusted chain knotted around its doors.

"Careful," Suzy warned, as Avery neared the barn. "So much as sneeze and the whole thing could come tumbling down."

"You break it, you buy it," Sam teased.

Avery wondered if there was a way inside. Around the corner, flies circled a puddle of mud, near a rusted ax stuck in a log. The flies swarmed Avery. As she swatted them away, prints in the mud caught her attention. They were paw prints. Small paw prints. Teddy-sized. Her eyes widened.

"You found something?" Suzy asked.

"Pawprints. Maybe from my lost dog?"

Sam lifted a broken shovel, as though she might find Benji underneath. She let it drop again into the dirt. "I thought he's not your dog."

"That's not the point," Avery argued in frustration. "These are Teddy's paw prints."

Sam eyed the muddy marks. "I don't know, Avery. Looks like rabbit tracks to me."

Riley sniffed at the tracks and sat at Sam's feet, as though in agreement with her on the matter.

"Rabbit? No, it's Teddy. We have to find him."

"We have to find Benji and Graham Cracker," said Sam, stubbornly. "We can look for your imaginary dog some other day."

"He's not make-believe. Benji, tell them," Avery said, instinctively looking to her best friend for support. He wasn't there. She bit her lip. "I mean, Benji can tell you."

"Yeah, when we find him." Sam glanced at the face of her sports watch. "It's already late afternoon. Why don't we split up? That way we can cover more ground."

"Are you sure that's a good idea?" Suzy asked, Pearl at her ankles. "I'm too scared to watch horror movies, so I wouldn't know, but that just seems like it's a bad idea."

"Fine, Suzy, you and the dogs come with me," said Sam, annoyed. "Avery, are you okay on your own? Or are you too scared?"

Avery's hands twinged, pulsing with heat. She'd never fit in. Being on her own seemed like it was her fate. "I'm fine," she said, stuffing her hands in her pockets. She was used to being alone, after all. She was an orphan. A dogless, orphan. . . . Unless she could find Teddy again.

It was better this way, being alone. She could do what she wanted and get things done.

She could save her dog.

CHAPTER 31

Barnhouse

Dead grass nipped at Avery's calves, as she circled the barn, following the trail of paw prints. Prickles ignited from the center of her palms, racing up her arms and into her neck. Was someone watching her? When she looked over her shoulder, all she saw were decayed fields and the abandoned farmhouse and silo.

Sam and Suzy had trekked off. But Avery didn't care. If they weren't going to help her find Teddy, she was better off without them. Fitting in wasn't everything it was cracked up to be if it meant not being able to do what was right. Sometimes, forging one's own path was the best way forward.

Avery came to a crack in the barn wall, where a wood plank bent from its frame. "Teddy! You in there?" she hollered. Titling her neck, she tried to poke her head in for a better view, scraping her scalp against the plank's rough edge.

"Ouch." She rubbed her head and stretched her arms. "Brute strength it is."

Avery gripped the loose board and heaved it aside with all her might, slivers slicing into her palms. Sweat formed on her forehead under her messy, black bangs. She heard a rustling in the barn. "Teddy?" she shouted, but there was no response. Avery popped the board free, then, exhaling, she sucked in her stomach and squeezed through the crevice.

From a hole in the roof, sunlight filtered in, illuminating dust motes suspended in a slow-motion descent. A bridle covered in cobwebs hung in a horse stall. Shadows played tricks, casting projections of tombstones on the crooked walls.

"Teddy? Benji?" Avery called out, her voice cracking. "Graham Cracker?" Her knees shook. A chill vibrated down her spine. She clasped her damp, sweaty hands together. Suddenly, she wished she wasn't alone, that Sam and Suzy were with her. Even if she didn't quite fit in with the girls. Even if they were off doing their own thing, looking for Benji. Avery was beginning to think fitting in had less to do with following a pack and more to do with being yourself but still having others to turn to when things got tough or scary. "Anyone?"

She climbed over a fallen rafter. A nail caught her shoelace and she fell forward, landing on her hands and knees beside a mountain of wooden debris. Then, the whole pile quaked. It erupted like a volcano, sawdust spurting into the air. Avery screamed and shuffled backwards.

A white mouse with beady red eyes peeped out from the rubble. It twitched its snout, as though laughing at Avery, before scurrying through a fox hole under a barn wall, vanishing.

Avery's heart pounded. "It was only a mouse," she said to herself, taking a deep breath. "Just a little rodent. The kind who would help a princess dress for a ball in a fairy tale."

She hoped Sam and Suzy hadn't heard her shrieks. "It's nothing to be scared of, Avery Isadora," she scolded herself aloud. "Nothing to jump and scream over. Nothing to—Ahhh!!!"

A hideous creature landed on her back, its claws digging through her t-shirt, whiskers bristling against her neck. She shrieked, flailing her arms wildly. Whatever the critter was tumbled to the floor, then pitter-pattered to Avery's feet, jumping up to put its paws on her knees, licking her fingers and howling for joy.

"Teddy!"

Avery almost couldn't believe it. Teddy's soft paws tapped her legs and face, as he crawled onto her, rubbing his cheeks against her face. He lovingly pressed his snout under her chin and whimpered with joy. He licked her nose with his bumpy tongue, tail motoring, then flopped onto his back, to soak up all of Avery's rubs. All the while, his loyal eyes stayed glued to Avery's, like he would never look away, ever again.

Avery embraced Teddy, petting his head, and rubbing his stomach as he twisted and turned. "I knew I'd find you."

"Aarr, arff." He hopped up and stretched back in a downward dog, wagging his tail.

Then, *swoosh,* a streak of light crossed the sky, flooding the barn with blinding brightness. Avery held

Teddy tight. With a crash, the barn rumbled, dust raining down from the rafters, as the light disappeared.

"What was that?" Avery asked.

Teddy growled, his tail between his legs, his attention fixed on the forest in the distance, visible through the cracks of the barn planks.

Avery's eyes watered. Something was burning. She walked towards the barn wall, followed by Teddy. Peeking between the wood planks, tendrils of smoke curled into the air beyond the tree line, forming shapes that reminded Avery of squiggling worms. Something, or someone, crashed into the woods. Had it been a meteor? Lightning? There were no storm clouds in the sky.

Then what had it been?

"The Scorned Slider." The words fell out of Avery's mouth.

Teddy suddenly scurried away, and before Avery could react, he was half under the fox hole, floppy ears and stomach out of the barn.

"Teddy! Wait!" Avery scrambled after him. By the time she made it to the hay-covered floor, Teddy was already outside, sprinting towards the forest. It wasn't a smart idea to run towards the crash, towards the smoke. Avery was perfectly safe inside the barn. But she couldn't let Teddy go off on his own. She had to stick by her pal because that's what being a friend was all about.

Avery crawled through the foxhole on her hands and knees. Pebbles scraped her skin and jagged wood planks scratched against her back as she pulled herself under the wall. She clambered to her feet, as Teddy disappeared into the plume of thick smoke streaming from the woods.

"Teddy! You're going the wrong way!" she shouted, chasing after him through the dead grass. "Home is the opposite direction!"

She didn't have a good feeling about this, but she had to go after him. She couldn't lose him. Not again.

An overgrown path led into the forest then snaked through fallen trees, misfit branches, and mossy roots, arching and twining. Avery pushed through the branches, slicing her arms and calves. The cuts stung. She could taste smoke, the air heavier, murky. "Teddy?" she called out into the abyss.

A branch snapped. Avery looked towards the noise and caught the sight of Teddy's jaunty tail hopping into a bush. "That's him." Without a second thought, she dove after him.

But behind the bush, the forest floor dropped unexpectedly down a steep hill, rolling into a meadow below. Avery lost her footing. She tried to dig her heels into the dirt, but it was too late for brakes. She launched downwards, tumbling head over heels. The woods, the sky, rocks, the sky—her world spun. With a painful smack, she collided against a prickly object. Dizzy, it took her a moment to realize she was no longer spinning. She had flopped against a toppled tree trunk. The wetness against her cheek was Teddy's snout, pressing his nose against her face, trying to rouse her.

Teddy whimpered. He nudged his snout against her shoulder, urgently. He bit the cuff of her t-shirt and tugged.

"Okay, okay," she said, pushing herself upright.

Her stomach tossed, and bile rose in her throat. But it wasn't just from the fall. A putrid smell overwhelmed her nasal glands. She gagged, covering her mouth, drool spilling onto her hand. As she turned her head to look past the tree trunk, she realized where she was. She froze.

There, at the bottom of the meadowy hill, a patch of grass smoldered, hot and smoky. It looked like a lightning bolt had crashed through the sky and landed smack dab in the middle of the mysterious meadow. Surrounding the smoldering grass was a circle of perfectly arranged smooth boulders. Boulders that towered like overseeing giants. It reminded Avery of photos she had seen of Stonehenge in England.

"Stone Circle," Avery mouthed.

The most haunted place on Beaver Island.

And there, in the center of the henge, was the Scorned Slider.

And she wasn't alone.

CHAPTER 32

Stone Circle

The Scorned Slider cowered before a looming man in a silver cloak. Her worm hair coiled into frightened spirals, the man's shadow falling over her. Embedded in the man's bald head, was a rusted crown, as though its spikes painfully protruded straight from his scaly skin. His beard was gristly and silver, winding at the tip into a hypnotizing curl. Even from afar, his eyes brewed with violent clouds, pupils pulsing with the power of a hurricane.

In his fist, he clutched the snath—the long handle of a dangerous scythe—the scythe's blade sharp and ready, glinting in the strange light.

Avery held her breath.

This couldn't be. . . .

There was no way. . . .

It was. . . .

"King Weird, your majesty." The Scorned Slider trembled, eyes down, as though she dared not meet the gaze of the menacing presence.

"Wornher," he said, his voice low and powerful,

rumbling from deep inside the Earth. "How dare you appear at my altar without the dog. Where is the terrier? Theodore Dogmore the Third, sworn guardian of the Dog Dimension? Where is HE? Answer me, Wornher!"

Wornher. So, that was the Scorned Slider's name. And Teddy's full name was Theodore Dogmore the Third, and he was from Dog Dimension. Had Avery heard that right? Then, who was Harmony? Confused and full of questions, Avery looked to the terrier at her side, hiding behind the upended tree trunk.

Teddy seethed—angry eyes, alert snout, stiff tail, and bared teeth focused on the figures in the stone henge below. Foam formed at the corners of his mouth. This wasn't the furball of cuteness Avery had come to know. Angry. Vicious. Who was he, really? And how could he, a tiny terrier, stand a chance against the towering King Weird and wicked Wornher? For a moment, Avery became wary of her furry friend. There was so much she didn't know about him. Yet, deep in her gut, she felt like she could trust him.

Wornher trembled as she scrambled to her feet. "Your majesty, I nearly had the terrier. I uncovered his hiding place, had him by the scruff of his tail, but then—"

"But then what?" King Weird roared.

Wornher lowered her eyes. She whispered, "He ran away." Wornher swallowed a lump in her throat. Bracing for his reaction to her words, she retreated into the folds of her cloak, hunching. She wrung the fabric with her warty hands.

"Outsmarted by a terrier? A yappy dog, the size of a large rat? Tell me, how many times has this tiny terrier foiled your Sacred and Wicked Mission so far, hmmm?"

"What happened last time was unexpected," Wornher pleaded desperately. "Poisoning the doggie water dish outside Beaver Dam's Good Ice Cream on the first day of Spring, why, I would have transformed every canine on the island if that terrier hadn't interfered. I never expected a dog could burn the whole shop down!"

Avery nearly gasped aloud when she realized—that's why Teddy had a glop of strawberry sauce in his fur when she first rescued him! That's why the ice cream shop was a smoldering wreckage the first day Aunt Laurel and she had arrived on Beaver Island. Because Teddy had stopped Wornher from poisoning the ice cream shop's doggie water dish by burning down the whole shop. Teddy had saved the day! He had saved the island's dogs from poison! He was a hero!

"All that ice cream wasted," King Weird said, longingly, as though grieving the lost frozen desserts. Rage flooded his features. "Tell me, why shouldn't I transform you into a mosquito this instant?"

"Because the Blood Moon isn't until midnight," Wornher groveled, desperately, folding her hands in supplication. "I still have time to succeed at my Sacred and Wicked Mission, to repay my debt to you, Your Majesty, for granting me refuge all these years after the Goodness Council kicked me out of my home dimension. You gave me until the Blood Moon. And technically, the Blood Moon doesn't reach its fullest until the clock strikes twelve. Just allow me that grace to complete my Sacred and Wicked Mission, my King."

"Mission?" Avery mouthed, silently.

King Weird scoffed. He paced around Wornher, his stature only trumped by the massive boulder slabs of Stone Circle. "You expect me to believe you'll capture Theodore Dogmore the Third and eliminate all the dogs of Beaver Island before midnight? You? A *loser*?"

"Yes. I will," Wornher insisted, voice laden with false confidence. "I have a brilliant plan. Simply ingenious this time. By the time the Blood Moon reaches its full size, Beaver Island will be a canine-free zone, once and for all."

An unsettling feeling surged in Avery's chest, rising in her throat. *What*? Did she hear that correctly? Wornher's Sacred and Wicked Mission was to eliminate all of the dogs on Beaver Island. Not just Teddy, but Riley? Pearl? Graham Cracker? Even Princess? They were all in danger.

She looked at Teddy, his mouth still quivering in a low growl. Then, it clicked. Wornher was chasing Teddy, but Teddy was also chasing her. That's why he had led Avery to Stone Circle. That's why he ran away from Cliff Cottage. It wasn't because he didn't love Avery, it was because he was trying to stop Wornher's plan from succeeding.

"You're trying to stop them, aren't you? From hurting the dogs?" She whispered, moving closer to Teddy's triangle ears. "That's why they're after you? And that's why you're after them?"

Teddy looked back at Avery, his button eyes serious. He nodded. At least, Avery thought she saw him nod. Yes, that was a definite nod, she decided. Avery was sure of it. Teddy was trying to save the dogs of Beaver Island. And she would help. No matter what. No matter how fast her heart was beating or how much her legs trembled. She needed to be brave.

"Trust me, my liege. Tonight, all of the dogs of Beaver Island are gathering for a Fourth of July party at a mansion on the cliff. With my energy poison," Wornher dug into her cloak pocket and brought out a green vial which she held between her thumb and forefinger. It pulsed with a radioactive green glow. "I shall turn all the dogs of Beaver Island into hot dogs."

Avery clasped her hand over her mouth so as not to gasp. Her palms were warm against her face. *Hot dogs*? She dreaded the thought of her favorite pooches transforming into concession stand snacks. What if they were smothered in onions and ketchup? What if seagulls descended in a hungry frenzy and ate them all?

Avery recalled Aunt Laurel's warning: "*We are forbidden from manipulating animate matter. . . . It will rot you from the inside out.*"

Is that why Wornher had become a Scorned Slider? Because she planned on manipulating the matter of living, breathing dogs?

Avery's heart pounded louder. She swore the whole world could hear it beating. They had to stop Wornher. But how? Suddenly, Avery wished Aunt Laurel had covered Slider lessons with her. She never thought in a million years that she'd long for her aunt's lectures, but here she was, surprising herself. Avery's hands felt prickly and itchy. She thought back to how she had lit the photos aflame. Could she do it again? If so, how? She hadn't really burned that photo with her bare palms, or had she? And if so, could she do it again?

King Weird glared. He slammed his scythe snath into the ground, a quake vibrated throughout the forest floor. Birds fled from their nests, escaping into the sky with squeaky protests. The blade of King Weird's scythe glistened red, mirroring his anger. "Your plan will never work, foolish Slider."

Wornher shook. "But, but, of course, it will, King Weird, I promise."

"Not unless you capture the mutt!" King Weird bellowed. "The terrible terrier. Theodore Dogmore the Third. He's thwarted you before, and he'll thwart you again. I want him eliminated. Understand me? He's a threat to us all while he's alive! He's vicious, he's brutal, he's—" King Weird froze. He flared his nostrils, as though he had picked up on a scent. He slowly walked around the perimeter of Stone Circle. With each footstep, he moved slower, smelling the air. He stopped in his tracks. "He's here," he said with a deliberate and quiet snarl.

Suddenly, he aimed his raging blade straight towards Teddy and Avery's hiding place behind the upturned tree root. A surge of energy blasted from the scythe blade, crashing against the tree trunk which exploded into a million bits of sawdust, leaving Avery and Teddy exposed. "Run!" Avery yelled as she rolled over onto a mossy patch and sprang to her feet, Teddy sprinting away in the opposite direction.

"It's him! It's the terrible terrier! Get him!" King Weird commanded.

Wornher stood upright and plucked a squiggling worm

from her scalp. She bit the critter, holding it in between her teeth as she stretched the creature until it was several feet long. With the rope-like worm, Wornher fashioned a lasso and threw its loop out and around Teddy. The terrier barked, snapping at the constricting worm.

"Let him go!" Avery ran to help the terrier. She thudded against a solid wall. No, not a wall, a strong body as sturdy as concrete. It was King Weird. In one motion, he twirled behind Avery, slicing the wood snath of his scythe under her chin, gripping her in a chokehold. Avery struggled, but it was useless.

"Well, well," King Weird taunted. "Who do we have here?"

Avery could hardly breathe, let alone answer.

King Weird smelled Avery's hair, slowly inhaling her essence. He reeked like a rotten corpse. "I know who you are." His words sent shivers down Avery's spine. "You're Wendy's daughter."

Wendy's daughter? No one had ever called Avery that before. The mention of her mom sent tingles through her spine.

"You," Avery struggled to speak, trying to pull King Weird's wooden snath away from her vocal cords. "You—knew—my—mom?" she managed to ask. Her hands throbbed against the wood snath of the scythe.

"Of course, I did," said King Weird. "Your mother was as Scorned as they come."

That can't be!

A surge of anger emitted from Avery's heart, flooding her body, then bursting free. Wisps curled from the snath under Avery's grip, smoke tickling her nose. She was searing the scythe's handle with her hands!

"Fire?" King Weird sniffed.

The wood snath of the scythe lit aflame, singeing Avery's chin and the ends of her black hair. King Weird dropped his weapon, and Avery ran as fast as she could towards Teddy, grasping her scalding throat.

"Stop her!" King Weird screamed.

That's when her entire body prickled with thousands, then millions of burning needles. Avery was on fire.

No, Avery *was* fire.

Her particles tore apart with a sharp sensation, and she was sprinkled into billions of pieces, orbiting around each other in dizzying galaxies of flame.

She could see Wornher and King Weird yelling, but she couldn't hear what they were saying above the whirling energy, as her infinite bits and pieces spun faster and faster until the entire world was a blur.

Suddenly, Avery evaporated into the gaps between space and time.

CHAPTER 33

Warp To Cliff Cottage

With a whipping pain, Avery's atoms melded into form. She touched her neck, red and blistered. *Ouch.* She flinched. High-pitch ringing echoed in her ears. She stumbled, dizzy, catching herself against a splintered, wood wall, her eyesight blurry and clouded.

Where am I?

Her senses blended and swirled in confusion. What was that awful smell, putrid as it sloshed in her saliva? *Snert?* She gagged. She tried to spit the odor from her mouth, but the smell coated her tongue, burrowing into her taste buds.

King Weird.

She panicked. Her throat constricted, as she remembered the snath of King Weird's scythe pressed under her chin.

You're Wendy's daughter.

Teddy.

Avery tumbled, coming to balance against another grainy wall, a few feet from the other. Her focus blurry, she couldn't figure out her surroundings, though with the walls so close together, it felt like she was in a rectangular box. Like a coffin. No, it was too big for a coffin. It was more like a closet or a pantry.

Shakily, she waved her hands in front of her like giant antennas. She felt a metal latch.

An exit! She fiddled with the hook, and it came loose, the door swinging open, light flooding Avery's blurry vision.

She fell to her hands and knees, onto a dirt path—the silhouette of a log cabin in the distance. She blinked, her vision finally clearing. Cliff Cottage's roof, poking through the birch, cedar, oak, and pine, comforted, yet confused Avery. She was no longer at Stone Circle.

What in the world? She panicked. *Where is Teddy?*

Plunk, plunk, plunk.

The wooden door, hook unlatched from its eye, bobbed against the outhouse's frame in the breeze.

Well, that explains the smell, Avery realized. She had mysteriously found herself one moment at Stone Circle and the next moment in the outhouse at Cliff Cottage.

Mysteriously or by sliding through space?

Avery felt ill.

She pressed herself to her feet. How of all places had she ended up in the outhouse at Cliff Cottage? Frantically, she looked inside the wooden shack. It smelled like a dump, a lavender candle on a dish in the corner unable to fend off stench with an unarmed wick.

"Teddy?" Avery shouted, her voice echoing in the woodsy interior. Where was he? She plugged her nose, and in vain, lifted the wooden toilet seat. Her stomach curdled, though there was nothing but endless darkness down the deep hole. "You down there?" she called. No response.

She barged outside, faced with the forest which encircled Cliff Cottage. The branches arched and swayed. "Teddy! I'm here! Come out!" The woods answered with the rustling of leaves and the cracking of branches. In other words, it was no help.

Avery ran down the path towards the cabin, desperately hollering Teddy's name.

"Avery!" Aunt Laurel appeared from around a corner, eyes puffy and swollen. She rushed towards her niece, embracing Avery in a tight squeeze. "Thank the Goodness Council. You're safe now." Aunt Laurel sniffed, chest heaving, as though she was holding back tears. "Everyone was looking for you. We found Benji and Graham Cracker on the side of the road, by Lurk Farms. Then, we found Sam and Suzy and their dogs. No one knew where you were. I was worried sick. I thought you were in danger." Aunt Laurel took in her niece's appearance, concerned: singed hair, blistered neck, arms and legs cut up from branches. Her expression twisted with concern and fear. "You *were* in danger. Look at you. Your knees. Your throat."

"I don't know how I got here," Avery confessed. As she shifted, her cheek brushed against Aunt Laurel's locket. The hot metal throbbed against her skin. She flinched and pulled away. It was as hot as Avery's hands had been when she burned King's Weird's scythe handle. A supernatural sort of heat.

Did the locket have something to do with it?

Swirls of confusion formed a picture in Avery's mind like clouds in a sky. Had her Aunt Laurel warped her to Cliff Cottage? Did she have Slider energy hidden away inside the tarnished locket she always wore?

"Wait, did you—did you bring me here?" Avery asked.

"Avery," Aunt Laurel lowered her eyes. She touched the locket, her fingers recoiling from the heat. She blew on the charm, as though to cool it, then, carefully, she pried it open with her fingernails to reveal a photo inside. It was Avery's mother. She seemed to smile, her eyes filling with a caring warmth. Aunt Laurel explained, "This necklace is powered with energy to keep you safe. It was your mother's. It sort of has a mind of its own, but yes, it let me know you were in danger. The rest was up to the locket."

Avery pulled away, angry. "But I nearly had him back! Now he's in danger! And I can't help him. All because of some dumb necklace charm!"

"Had who back? Help *who*?"

"Teddy!" Avery burst.

"The dog did this to you?" Aunt Laurel assumed, accusingly. Her forehead scrunched with scorn. "This is war. Sliders versus dogs. I'll write to the Goodness Council at once. They'll send troops. A canine cannot harm one of us without consequence."

"What? Teddy didn't hurt me. He's trying to save dogkind from Wornher's plan to transform all the dogs on Beaver Island into hot dogs!" Avery shouted. "And we had nearly escaped. Sure, King Weird had me in a chokehold with his Grim Reaper blade, but I broke free all on my own. Without you. Without your useless locket. I would have saved Teddy too, but then, your locket charm zapped me into the outhouse of all places." Avery caught her breath, exasperated. "I left Teddy all alone, with Wornher and King Weird, with no one to protect him. And he is the one terrier who can stop Wornher from fulfilling her Sacred and Wicked Mission before the Blood Moon."

Aunt Laurel's face went blank and still, her Orion constellation shrinking. For a few moments, she stood still as a statue. Then, she came to, as though waking up from a brief sleep, a mental checkout. She blinked. "I may have just blacked out. Can you repeat what you said? All this stress must be getting to me. Selling Cliff Cottage because Ghizwhisch Fiddlesticks is sabotaging my store. Gearing up for a bake-off to save my business and this cabin. Rescuing Joseph and Benji from their sinking boat. Having to deal with ghosts from my past. Etcetera, etcetera."

Avery, annoyed, stomped in the dirt. "I — was — just — about — to — save — Teddy — from — Wornher — and — King Weird."

Aunt Laurel blinked again. "King Weird?"

Avery spoke urgently. Why couldn't her Aunt Laurel follow along? They didn't have any time to spare, the full moon was already glowing in the early evening sky. "Teddy led me to Stone Circle. Wornher, the Scorned Slider, is going to turn all the dogs from Beaver Island into hot dogs. At Freedom Fest. Tonight. Before the Blood Moon."

Aunt Laurel's skin greened. Her constellation of stars was lost now in a toxic, gaseous fume. "Did you say King Weird?"

"For the billionth time, *yes*. He's going to transform

Wornher into a mosquito if she fails at her Sacred and Wicked Mission. And if she succeeds, then it's game over for all of the dogs on this island. Graham Cracker. Teddy. Pearl, Riley, and even Princess. All of them."

Aunt Laurel trembled. "You saw King Weird? And survived?"

"I got away from him." Avery wiggled her fingers. "Guess I'm coming into my abilities after all. And I would have escaped with Teddy too, if it hadn't been for your junky locket."

"We're leaving. Now," Aunt Laurel snapped. "We are packing the jeep this instant and heading out on the next ferry. King Weird is ruthless, he's vicious, he'll never stop until he gets what he wants."

Aunt Laurel fumbled her phone as she slipped it from her pocket, dropping it to the grass. She picked it up and rubbed the dew against the sleeve of the mauve hoodie tied around her waist.

"Didn't you hear me, Auntie L?" Avery asked, frustrated.

Aunt Laurel ignored her niece, hunching over her phone and talking to herself, as though she was her own coach, "You can fix this, Laurel. Everything's going to be okay. Just get the heck off this island. You should have listened to your mother and never have come back here. Oh, Goodness Council, my mother was right all along."

"Hello. Earth to Aunt Laurel. We can't leave. We have to save Teddy. We have to save all of the dogs! Do whatever it takes to stop Wornher."

"Avery, it's too dangerous. It's out of the question."

"Did King Weird have something to do with my parents' disappearance? With the disappearance of the beagle we had when I was a baby?"

Sadness flooded Aunt Laurel's grey eyes, like tsunami waves of pain. "Why would you ask that?"

"King Weird knew I was Wendy's daughter," Avery said. "He said she was Scorned. That's not true, is it?"

"Avery, this isn't the time," Aunt Laurel interrupted, focused again on the screen of her phone. "There's no ferry spots open until tomorrow." She fiddled with her locket, forgetting its pulsing heat. She cringed. "We won't go to the party. We'll stay inside with the doors locked and the curtains shut until dawn. Then, we'll leave first thing in the morning."

"It won't make a difference," said Avery. "If we don't stop Wornher, she'll manipulate the matter of all of the dogs on this island and turn them into hot dogs. What do you think the party guests will do once Wornher transforms their dogs into concession stand snacks? They'll grab pitchforks and torches and hunt for the Weirdies who did this! Just like they did to Great-Grandma Elsie. Guaranteed."

Aunt Laurel tensed. The fine worry lines on her forehead sunk into deep trenches. "What do you expect me to do, Avery?"

"I expect that together, you and I will save the dogs," Avery rallied. "That we find Teddy and stop Wornher. King Weird said it himself, Teddy is the one canine who can thwart Wornher's plot. He's stopped her before."

"We can't help the dogs, they're our sworn enemies.

We're at war!" Aunt Laurel argued.

"You've broken the rules before, Auntie L," Avery pointed out. "When you came back to Cliff Cottage against your mom's rule."

"That's different."

"The night we lost Teddy, you said that sometimes, doing what's right makes it impossible to follow the rules."

Before Aunt Laurel could answer, a scampering of paws sounded from the dirt path. Graham Cracker stampeded towards Avery. The Golden Retriever leaped up, paws resting on Avery's shoulders, giving her a big, furry hug. Graham Cracker licked Avery's nose, then hopped up and down, howling excitedly.

"Someone sure missed you," Aunt Laurel noted. Avery swore she heard a crack in her aunt's voice.

"I missed her too," Avery kneeled to rub Graham Cracker's head. The Golden Retriever mix pressed her snout against Avery's chin, lovingly. The moment melted Avery's heart. How could she let anything happen to her fur friend? How could her aunt? Avery looked up to Aunt Laurel, eyes pleading, "We can't let Graham Cracker become—" She placed her hands over Graham Cracker's floppy yellow ears. "A hot dog."

Aunt Laurel's constellation swelled. For a moment, Avery thought she spotted tears welling in her aunt's grey eyes. Slider or not, Avery knew her Aunt Laurel had a heart, that she cared for Graham Cracker deep down. She had to. Avery thought of all the times Graham Cracker sat eagerly at Aunt Laurel's feet, tail wagging, waiting to perform a trick for a Barkleby Biscuit at the chef's command. How

Aunt Laurel's constellation seemed to twinkle when Graham Cracker happily produced her paw for a high five.

Aunt Laurel massaged her temples. "I'll write to the Goodness Council. I'll explain that they need to do something to stop Wornher."

Avery's jaw dropped with dismay. "You're leaving it to politicians to save the day?"

Graham Cracker barked, as though to agree with Avery's protest.

"Your point is duly noted," Aunt Laurel sighed. "But we're desperate. It's the only way."

"It's not," Avery said. She looked to her own palms, itchy with prickles, then to Aunt's tarnished locket dangling around her neck. Maybe the necklace wasn't the only place Aunt Laurel had energy hidden away. "We're Sliders, remember?"

"It's too dangerous," Aunt Laurel warned. She clutched her rusted locket, the charm energized to protect Avery. "My whole life has been about keeping you safe."

"And look, I'm still standing. Now, it's time to let me grow up." She softened her voice, "You kept me safe my whole life so far, now it's time for us to keep each other safe. And save the dogs of Beaver Island. Deal?"

"I can't believe I'm saying this," Aunt Laurel twisted the necklace chain around her fingers, eyes panning from her niece to the Golden Retriever mix with the puppy dog eyes. "Deal."

Graham Cracker howled.

CHAPTER 34

Slider Time

In a frenzy, Aunt Laurel ran to the cabin, Graham Cracker at her heels. "Did Wornher say how exactly she was going to transform that many dogs into hot dogs?"

Avery tripped over her undone laces as she ran after them. Too jittery to tie her shoelaces in a neat bow, Avery instead messily stuffed them in the sides of her shoes and jumped back to her feet, dusting off her hands. "No." Then the image of the green toxic vial flashed in her mind. "But she had a concoction of some sort. A poison!"

Aunt Laurel halted at the cabin's back door. "The canine cookies. I bet she's going to poison the batter. We have to convince Ghizwhisch Fiddlesticks to cancel the bake-off."

"But what about Cliff Cottage? And Barkleby Biscuits, your shop?" Avery asked. She knew the cabin didn't mean anything in comparison to the lives of the island's dogs. But still. It was the first time Avery considered that saving dogkind would have consequences she hadn't thought of before.

"It's the only way," said Aunt Laurel, hand on the doorknob. "Sometimes, doing what's right comes at a big cost."

Before Avery could make it past the stoop, Graham Cracker bulldozed into the cabin, kicking up the pilly carpet in the living room with her paws and then plummeting through stacked boxes, as though rushing to tell Joseph about the good news that Avery was back.

"Avery." Joseph popped up from his mountainous mess of Dog Lingo 42 parts on the kitchen table. He wore a hat with a built-in headlamp and magnifying glasses, his green eyes appearing twice their usual size behind the lenses. "You're found! It's a discovery of the most extraordinary nature." He tripped over the garden hoses and ventilation tubes on his way towards Avery and Graham Cracker.

"Yeah," Avery shrugged, "Turns out I was just in the outhouse the entire time."

"Really?" Joseph asked, astonished. "You know, I was trying to get the Dog Lingo 42 running again so I could interrogate Graham as to your whereabouts."

Then another voice. "Avery! You're okay!" Benji's feet echoed through the cabin as he hopped down the stairs. In his hand, he held a piece of paper and an orange marker. "I was making Lost Avery posters," he confessed, showing Avery his work.

Avery squinted and tilted her head. "Looks more like a skunk from this angle."

Benji rolled his eyes.

"She was in the outhouse the entire time," Joseph explained.

"Really?" asked Benji, confused. "How? I was with you at Lurk Farms. It's a two-hour walk."

"I jogged?"

Benji scrunched his nose, perplexed. "But, why?"

"Ah," Avery hesitated. She didn't have any explanation but Aunt Laurel's locket. She stuffed her hands, tingly, into the pockets of her tangerine shorts and shrugged. "When you gotta go, you gotta go."

Then Aunt Laurel looked at her wrist, even though she was not wearing a watch, and said hurriedly, "Well, would you look at the time. Chop, chop, let's get going, Avery. I have a bake-off to call off."

"Call off?" Joseph repeated, confused. "Well, that's all right if you got stage fright. We can focus on the party festivities and pitching my invention to Mrs. Fiddlesticks for a sizable investment."

"Sorry, Joseph, Avery and I are going to Freedom Fest alone. I'm sorry." She choked on a lump in her throat. She averted her eyes. "You weren't invited."

Joseph's jaw dropped. "Laurel, you can't be serious," he forced a chuckle, awkwardly. "Every dog on this island is going."

"We need their help," Avery pleaded to her Aunt Laurel. Besides, Joseph and Benji were their closest friends. Friends helped each other out, and even so, sometimes it was very hard to ask for help. But if they couldn't rely on their friends now, when they needed them the most, then when?

"If every dog on the island is invited," stated Benji, matter of fact in his tone. "That would include Graham

Cracker, would it not?"

Aunt Laurel dug her ankles in. "I'm not changing my mind. This—this is serious."

"Please, Auntie L," begged Avery. "We should stick together."

"It'll only put them in danger."

"Danger?" Joseph questioned, taken aback. "I mean, sure, the kids might get a bit sugar high, but it's a national holiday."

"It's not that," Aunt Laurel said. "I can't explain, not now. Trust me, Joseph. It's the right decision." She unfurled the cabin's key from her keyring. She placed it in Joseph's hand, squeezing his palm shut. "Lock the doors. Whatever you do, don't let anyone in. Especially if they have pitchforks or torches. Or if they smell like pea soup without a good reason."

Joseph lowered his eyes at the rusted key. "I get it. I'm an embarrassment, aren't I?" His green eyes pooling with tears behind his eyeglasses. "You don't want to be seen in public with me."

"No, Joseph, please, it's not personal," said Aunt Laurel.

"It's not me, it's you. Right?" Joseph ran his greasy fingers through his hair leaving a streak of slick in his floppy mane. "I know I'm not exactly arm candy, but I thought we were friends."

"We are," insisted Aunt Laurel. "That's why I need you to stay behind."

"Are you afraid that you might lose the bake-off, Miss Laurel?" Benji asked. "Because you're the most amazing canine cookie chef in all of Chicago, and even if you did fail, who cares? We'll still be there for you. We'll cheer you on, no matter what."

"That's not true," Aunt Laurel muttered.

"Of course, it is, Laurel," agreed Joseph.

"No, you say that now, but the moment that you find out who I really am, you'll turn on me. Just like the villagers turned on my Grandma Elsie. Just like they ran her off Beaver Island."

"Wait," Joseph stopped. "What are you saying? Was your grandma. . . one of those Weirdies?"

The accusation hung in the air. Aunt Laurel finally took a breath. "Yes." She cast her eyes down to her motorcycle boots, unable to look at the reaction on Joseph's face. She wrapped her locket in her first. "I come from a long line of Weirdies. Same with Avery. We call ourselves Sliders. We come from another dimension. But we're still God's children, just like you."

"And we're not bad," Avery interrupted. She wanted to clear the air straight away. They weren't dog-hating Scorned Sliders. They were going to save the dogs of Beaver Island, after all. Even though they were breaking the rules, Avery figured they wouldn't rot from the inside out. Not when they were doing what was right. "At least, most of the time. Sometimes, we break the rules, but we would never eat dog stew! You know that. Right, Benji? We love dogs." She caught Aunt Laurel's glance. "Even Auntie L. She just pretends not to."

"It makes sense," said Joseph, cheerfully.

"It does?" Aunt Laurel asked, off guard.

"I always knew there was something special about you. Consider that data confirmed."

Aunt Laurel's constellation flooded with pink, swelling in shape so her stars beat like mini hearts on her cheek. Joseph's eyes twinkled, the two of their faces like galaxies orbiting, caught up in each other's gravitational pull.

Avery looked over in the direction of Benji and Graham Cracker, too nervous to meet their eyes. "And Benji? Graham Cracker?" She stuffed her hands back in her pockets. "Will you still be my best friends? Even though I'm a Slider?"

Graham Cracker placed her paw on Avery's tangerine sneaker. The dog's big brown eyes appeared loving and kind.

"Graham Cracker doesn't seem to mind," Benji noted.

"You know what they say," said Avery, "A dog will always be your ally."

"And I'll always be your best friend," said Benji.

Aunt Laurel turned to Joseph, hands fiddling with the chain of her tarnished locket. "So, you're not scared of me?" She tilted her head towards Avery. "Of us? Even though we're different?"

"Goodness no! We're kindred folk," Joseph explained. He placed one arm around Aunt Laurel's shoulder, like she was his buddy, and pulled her close. "Scientists were once considered outcasts too. Just think of Copernicus! He was called wicked for discovering the Earth goes around the sun and not the other way around." He hesitated, his face falling into a frown. He dropped his arm from Aunt Laurel and stuffed his hands in the pockets of his wrinkled cargo shorts. "Not that I'm on the same level as Copernicus. I am, after all, a failed inventor, not a world-famous one."

"Joseph," Aunt Laurel started, her voice shaky. "There's something I need to tell you." She took a deep breath and bit her lip, twisting the locket chain around her fingers so tightly her knuckles went white. "It's bad."

"Laurel, I accept you for who you are," he said. "You're an amazing friend. And that's all that matters."

"I'm not," she said. "I've done something horrible." She cast her eyes down to the ground. "I promise, my intent wasn't to hurt you, I was just so scared of you finding out Avery and I are Sliders, and the dogs on this island know so much, I couldn't risk them revealing our secret. They can smell us from miles away! So," Her face turned green as though she was about to hurl. "I sabotaged Dog Lingo 42."

"You what?" Joseph's eyes welled with tears. Avery thought she could hear his heart shatter in pieces. He took off his eyeglasses and rubbed his face.

"I stole a curly red wire from your invention." Aunt Laurel hung her head. "So, it wouldn't work."

Joseph perked up, as though a light bulb went off in his mind. "That's it!" He ignited, his face beaming with joy. "The *thingmajig*. I knew something was missing."

"You're not mad?" Aunt Laurel shifted her weight. "Angry?"

"This is wonderful." He wrapped his arms around Aunt Laurel, embracing her in a tight hug. He pulled back, looking her in the eyes, enthusiastic and full of life. "You understand what this means? I'm not a failure. The Dog Lingo 42 works. Well, it will work once I reconnect the *thingamajig* to the *whatsitmacalled.* I forgive you, Laurel. Now, let's get that wire hooked up."

Aunt Laurel grimaced. "I threw it out."

"No," Joseph gasped. "Please, don't say that. It was a cross conducive, electro magnetized, rare curly red wire. I won't be able to find anything like that around, not unless I'm in a big city like Chicago."

"I'm sorry," Aunt Laurel picked at her fingernails.

"Is this what you're looking for?" Benji asked, dangling a red spiraled *thingamajig* in his hand, his tan fanny pack zipped open.

Joseph's eyes widened. "Yes, that's it." He ran to his son and scooped the wire in his hands. He inspected it up close, admiring the object.

"See, my scavenging comes in handy," said Benji. "It was in the recycling bin."

"Brilliant." Joseph clapped. "The Dog Lingo 42 will change the world. Finally, humans everywhere will be able to communicate with their fur friends. Understand exactly what they mean with each bark, whimper, or song. It will usher in a new age of our relationship with canines."

"Um," Avery interrupted. "That is if we can stop Wornher from transforming all the dogs of Beaver Island into hot dogs before the Blood Moon."

"What?" Joseph and Benji asked at the same time.

Graham Cracker whimpered and sat protectively at Joseph's feet.

"We have a lot to catch you up on," noted Avery.

"But we really don't have time," Aunt Laurel rushed. "Everyone, into the jeep! We'll brief you on the drive over to the Sugar Shack."

As everyone scrambled into the vehicle, Joseph pushed the Dog Lingo 42 in a wheelbarrow towards the cargo door of the Jeep.

"Can you all lend a hand lifting my invention into the Jeep?" He asked, sweat on his forehead. "I think it may come in handy."

After loading the Dog Lingo into the vehicle, Aunt Laurel gave a final warning to Avery and Benji as she turned on the engine, "Buckle up, it's going to be a bumpy journey."

What no one noticed was that as they had been revealing themselves to Joseph and Benji, and as Toast slept inside Cliff Cottage, Butters, the black cat, had snuck in the jeep, and was now hiding in the cargo hold under the Dog Lingo 42's tentacle arms.

CHAPTER 35

Bake It Off, Bake It Off

Under the waxing moon, bright in the sky, the jeep rolled by the brick pillars of the entrance to Sugar Shack, the shiny gate wide open in invitation. Elaborate helium-filled balloon arrangements in the shape of red, white, and blue poodles flanked the driveway. All four humans and Graham Cracker nervously sat in silence in the vehicle, Butters's presence undetected as the black cat dug her claws into the cargo area carpet, hidden under the Dog Lingo 42.

"Here we go." Aunt Laurel downshifted a gear as the jeep bumped down the golden brick road to the circular driveway, winding around a fountain spewing pink bubbles. Topiaries of sharks swam in the gardens, a quartz mansion shimmering on the lawn of green and gold. "Let's put an end to this bake-off!"

On the grand marble staircase leading to Sugar Shack's even grander rose-gold doors, families and their dogs excitedly chattered as they filtered into the party scene. Guests wore red, white, and blue, some in silly hats and sunglasses with tinsel and poms-poms, and kids' cheeks marked with face-painted stars and stripes. Dogs wore sparkly collars and special costumes: a bulldog in an Abraham Lincoln hat and beard, another dressed like a hot dog in a bun. At that sight, Avery gasped, her heart skipping a beat. She took a deep breath. It was just a costume. There was still time to stop Wornher from using her poison. Still, Avery's stomach spun.

"What if Mrs. Fiddlesticks doesn't listen to us?" Anxiously, she peered out of the window, looking closely for Teddy in the sea of pooches and their human pals.

"Then maybe she'll listen to Graham Cracker," Joseph said, confident that his invention would now work, and Graham Cracker howled.

Avery noticed something unexpected outside. Movie cameras. People in head-to-toe black, scuttling in the shadows of the mansion's columns and hedges, mumbling into walkie-talkies, holding clipboards, and coffee cups. Bright lights on sturdy stands. Hovering boom mics. It was as though the mansion's exterior was secretly the set for a film.

Tap, tap, tap.

Marcus the Butler knocked his white-gloved knuckles against Aunt Laurel's window. He wore his typical butler's uniform, along with an earpiece that coiled behind his neck, disappearing into his tuxedo as though he moonlighted as a secret service agent. He spoke into the earpiece's mic, "The guppy is in the shark tank. I repeat, the guppy is in the shark tank." He tapped again, gesturing to Aunt Laurel to unroll her window.

"Ahem," he said, "It's seven-fifty-nine p.m. Filming

starts in precisely one minute."

"Filming?" Aunt Laurel raised her eyebrows.

Marcus the Butler reached over the steering wheel and turned off the ignition. "Chop, chop." He hurried, tossing the key ring to one of the shadows in head-to-toe black. "Jenny Number One will take care of parking this. . . ," he glared down at the rusted jeep, ". . . monstrous tin can. The rest of the Jennies will take your things into the kitchen to set up for the bake-off. Let's get you into hair and make-up! Jennies, *assemblé, si vous plait.*" He snapped his white-gloved fingers.

"There's not going to be a bake-off—" Aunt Laurel protested.

Before she could say another sentence, an army of production assistants—all answering to the name Jenny, at the beckoning of Marcus the Butler—swarmed the vehicle, like ants attacking a picnic basket. They popped open the jeep doors and led Avery to a Jenny who puffed a brush on her cheeks, pink blush erupting in a plume. Avery sneezed.

"I don't need face paint," Avery said, trying to dodge the Jenny's makeup brushes.

"Everyone needs a touch-up before going on camera," another Jenny replied.

"Camera?" Avery asked.

A Jenny ran a comb through Benji's hair, rearranging his mane in a severe side part that made him look like an old man, while yet another Jenny misted Graham Cracker's breath with a mint spray. A fourth Jenny came towards Joseph with a wand of mascara. She took off his eyeglasses, a spidery blur swinging towards his eyelid.

"I can't see." Joseph stumbled, out of sorts.

"Hold still," a Jenny snapped.

"Butters?" From the corner of her eye, Avery thought she saw a black cat's slinky tail leap from the back of the jeep and disappear into a hedge. Avery couldn't turn her head to look, as a Jenny smearing foundation on her chin blocked her view. "Auntie L, did you just see Butters?"

Aunt Laurel nudged a Jenny who was armed with a comb, away from her wild wheat shuck hair. Another Jenny tried unclipping the locket around her neck. Aunt Laurel clutched the charm tightly. "Hands off."

"That's our cue." Marcus the Butler snapped his white-gloved fingers, his other hand pressed to his earpiece as though he was responding to a command. "Swim the guppies into the shark's jaws. The bait is set. I repeat, the bait is set!"

Marcus the Butler and the Jennies ushered Avery, Benji, Joseph, Aunt Laurel, and Graham Cracker up the marble staircase to the mansion's rose-gold doors.

"And don't forget," Marcus the Butler advised, as they stood before grand sparkling doors to Sugar Shack. "Smile. It distracts the audience from the ten pounds the camera adds."

The grand doors opened to reveal the marvelous marble foyer with cameras and film equipment stationed about. A crystal chandelier glinted, blinding Avery's view when it caught the light pouring in from the glass atrium ceiling. She blinked, then shielded her eyes with her hand like a visor to see Mrs. Fiddlesticks posing on top of a double staircase mezzanine.

"Laurel Foster," Mrs. Fiddlesticks's voice boomed from her perch. "What a pleasant surprise. I was just in my bedroom writing inspirational letters to retired seeing eye dogs who live in remote, mountain villages." Mrs. Fiddlesticks coughed, directing the camera people to focus on her. She cradled Princess in her arms, the Maltese constrained in a jumper meant to look like a chef's jacket, and a floppy chef's hat decorated with pink bows. As Mrs. Fiddlesticks glided down the stairs, Princess snarled, struggling to break free from her owner's embrace.

"You were writing letters in your apron?" Benji asked, confused.

Avery snorted.

"One must always be prepared for a bake-off," Mrs. Fiddlesticks advised, her mouth stuck between an annoyed sneer and a fake smile. She reset, angling her chin as though trying to present the cameras her best side. "Are you ready to lose your cookie shop *and* your cabin, Laurel?"

"We can't do this," Aunt Laurel stated. "That's why I'm here. We have to cancel the bake-off, there are bigger things at play."

"Ha," Mrs. Fiddlesticks laughed. "Typical. I knew you'd chicken out. If you break our deal now, I win. See you in the kitchen, Laurel, if you can handle the heat."

"Cut," yelled a Jenny.

Suddenly, a swarm of Jennies came out from behind the lights and cameras, reapplying everyone's makeup and fixing everyone's hair, repositioning lights, and boom mics.

Director Jenny in a French beret clapped her hands. "Amazing work, Mrs. Fiddlesticks. Truly captivating. What do you say we try that again from the top?" She turned towards Aunt Laurel and Avery, "But this time, I'd like more energy from our antagonist and her little ragamuffin sidekick. I want to feel your pain. Remember, you're about to lose everything. Alright?"

"Excuse me?" Avery scrunched her brow.

"What's going on?" Aunt Laurel questioned.

"Oh, didn't I tell you," Mrs. Fiddlesticks cooed. "They're filming my reality TV show, *The Sultaness of Sugar Shack*. It's not like the good ol' days when being a self-made, multi-million-dollar business mogul was enough. There's this whole fame game nowadays that I, like anyone else who wants to be worth remembering, need to play. We'll shoot a few scenes to escalate the tension before we set up in the kitchen auditorium before a live studio audience of all my party guests and their dogs. Then, they can all watch as the dogs of Beaver Island choose my canine cookie over yours. Even viewers at home."

"I'm not sure what's going on here," Director Jenny said, waving her hand in front of Joseph's face. "He's handsome, but in a homeless busker sort of way. He'll make your mom viewers uncomfortable, and moms need to feel comforted by your brand."

"I'm not homeless." Joseph adjusted his eyeglasses, offended. "Well, I guess, I sort of am. But just for the moment, while my motor trawler sits sunken in the bottom of the bay. I'm an inventor. A successful one. Why, I can even show you my world-changing invention, the Dog Lingo 42. I happened to bring it along if the Fiddlesticks Cookie Empire is interested in investing."

"Cut him," Mrs. Fiddlesticks hollered. She flung her diamond-clad wrist in Benji's direction. "Take his offspring too. And the Golden Retriever mutt. It's going to be easier to portray Laurel as the dog-hating, dog cookie chef if she doesn't have such a gosh darn cute dog around."

As Jennies directed Benji, Joseph, and Graham Cracker away, Avery called out, worried, "Where are you taking them?"

"Relax. They're going to a green room. There's candies and magazines."

Director Jenny stood in front of Avery, blocking her view of her departing friends, as the director eyed the girl from muddy sneakers to blush smudged cheeks. "And is the ragamuffin necessary? Or can she go too?"

"She's an orphan," Mrs. Fiddlesticks noted. "So, she'll win us sympathy points with our viewers. Especially when I crush her aunt in this bake-off and take away their shop and their cabin."

"I'm not doing the bake-off," Aunt Laurel said, her tone final.

Director Jenny ignored Aunt Laurel's protests. "Absolutely, genius observation Mrs. Fiddlesticks. All right. Let's reset Mrs. Fiddlesticks on the top of the staircase. Laurel and the orphan go back to the entrance."

"Stop!" Aunt Laurel yelled, swatting away a swarm of Jennies. "Is anyone going to listen to me? All your dogs' lives are at risk!"

"Exactly. That's the passion I want to see." Director Jenny clapped. "Now, make sure the camera can't pick up a single one of those freckles on our villain's cheeks. Freckles are far too cute on a character our audience is meant to hate."

Suddenly, the Jennies attacked Aunt Laurel with all sorts of make-up brushes and swabs. Avery tried to pull her aunt from the crowd, but it was no use. The Jennies circled Aunt Laurel, leaving Avery on the outside.

How would they ever stop Wornher if they couldn't even get away from the cameras? That's when a tendril of sour smell tickled Avery's nostrils. Avery whipped around to see a figure crossing the archway to the hallway at the end of the foyer. The figure moved quickly, appearing briefly in the arch's frame. But Avery knew exactly who it was.

Wornher.

Little girly, be normal. . . . Turn around. . . . Be normal. . . . Go home. . . .

The voice erupted in Avery's head. It drowned out any other thoughts she had. She covered her ears. Her feet began to move. It was as though the voice controlled her body, like a parasite taking over her movements. Her legs. Her sneakers. Her steps.

But there was another voice, even deeper down, advice burrowed in Avery's mind far beyond where Wornher's voice rang. It was her Aunt Laurel.

If you see a Scorned Slider, run.

And this time, Avery obeyed.

She ran.

Following the Scorned Slider.

CHAPTER 36

Kitchen Party

Avery went through a set of black doors, still swinging in Wornher's wake. She found herself in the shadows of velvet curtains, cables snaking throughout the sprung, black floor, over and around traces of peeled electrical tape and powdery rosin. Overhead, stage lights pulsed with heat. *It's like backstage*. She held her breath.

The kitchen auditorium.

The smell of snert worsened, as though Avery was walking through a pea soup factory. Her knees shook. Her stomach curdled. Her palms itched with prickles. She tiptoed to the curtain and cautiously pulled it back, stiffening, fearful her heartbeat would give her away. *Beat, beat, beat. Beat, beat, beat*. It pounded like the percussion section of an orchestra.

"Avery, you're just in time," Wornher greeted, her tone eerily welcoming. She wore the disguise of a chef. Her reddish-brown hair seemed to squiggle out from underneath her poofy white hat.

Under the hot yellow and white stage lamps, the kitchen set sparkled and gleamed like pirate treasures. Spotlights focused on two baking stations, each with its own island, mixer, oven, sink, and fridge. Offstage, the chairs in the auditorium were empty, awaiting the live audience of guests and their dogs.

At the far station, Wornher hovered over a shiny, metal bowl. Between her forefinger and thumb, she held the vial of electric green ooze.

The poison.

"I know what you're doing. Poisoning Mrs. Fiddlesticks's canine cookie batter. You won't get away with it!"

Wornher smirked. "How clever of you, little girly." She slipped the vial into her apron pocket and twirled a wooden spatula until it transformed into a long umbrella with a hooked handle. "Of course, I wouldn't expect anything less from Avery Isadora, daughter of Wendy Foster Warwick."

My mom.

Avery wanted to know more. How did Wornher and King Weird know her mother? It was a trap. A way to distract her. Avery shook her head. "Where's Teddy?"

"The terrier mutt? Our sworn enemy?" Wornher cackled, high-pitched. "You're choosing the wrong side of the war, Avery. It's Sliders versus dogs. Need I remind you, you're a Slider?"

"Your plan will never work."

"Tsk, tsk," Wornher dismissed. As she popped open the umbrella, an intense wind blew off her Chef's hat to reveal a scalp of squiggling worms, the invertebrates viciously preening and twisting. At the same time, her Chef's outfit flapped out into a black cloak like the wings of a bat, hot air bursting towards Avery's face. Wornher was fully returned to her Scorned Slider form. She slowly twirled the umbrella, its white-and-black spiral pattern hypnotizing, lulling Avery into a strange calm again. Wornher's voice burrowed deep into Avery's mind.

My plan will work. I shall succeed at my Sacred and Wicked Mission before the Blood Moon. And I know this as a fact. Because with you helping me, there's no way we'll fail. You want what I want, little girly. You want the dogs of Beaver Island to transform into hot dogs, as much as I do. After all, it's your destiny.

Averting her eyes from the spiraling umbrella felt impossible to Avery, it drew her attention. Watching the umbrella's black-and-white swirl was all that mattered, along with the melody of Wornher's words. But there was something about them that were wrong.

Completely wrong.

With all her might, Avery threw her hands up in front of her face, breaking her sight of the umbrella's enchantment. Free to speak, she yelled, "Your plan will never *ever* ever work, and I will never ever *ever* help you. And even if you do get away with poisoning Mrs. Fiddlesticks's batter, the dogs will choose my Aunt Laurel's biscuits over hers. They'll never eat the poisoned cookies!"

"Oh, Avery Isadora," Wornher chimed in her hypnotizing, singsong voice. "That would be a problem, except Mrs. Fiddlesticks has the very same recipe as your Aunt Laurel. The one stolen from Dog Dimension. Given to Mrs. Fiddlesticks by me, who was given it by none other than your mother, Wendy Foster Warwick, from your

Great-Grandma Elsie."

"What?" Avery lowered her hands, thrown suddenly off-guard. Her eyes fearfully froze on the umbrella.

But Wornher zipped the canopy shut, tucking her umbrella under her armpit. "I don't need hypnotism to convince you to join my Sacred and Wicked Mission. After all, this is what your mother always wanted."

My mom wanted what?

No. Avery's mom loved dogs. The photos of her mom with the beagle at Cliff Cottage were proof of that. "That's impossible."

"Wendy was the most powerful Scorned Slider there ever was," Wornher explained. "I should have taken a page from her playbook long ago. This one, now this one, is particularly devious."

"My mom loved dogs. You're lying."

Wornher shrugged. "I'm not surprised your instinct is to assume adults aren't telling you the truth. Your Aunt Laurel lied to you for so many years. Kept you away from your roots, from your destiny. From your proper place in this world as a Scorned Slider. From joining King Weird's Army."

Avery's stomach caved inwards. She wanted to throw up. "It can't be. You're lying."

"Lying? No, little girly. It's your Aunt Laurel who's the liar." Wornher went on. "You know your mother lived at Cliff Cottage, don't you? She went back despite your Grandma Isadora's rule. Under the protection of King Weird, your mother made Beaver Island her home, embracing her destiny as a Scorned Slider. Plotting against dogkind. And she would have raised you to follow in her footsteps if your aunt hadn't interfered."

"What do you mean? Interfered?" Avery's knees trembled.

"Your Aunt Laurel couldn't stand the humiliation and shame of having a sister who was a Scorned Slider. It tarnished her perfect reputation with the Goodness Council, you see, the very same concern shared by Isadora. They are very much alike after all, your Grandmother Isadora, and your Aunt Laurel. They're both strict. Stern. Rule-abiding. Any of this sound familiar?"

Avery shook her head. She wouldn't give into Wornher's lies. But there must be some truth in them, didn't there? Avery had seen the photos herself. Her mother had lived at Cliff Cottage. Which meant she had broken Grandma Isadora's rule. Which meant she would have been kicked out of Slider Realm, their home dimension, like Aunt Laurel. So had Avery's mom been a Scorned Slider? Avery's head pounded.

"When you were born, your Aunt Laurel vowed to do whatever it took to ensure you'd blossom into a Lawful Slider instead of following the destiny ordained by your own mother. No matter the cost."

"What do you mean?"

"Your Aunt Laurel pressures you to follow the rules, doesn't she? She expects you to be perfect and will settle for nothing less. Have you ever wondered what lengths she would go to, to get what she wants? Or perhaps what horrible crimes she's already committed to get her way? She kidnapped you, Avery. She's responsible for the disappearance of your mother and your father."

"That's not true," Avery muttered. Her head clouded with confusion. Her aunt wasn't responsible for her parents' disappearance. That was impossible. Wasn't it? "My parents disappeared in a float plane accident."

"A mysterious crash where the plane was never located? You really believe that fairy tale?"

"It's a lie?"

"Bingo," said Wornher. "Are you ready to learn the truth? About what *really* happened to your mom and your dad?"

"I don't believe anything you say," said Avery, clutching her hands in fists, trying to will the heat to return, whatever energy she had tapped into at Stone Circle. But she felt nothing except her nails digging into her palms.

"You don't have to. I'll show you. Ready for a trip through time? I got a two-way ticket to Cliff Cottage. To the night your aunt kidnapped you, so you can see for yourself."

CHAPTER 37

The Truth About Cliff Cottage

"I can teach you, Avery," Wornher tempted. "I can train you to harness your emotions to create energy. I can show you how to manipulate matter to travel through space and time. Like this. WARPI-WARP, portal to the past!" Wornher bellowed. Her umbrella glowed amber, starting with its ferrule tip, then igniting in sparks down to the handle. Suddenly, the kitchen auditorium filled with dark rain clouds even though they were inside. Thunder rumbled. Lightning bolts shattered through the air.

The heat warmed Avery's cheeks, sweat forming on her brow, as Wornher seemed to collect the lightning's energy with her umbrella and cut a circle in the sky, slicing through space and time to reveal a portal, a gateway that looked like an endless tunnel of whirring energy leading into a dark abyss.

"Ready to find out what happened the night your mother and father went missing?" Wornher's black cloak flapped out like bat wings as she swished around to face the tunnel. She looked over her shoulder, her worms desperately squiggling, preening for skin flakes. "After me."

Avery hesitated. Was Wornher lying? How could Aunt Laurel ruin her family over a silly thing like her reputation?

Protective, paternal Aunt Laurel. Overwhelmed, overbearing Aunt Laurel. Strict, stubborn Aunt Laurel.

Avery would never know the truth, she realized.

"Tell you what," Wornher said with a crooked smile. "Follow me to find out what really happened. Then, if you still don't want to join my Sacred and Wicked Mission, I'll back off. Leave you alone. But chances are, you'll be poisoning the batter yourself once you see the past."

Then, against Avery's better judgment, against the achy feeling in her gut, Avery found herself once again following Wornher. This time, straight into the whirring portal.

Darkness.

Avery's molecules spun apart, then swirled together again like paint blending on a canvas. With a harsh snap, she solidified into something kind of like an eleven-and-a-half-year-old girl. She was Avery-size and Avery-shape. Only she felt lighter than usual. Almost like she was floating.

But she wasn't floating. She stood on a stone pathway, surrounded by lavender fields, roses, and sunflowers. The pathway led to a familiar-looking cabin, smiling like a cheerful cherub. The fresh paint absorbed sunlight. The cabin was fitted with bright blue curtains.

It was the smiling-faced cottage from the photos. And there was no denying it was Cliff Cottage. It was the same shape, size, and the trail curved this way and that in all the same directions that Avery had become familiar with over the past few days. But why did it look so shiny and new? Happy and alive? It wasn't the dilapidated, sad shack Avery helped pack up with her aunt. It was like the cabin from the photo.

"Looks different than what you're used to?" cooed Wornher, as though reading her mind.

Avery couldn't believe her eyes, not just at the sight of Cliff Cottage, but also at Wornher's appearance. She flickered like a staticky TV signal. Avery could see right through her, as though she were a hologram.

"Yeah," Avery muttered. She looked down at her own hands, also transparent like those of a ghost. The world around them was bright and colorful, but Avery and Wornher were monochromatic and transparent.

"When your mother moved into Cliff Cottage, she used her energy to give the place a facelift. A *zap* here, a *zip* there. Sadly, her improvements will begin to fade with her disappearance tonight. Cliff Cottage will revert into its sad, shacky state which you've come to know. It will look exactly like it did the night your Grandma Isadora discovered your mother's and aunt's betrayal, that they had been sneaking away from the Slider Realm to spend time at this cabin as teenagers, the night she finds them playing board games, eating popcorn, and painting their toenails inside, and compels them to leave in a rush. The next time anyone would step foot in this cabin, it would be your mother. Returning to start her life as a Scorned Slider."

The board game spilled over the pilly rug. The withered popcorn kernel Avery had licked. The spilled nail polish bottles. She replayed the moment Aunt Laurel and Avery walked into Cliff Cottage.

I wasn't expecting this, Aunt Laurel had said, dropping Toast to his paws.

The mess throughout the sitting room. The kitchen table. The bedroom upstairs. That mess had all been left over from the night Grandma Isadora discovered Aunt Laurel and Avery's mom, Wendy, at Cliff Cottage. The night she banned them from ever stepping foot on Beaver Island again.

But Avery's mother had come back, improved the place with Slider energy, and started a new life. Her life with Avery's dad. With Avery. With their dog?

It hit Avery. *My mother is still here. She's not gone yet. Where is she?*

"Can I save her?" Avery asked, desperately.

"No," Wornher replied. "We're mere visitors to this era. We can't change anything. We're useless as ghosts. We can't even blow dandelion seeds from its stem. Go ahead, try to pick one."

Avery's hand slid through the weed.

"Fortunately, for our purposes, someone's already broken in," Wornher gestured at the front door, swinging ajar in the slight breeze. "We must make haste. Haunt the past too long and the past begins to haunt you. You can stay stuck forever if you wallow too much." Wornher slipped inside.

Avery's stomach tumbled. It felt like she was on an upside-down roller coaster, without a safety harness to hold her in. What if her parents never went missing in a float plane accident? What if Aunt Laurel was responsible for their disappearance? What if Avery walked through those doors and witnessed her very own Auntie L doing the unthinkable? Would her world fall out from under her? Would she tumble into a dark and endless abyss, never able to crawl herself out? She clutched her hands in fists.

She exhaled and followed Wornher.

Upturned furniture and smashed decorations met Avery in the sitting area. The bluebell sofa was tipped on its back, a chewed doggie toy underneath. A planter of herbs splayed out over the pilly carpet, and traces of the dirt scattered up the stairs. A lamp laid in shatters. "What happened?" Avery asked.

Wornher bowed her eyes, solemnly. "We're too late."

"My parents? They're already—?" Avery couldn't finish the sentence.

"It's best you didn't see what your Aunt Laurel did to them."

"Did she hurt them? Where are they? Where is she?"

"Sssh," Wornher hissed. She pointed up to the ceiling with her closed umbrella. Footsteps hammered over the floor above them. Someone was upstairs. "It's your Aunt Laurel. She's about to take you away."

"Why?" Avery asked. "Why would she hurt my parents to kidnap me? She's annoyed with me, all of the time. I thought she'd rather live without me. That I'm a nuisance to her."

Wornher smacked her dry lips. "Like I said, your Aunt Laurel was ashamed Wendy chose the life she did. She couldn't bear that her sister was raising you as a Scorned

Slider too. Your reputation would damage her own."

Avery's limbs felt heavy. She couldn't breathe. Her lungs squeezed in her chest. Her head rattled with static as sharp as nails. "That's not true?" Her voice cracked as what was intended as a statement transformed into a question, her whole world quaking.

"See for yourself." Wornher invited Avery up the stairs.

Despite how sluggish she felt, the steps didn't creak under her weight. She grasped the railing to help her up, but her hand slipped right through the wood. She truly was a ghost, her sadness and grief haunting Cliff Cottage with her colorless soul. Her body wouldn't leave lightly, if it could depart at all. Avery understood now how easy she could slip into the past and hover in this sad moment forevermore.

As she reached the hallway on the second floor, the door to the spare bedroom was wide open. Inside, it wasn't the bunk bedroom she had slept in, with Teddy curled at her toes. Instead, there was a wooden crib perched under tangerine curtains. It was her room. From when she was a baby.

And leaning over her crib, was none other than Aunt Laurel, her blonde hair frizzy beneath an eggplant purple cloak. As Avery walked closer, Aunt Laurel's hood fell, revealing her face, eyes swollen and puffy, the constellation of Orion twinkling on her cheeks. "Auntie L?" Her Aunt Laurel didn't respond. She crouched over the crib and scooped the infant baby in her arms.

The baby cried and cried and cried. Her little limbs

kicked and struggled, as though she knew she was in the midst of being kidnapped by the Slider who caused her parents' disappearance.

"It's okay, Avery," cooed Aunt Laurel to the baby. "I'm with you now. Everything will be fine. Everything will be good."

"No," ghostly Avery shouted, but Aunt Laurel couldn't hear her. "No, it won't."

How could this be? All this time Aunt Laurel had been lying to Avery about her past.

Aunt Laurel had been responsible for everything bad about Avery's life!

It was all her fault!

To think, if it wasn't for Aunt Laurel, Avery would be living at the smiling-faced Cliff Cottage, with her mom and her dad. She would never have been an orphan. She'd be loved and cared for by a real family.

"Convinced yet to join my Sacred and Wicked Mission? To embrace your destiny as a Scorned Slider like your mother would have wanted? To eliminate the dogs of Beaver Island?" tempted Wornher.

"But," Avery felt numb except for the ache in her heart. "I love dogs."

"Dear child, you don't love dogs. You love the idea of having a dog, of having someone to talk to. Someone eagerly waiting for you at the door when you come home from school. Someone to protect you, and cuddle with when you're sad. It's not a dog you crave, Avery, it's family. And King Weird's Army can be your new family. If you join us."

Avery's head spun. Wornher was right.

She wanted a family.

Avery wanted acceptance. She wanted to be herself. She wanted a home. So, what if that home was with King Weird's Army as a Scorned Slider?

Tiny, sharp teeth pierced Avery's ankle. Avery looked down at her sneakers, finding a slinky black cat attacking her socks. "Butters!" Avery shrieked. "Get off me." Avery shook her foot, trying to rid the cat from her ankle.

"Demon!" Wornher screamed, wielding her umbrella like a sword but its handle passed through the cat like the wind.

"It's Aunt Laurel's cat, Butters, " Avery said, hopping on one foot, trying to loosen Butters's grip.

"It's not an ordinary feline. See how it latches onto your shoelaces, while everything else goes through you? It can trap you here, in the past. Demon cats do not abide by the rules of matter."

"Butters is surly, and sometimes a pest," Avery admitted, looking down at the black cat's determined face. "But calling her demonic is a stretch."

"Ditch the demon now. It's time to go and take care of the dogs of Beaver Island once and for all." Wornher's umbrella glowed a fiery red and with its ferrule tip, she ripped a tunnel in time in the hallway. The portal whirred with fiery energy. "Before it's too late. Before we're trapped in the past by the demon feline."

"Stop it, Butters." Now the cat was tugging on Avery's shoelaces, trying to drag her back into the spare bedroom. "You're pulling me. Ouch!" The black cat persisted. "Wait."

"This way, now," Wornher commanded, head cocked towards the portal.

Avery bent down to the cat with a realization. Butters wasn't trying to attack Avery, she was trying to get her attention. "She's trying to tell me something. Lead me somewhere. Go on, Butters. What is it?"

"You dare disobey my direct order?" Wornher seethed.

The cat meowed and turned her tail on Avery, brushing her cheek against the open bedroom door. "You want me to go into my bedroom?" Avery asked, watching the cat slink towards Aunt Laurel.

"Avery Isadora Foster Warwick!" screamed Wornher. "This is your last chance. Follow me into the portal or I shall leave you here to perish. To exist as a ghost haunting the past forevermore."

Family stays by each other's side.

"Some family you are," Avery said.

She looked into the bedroom to see Aunt Laurel bouncing infant Avery in her arms. Her real family. Her aunt who had been there for Avery since the beginning. Since this very moment Avery was witnessing now. Love swirled in Aunt Laurel's grey eyes as she comforted the crying infant.

How could she have been so blind?

"Ssh, don't cry, I'm your Auntie L. I'm here for you," Aunt Laurel cooed. "You're safe. That's all that matters." The infant shrieked as Aunt Laurel placed her back into the crib. "Oh, what do I even do with a baby?" She twirled a lock of her hair as the baby's wails grew louder. "It's okay,

Avery," Aunt Laurel reassured. "I'll find your mom and dad. I'll be right back. I won't go far. I promise." The baby responded with a loud scream. "Fine. I won't leave your sight."

Rule one, thought Avery. *No leaving my sight.*

Aunt Laurel scooped up the baby against her cloaked chest, and hurried into the hallway, running straight through Wornher, as though the Scorned Slider were nothing more than a cloud, as though the whirring portal was merely air.

Wornher fumed with anger, "You weren't supposed to see this."

Avery brushed by Wornher, after her Aunt Laurel.

Aunt Laurel looked in the main bedroom. "Wendy! Widmore!" she called. "Where are you? I got your distress signal."

"Distress signal?" Avery repeated. Then, it clicked. "She's looking for my parents."

Aunt Laurel found a newspaper on the nightstand, next to a pencil. She gently placed baby Avery on the blue pillows of the big bed. She tore open the newspaper to the Crosswords section.

"A crossword? Really? Now?" Avery watched on, confused. As she looked over her Aunt Laurel's shoulder, she saw her aunt was writing in the grid: SOS Wendy and Widmore. SOS. Send help now.

"*Warpi-warp*, crossword to the Slider Realm," Aunt Laurel concentrated on the flimsy paper. "Attention of the Goodness Council."

Suddenly, the crossword ignited in a zap of electricity

and disappeared.

"Avery, the portal is closing," shouted Wornher from the hallway.

"My Aunt Laurel didn't harm my parents," Avery said, approaching Wornher. She faced Wornher head-on, the heat of the portal warming Avery's cheeks. "My Aunt Laurel came to save me."

"You foolish little girly," Wornher snarled. "You could have had everything and instead you choose the truth. May you haunt the past forevermore."

With that Wornher took her umbrella, leaped into the portal, and with the umbrella's tip, began to zip up the portal's entrance as though it were a sleeping bag. Avery watched in horror as the path back to the present closed before her eyes.

It's over.

She would be stuck in this moment for eternity. At least she could find love there. In her Aunt Laurel's eyes.

But it was over.

That is, until Butters launched her furball body like a cannonball from across the hallway, blasting a hole into the portal's remaining slit entrance, arcing up onto Wornher's neck, clawing her fangs into the Scorned Slider's warty skin. As Wornher screamed, the portal burst open with light, swallowing Avery and all of Cliff Cottage whole.

CHAPTER 38

All Along

Light twisted and twirled around Avery particles as she zapped through space and time, flying from Cliff Cottage into an unknown vastness of nothingness, a gooey sea of anti-matter. As she hovered in the in-between place where essence ceased to exist, her mind cleared.

She had discovered some truth about her past. Witnessed it first-hand. Someone had invaded Cliff Cottage and caused her parents to disappear, but not before Avery's mother sent out a distress signal to Aunt Laurel.

Even though returning to Beaver Island would break Isadora's rule and cost Aunt Laurel everything—her perfect life, the favor of her mother, Isadora, belonging and acceptance as a Lawful Slider—Aunt Laurel risked it all to help save Avery.

All along, Aunt Laurel wasn't just Avery's guardian, but her guardian angel.

Which made Butters her fur angel. All along, that annoying cat was a blessing in disguise, guiding Avery towards the truth.

Without Butters, Avery would have only discovered what Wornher wanted her to see—a distorted version of the past. She would have never known the full story—that Aunt Laurel was at Cliff Cottage that evening to save Avery, not take her away from her parents.

That's when Avery realized, she didn't need a dog to protect her. She didn't need a dog to love her and provide her with support and affection and unconditional love. She already had Aunt Laurel, Butters, and her other cat, Toast. They were her family, no matter how strange they seemed. They had been by her side all along. And that was enough. That was all that mattered.

As for who harmed Avery's parents, there was only one explanation. Wornher. How else would the Scorned Slider know exactly the time and place Avery's parents went missing? Known exactly the sliver of time to show Avery to support her lies? But why? Why had Wornher harmed them? Avery's mind flashed to the photos of her parents at Cliff Cottage with the beagle. Had Wornher taken action because her parents had a dog?

Before Avery could make sense of her swirling thoughts, a portal suddenly sucked her particles back down to Sugar Shack. Her molecules knotted together with a sudden and violent tug. She tumbled from the sky, landing on her hands and knees on the cold auditorium stage. Her fingers were a peachy pink. She was no longer a translucent ghost.

She had made it out of the past. She was in a time and place where she was loved by her Aunt Laurel, her cats, and all of her friends and their dogs.

If only she could keep them all safe.

If only she could save Teddy.

"Avery," a soft voice chimed. The voice was soothingly melodic, like music to Avery's ears, as though it plucked at her heartstrings and settled her soul. Avery noticed the tip of bluebell shoes at the top of her frame of vision. She pressed herself upright, raising her eyes. Standing before her, was a lovely woman who Avery instantly recognized.

She choked. "Mom?"

"Yes, it's me, darling."

Avery trembled. How was it possible that the image from her photo, the one she kept by her bedside, the one she spoke to when she was lonely, the one who watched over her while she slept, was now standing before her, in the flesh? After all these years?

The woman's dark hair framed her heart-shaped face, the strands straight and shiny as crow feathers, just like Avery's. Slim, the woman wore a simple outfit of dark pants and a matching shirt. Something about her silhouette, the slight arch of her lower back, the noble reach of her neck, seemed almost feline-like, reminding Avery of a cat.

She knelt and flung out her arms to embrace her daughter.

"I'm so proud of you Avery," said her mother, holding her tight.

Was this real? It had to be real.

Love coursed through Avery's veins, warm and vibrant. Her mom's heartbeat thrummed against her own. Avery's mind raced with thoughts and doubt interrupting her heart's expression.

How was this possible?

Where had her mother been all this time?

As though sensing Avery's questions, mom pulled back and locked eyes with her daughter, her hands on Avery's shoulders. It gave Avery a chance to examine her mom. Up close, her mother's skin was marked with crow's feet and fine smile lines, details not visible in the photo Avery cherished. Yet, there was something so familiar about her mother's eyes, about the swirls of love that surrounded her pupils. Avery swore she recognized those eyes. That she had seen them many times before, not just in photos.

"You've flourished into such an independent and courageous young Slider," said Avery's mother, smoothing hair out of Avery's eyes. "I couldn't have raised you better myself, really. I love you so much. I always have and I always will. I never stopped. Not for a second."

It was all Avery had ever wanted to hear, yet she couldn't absorb it. It felt unnatural, like a plant rejecting sunshine.

Avery bit her lip, trying to hold back tears. "Where have you been?"

"With you darling," her mother answered. "I've watched you grow up. I've been by your side this whole time."

Avery sniffled. "I don't understand."

It didn't make any sense. Surely this was one of those strange adult sayings, like "I'll keep you in my thoughts." It didn't mean someone actually stored you in their brains as though a toy in a box, it just meant that the person may think of you from time to time. Avery's mom hadn't actually been with Avery all along. Had her mother been watching her from the photos this whole time?

Her mother exhaled a long sigh. "It's not what you think. The night Wornher invaded Cliff Cottage, I was transformed. Into a cat. Same as your father."

"What?"

With a jolt, everything clicked.

The jeep ride to Charlevoix: *I guess they're just excited to visit her hometown. Butters and Toast are from Beaver Island. Found them in a foxhole.*

Wait, Avery froze as she held the final puzzle pieces in her mind. *Did that mean—?*

Avery gasped.

"That's right," her mother nodded. "I was Butters all along. The longer I was a cat, the more my feline instincts took over. But I remember everything. I'm so thankful for the blossoming Slider you've become."

Overwhelmed, Avery dug her nails into her palms to stop from crying. "I don't want to be a Scorned Slider," she cried. Her mom had to know that Avery wasn't going to join King Weird's Army. She wouldn't join their war against dogkind. Even if Avery was destined for a life as a Scorned Slider.

"Oh Avery," Her mother pulled her close again. "It's not a label that determines if you are good or bad, it's what's in your heart, and how well you listen to your heart's sounds."

"We have to save them," urged Avery. If she listened to her heart, that was the message loud and clear beating from her chest. "Wornher's planning on transforming them all into hot dogs."

"Sssh, it's okay, Ave," said her mother, smoothing Avery's hair once again. "We don't have to worry about Wornher. She didn't make it back from the past. She's trapped there. Her energy no longer has any effect in our present. It's why I'm no longer in cat form."

"Wornher trapped you as a cat? Why?"

Her mother looked downwards, sad. "Wornher and I were once close friends."

"You were friends with a dog-hating Scorned Slider? Do you hate dogs too?"

"No, of course not." Her mother bit her lip. "I admit, I've made some mistakes, Avery. I've never been good at following orders. My mother, Isadora, forbade me from visiting Beaver Island but I couldn't obey. I had already met your father, a human, and fallen in love. I followed my heart, we got married, and we moved into Cliff Cottage. That's when Wornher recruited me to join King Weird's Army. She made me feel like I still belonged within the Slider community. She led me to believe it was my life's calling to fight in the war of Sliders versus dogs. But everything changed when your father and I met Barney the Brave Beagle from Harmony Corps."

Through the audience doors at the back of the auditorium, barged in a monstrous beast with a giant horn and long tentacles snaking from its hunched back. Was it a robotic horned octopus?

"The war is over! The war is over. I repeat the war of Sliders versus dogs is officially over."

The announcement repeated on loop like a broken

record skipping, the voice was muddled with static, as though not quite tuned onto the correct radio frequency. The monster clanked and cluttered as it moved.

It took Avery a moment to figure out what was happening.

The Dog Lingo 42! Joseph's invention!

The monster's horn was the curve of the gramophone, strapped to Joseph's back, as he hunched, huffing and puffing down the aisle as though a mountaineer. The tentacles were the insulated tubes and wires connecting the Dog Lingo 42's parts dragging behind.

A cracked computer monitor waddled up to Joseph, with an unusually staticky mane of brown hair wisping from its upper crevices. It wobbled, turning to the side, revealing Benji cradling the monitor. The small boy's arms shook. "Dad, ever heard of an invention called wheels? Discovered by our forefathers, millennia ago?"

"Avery!" Joseph waved, a microphone in his hand, its wire snaking around his gramophone backpack. "We found you! It's my moment!" He gasped for air. "A time for me as an inventor to truly shine."

Joseph grinned proudly as though he had summited Everest.

"We have an important message to deliver," Joseph declared, "Someone furry has been wanting to talk to you for *quite* some time."

Rrrrawrrawrawwrawrawww, a Golden Retriever mix popped out between Joseph's legs, holding a keyboard in her mouth, tail wagging.

Avery's heart erupted with joy. "Graham Cracker!"

She smiled, happy to see a happy dog instead of a wiener in a hot dog bun.

"Not that someone furry," Benji corrected. "This one."

All of the sudden, a raggedy tuft of fluff hopped onto the monitor and excitedly barked, his silver tuft of hair even more messy than usual.

"Teddy!" Avery rejoiced.

With the added weight of the puppy, Benji's arm quaked, and he dropped the computer monitor with a thud. Teddy dropped like an elevator, then continued to jump up and down, yelping loudly at Avery as though he had a lot to say.

"Wait, Teddy, the mic," Joseph crawled over on all fours, the gramophone flat on his back. He held out the broken microphone, the wiring dangling before Teddy's snout. "Now, speak Teddy, speak."

"Princess Avery! Princess Avery! It's me. Your fur friend, Teddy!" The audio boomed throughout the auditorium, so loudly, that everyone covered their ears.

"Woah, woah, let's adjust the volume, shall we, Benji?" Joseph pulled the microphone away from Teddy and winced, while Benji fiddled with a knob on the gramophone. "Okay, let's try that again." He placed the mic before Teddy.

"Princess Avery, I have good news. The war is over. We can be friends forever. I'm so happy because you're my favorite Slider in all the dimensions. You play the best fetch. And you let me eat your socks."

"Ted—Ted—Teddy," Avery fumbled on her words. "Teddy, you can talk?"

And what was he speaking of? *Princess* Avery? Her head spun.

"It's my dad's invention, Ave. The Dog Lingo 42," explained Benji. "It works! I never thought in a million billion gazillion years that one of my dad's whacky ideas would actually amount to a scientific breakthrough that would forever change humankind's relationship with canines! Isn't that absolutely unbelievable?"

Joseph tilted his head, shakingly balancing the gramophone on his back while steadying the microphone for Teddy. "Well, it's not that unbelievable. I mean, I always had it in me. It took Edison ninety-nine attempts to get the light bulb right."

"Princess Avery, I love socks. I mean, I love, love, love socks," Teddy continued through the gramophone. "I love the way they smell, and the way they taste. Princess Wendy? Is that you? Princess Avery's mom? Your Majesty." Teddy sprinted from the microphone down the aisle, jumping onto the kitchen stage, and immediately rolled over onto his back in front of Avery's mom, tail wagging.

"Hello Theodore," Avery's mom said, rubbing the terrier's pink tummy. "How is Barney the Brave these days?"

Teddy barked, but without the Dog Lingo 42, it was less easy to figure out what he was saying though Avery could imagine.

"You two know each other?" she asked.

Avery's mom's eyes twinkled. "I knew Teddy's trainer. Barney the Brave from Dog Dimension who worked for Harmony Corps."

"Harmony isn't a person?"

Avery's mom chuckled. "Harmony Corps is a peacemaking agency, made up of the best dogs from Dog Dimension. Before you were born, Barney the Brave came to me at Cliff Cottage. His snout led him straight to the cabin's kitchen. I was baking a batch of canine cookies from the recipe stolen by your Great-Grandma Elsie. Barney's mission was to return the recipe to the Dog Dimension."

"The recipe you gave to Wornher?" Avery asked with a tremble in her voice.

"Wornher must have copied the recipe," Wendy explained. "I planned to enchant the dogs of Beaver Island using the cookies, but when I met Barney the Brave, everything changed. He was sweet, caring, and kind. Best of all, he loved you. One sniff of my pregnant stomach and he followed me around like a shadow, protecting my every move."

"He became your pet?"

"More like a guest. A very hungry guest." Wendy smiled. "When we figured out how to speak each other's languages, we realized just how silly the war between Sliders and dogs was. No one could even remember why, or who exactly, even started it. Nor could either of us come up with a good reason why our rivalry should endure. So, Barney and I created a peace treaty, a resolution to bring peace to Sliders and dogs throughout all the dimensions."

"You ended the war?" Avery asked as Teddy rolled over and pressed his snout against her hands, as though begging for rubs. Avery kneeled and patted his silver tuft, Teddy responding by covering her hand in licks. "You can do that?"

"Yes," said Avery's mom. "As a Princess of the Slider Realm, it was within my authority to do so."

Avery froze. "You're a Princess?"

"Our Great Grandfather Edmund took the throne when his older brother, King Weird was exiled to Beaver Island."

"Older brother?" Avery shuddered. "You're telling me, we're distantly related to King Weird?"

"From the good side of his family," Wendy emphasized. "And that makes us royalty."

"I'm a Princess?" She shook her head. She realized none of this mattered, as much as another very important and pressing question. "Does this all mean I can get a dog of my own?"

"Joseph! Benji! Have you seen Avery? I'm worried she's in trouble." It was Aunt Laurel, out of breath, at the back of the auditorium. She held the locket tightly in her hand. As Joseph and Benji gestured towards the stage, Aunt Laurel's jaw dropped. "Wendy? What? Where? How? Why? Uh—"

"Hi, Laurel," Avery's mom blushed with a wave.

"What in the world?" Aunt Laurel scuttled down the aisle and climbed onto the stage. "Thank the Goodness Council!" She wrapped her arms around her sister and squeezed tight, as the constellations on her cheeks sparkled more radiantly than any stars in the sky. "I got your distress call all those years ago. I came down to Cliff Cottage as soon as I could, but I couldn't find you anywhere. I took Avery. I raised her."

"I know what you did," said Avery's mom, voice melodic with gratitude. "You've been wonderful to us both. Thank you for taking care of Avery. It hasn't been easy, balancing your goals and dreams along with raising your niece. Yet, you've done such a great job with Barkleby Biscuits while acting as Avery's mom."

"How do you know about my cookie shop?" Aunt Laurel asked, startled. "Where have you been?"

"There's a lot to explain," said Avery's mom. "It starts with a dog. And it ends with a dog."

"And maybe there's an epilogue?" Avery added. "So, I can get a dog of my very own."

CHAPTER 39

Sam and Suzy Reprise

From the box theatre seats raised above the auditorium stage, Sam played over the events she'd witnessed. Their dogs with their families, Sam and Suzy had snuck inside the kitchen auditorium and found the coolest seats up a few flights of stairs. They had watched an unbelievable scene unfold.

"Weirdies. . . they're. . . they're real?" Shell-shocked, Sam could hardly form a sentence.

Suzy's face illuminated like a light bulb. "Weirdies are real, Sam. And they aren't scary at all."

"Ah, yeah, that's, ah, right," Sam said, and then she fainted in her chair.

CHAPTER 40

He's Toast

Meanwhile, at Cliff Cottage, Avery's father found himself very confused when woke up in an empty packing box, his human body curled up in a ball.

He stretched and yawned. He had a sudden craving for a can of tuna.

CHAPTER 41

Avery's Epilogue

Even though winter was brewing, the sidewalks were icy and the air frigid, family after happy family, happily lined up outside Barkleby Biscuits, their happy dogs in tow. Customers wore snow-dusted winter coats, mitts, and hats, while some of the smaller and skinnier canines wore wool sweaters and boots to keep them warm. Everyone buzzed with excitement.

It was a special day in December—the shop's Christmas charity drive. A new animal shelter had opened in the neighborhood, and Avery signed up to volunteer. On weekends, she cleaned kennels, brushed coats, and took dogs for walks to the park. She liked taking care of the furry creatures while they waited for their forever families to find them. Avery wanted the orphaned animals to feel loved, like they were still part of a bigger picture even though they hadn't found their particular pack yet. The idea struck her. What if she could bring Christmas to the dogs?

Now, on the snowy December sidewalk outside Barkleby Biscuits, moms, dads, foster parents, aunts, uncles, sisters, brothers, and grandparents, stood in line with their hungry fur friends, lugging bags and boxes of pet toys, dry food, doggie beds, and more, for donation to the animal shelter. Any customer who dropped off a donation got a free box of freshly baked canine cookies made by the lovely Aunt Laurel herself. That promise alone drove up the crowd.

"Merry Christmas." Avery handed a box of biscuits to Mrs. Sierra, a local librarian who used a wheelchair. Mrs. Sierra's old service dog licked its lips as the smell of goodies whiffed by its powerful, wet nose. "Thanks again for these rubber hoops and bones. There's a litter of teething puppies at the shelter that will love these chew toys to pieces. Literally."

"No, thank *you*," Mrs. Sierra said. "These cookies usually sell out in hours. How your Aunt Laurel is keeping up with demand today is beyond me."

"She's truly special," Avery smirked. "My mom and dad are helping too."

The greying service dog spoke, barks translated through the Dog Lingo 42 collar it wore. "Nothing is as satisfying after a day of work as a Barkleby Biscuit. I give them five out of five fire hydrants. Absolutely remarkable."

Joseph's invention was an overnight success, it seemed that dogs everywhere used Dog Lingo 42 to communicate with their human companions. Naturally, word spread quickly canine-to-canine about Aunt Laurel's cookies. With the biscuit business booming, they could afford to give back, and what better a cause for them to rally behind than Wornher's animal shelter.

"Last batch of cookies coming in hot," Aunt Laurel

announced triumphantly as she bounced the swinging door open with her hip. She slid the baked goodies onto cooling trays.

"Not necessarily," said Joseph. He tinkered with a human-sized robot behind the counter. "My Robbo Dobbo has the potential to create an unlimited supply of doggie biscuits with a fraction of the effort. Simply feed it a spoonful of batter," he scooped a measuring spoon into a mixing bowl and plopped the doughy mixture in the robot's mouth. "Then hit the baking switch, set a timer, and *voilà*!"

The Robbo Dobbo beeped on, its metal torso lighting aglow like the inside of an oven. Tendrils of smoke seeped from its surface.

"Until your Frankenstein does more than burp out burnt dough balls, I plan on baking the old-fashioned way," Aunt Laurel said.

As though on cue, the Robbo Dobbo belched and spit out a flaming handful of dough. Graham Cracker barked at the mess, as Joseph beat out the simmering goop with his gloved hand.

With tongs, Aunt Laurel divided the canine cookies from the cooling rack into cardboard boxes. She brought them over to Avery at the donation drop-off table.

"Just enough for your friends, then we close up for the night," Aunt Laurel said. "I'm proud of you, Avery. This is quite the donation haul."

Mountains of blankets, food bags, pet puzzles, fetch gadgets, and more, were piled on and around the table. Benji came out from behind a doggie pool and opened his notepad to a fresh page, pencil sharp and ready. His eyes glistened behind his glasses. "Cataloguing all of these donations for our records will take hours. It's my Christmas dream come true. Could life get any better?"

It could.

Bells chimed as Sam and Suzy walked into the shop with Pearl and Riley on leashes, both dogs sporting their Dog Lingo 42s. The cold air had pinkened the girls' cheeks, snow hitchhiking on their boots.

"Sam, Suzy, you made it," Avery greeted, excited to see her friends.

Since the night of the Fourth of July, Avery hadn't cared so much about fitting in. As soon as she embraced what made her different, her friends did too.

"Hi, Avery. Do you want to play fetch?" Riley galloped forward, marking the linoleum floor with paw prints. "I have a rubber ball, a tennis ball, and a squishy ball at home. I found a stick by the marina, but Sam said to leave it in the park. I still know where it is. Want to go get it? You can follow me."

Riley leaped in a circle.

"Did someone say ball?" Graham Cracker yelped from behind the counter. "I love ball."

"I prefer to chase my tail," said Pearl. The tiny fluff of black fur spun around like a tornado. "It's always there, no matter how hard I run. Endless entertainment."

"Yes, just like you, Pearl," said Suzy. "Since you got your Dog Lingo 42 collar."

"Riley likes to talk about sticks and food," noted Sam, as though a proud parent.

"Pearl loves chatting about smells and sounds."

"How's your trip going so far?" Avery asked Suzy and Sam, as the dogs snacked on Barkleby Biscuits.

"Amazing. I love Chicago," Suzy said. "We went to the Field Museum and saw an exhibit about bugs. It was so cool."

"You like museums?" Benji asked.

"No," Suzy replied. "I *love* them. I want to start my own museum one day."

"Really?" asked Benji, blushing.

"What about you, Sam?" Avery asked, changing the subject. "What do you like about Chicago?"

"The pizza. I had pizza for breakfast, pizza for lunch, and I can't wait for pizza dinner tonight. We'll meet you at the restaurant with your Aunt Laurel and Benji's dad, right?"

Avery's stomach growled. "I'm hungry just thinking about it."

"Did someone say food?" Riley piped up from his pile of cookie crumbs.

"Food, where?" Pearl echoed.

"I love food," Graham Cracked added.

"Sounds like we better get back to our hotel to feed the dogs," Sam said. "Our parents went for coffees across the street. They're probably done. We should get going."

"See you at dinner." Suzy waved goodbye. "Benji, maybe we could sit together?"

Benji's cheeks deepened in color. "That sounds nice," he said, nervously.

As Sam and Suzy left the shop with their dogs, Wornher entered.

CHAPTER 42

A New Start

Wornher's cheeks were flushed from the wintery weather, her crescent moon birthmark glowing. Flakes of snow dusted the hat that covered her head, her wavy tendrils of ombre-colored hair escaping from under the knitted cap.

"Brr, it's cold out there," Wornher shivered.

"Wait until you see the final donation haul. The shelter will have enough dog food for months," Avery boasted. "Speaking of which, any cuties come in today that I can adopt?"

"How about a pair? We rescued two Sheepdogs. They're no bigger than Teddy Bears, but they'll grow to be bigger than you, Avery. They could use a happy home."

Wornher's grey eyes warmed as she talked about the furry orphans. Avery couldn't believe this was the same Wornher, who only six months earlier, had tried to transform all of the canines on Beaver Island into hot dogs.

Then again, a lot more time had passed for Wornher

than the rest of them. The Scorned Slider had only escaped the past by living through it to the present. All that time to think and watch her past actions play out had changed her, softening her heart, and leading her to dedicate her present to seeking forgiveness and spreading love. And a strange thing happened. Her worm hair and warts disappeared. Her snert smell dissipated, replaced with the fragrance of fresh herbs.

But that was a story for a different day.

"What do you say, Aunt Laurel? Can we adopt them?" Avery smiled, innocently.

"Talk about it with your parents," Aunt Laurel said. She took a compost bag out of its bin, tying the end closed. "On your way to bring out the compost."

"Do I have to?" Avery moaned.

She knew the answer without needing to wait for Aunt Laurel's response. Avery took the green bag of food trimmings and pushed through the swinging door to the shop's back kitchen and office area. The smell of gooey peanut butter and crisp apples hung in the air, the room still hot from the oven's long shift. Avery took in a deep whiff, pleasant until the smell of rotting scraps from the compost bag made its way to her nostrils.

After the kitchen, she made her way through the dry storage. She turned the corner around the pantry shelves, where Aunt Laurel's bookkeeping desk hid. An old TV, perched on a windowsill, played commercials. As the programming returned, Avery recognized the show. She turned up the volume in time for the slick-haired host to announce, "Welcome back to Issue Island, where we take overachieving moms and their underachieving sons to a deserted island to live for ninety days. On tonight's episode, watch as Cookie Empress, Mrs. Fiddlesticks, and son, Tomin, rely on each other as they learn to forage for food and build a shelter." An episode preview played short clips.

Luckily, with a bit of Slider hypnotism, Wendy had convinced Mrs. Fiddlesticks to forget about Great-Grandma Elsie's canine cookie recipe. The Cookie Empress turned to other goals, such as connecting with her son and winning over reality television audiences across the country.

"Hey, Mom! Dad!" Avery hollered, flicking off the TV. "I got a question for you."

Avery caught her parents in a warm embrace. As Wendy turned to Avery, she revealed her grey eyes, full of love. She asked, "What is it darling?"

"Can I adopt a dog?"

"Ask your father," she smiled.

"Dad?"

"Hmm," her father stopped on a thought. "I wager I'm more of a cat person."

He pulled his daughter into a toasty hug.

Everything was almost perfect.

And even though Avery didn't have a dog of her own, she felt weirdly complete.

Outside, in the alleyway, Avery lifted the lid on the compost dumpster, recoiling from the putrid smell escaping from the bin. That's when she saw a furry mop of black and white digging into a bag of stale canine cookies.

"Rosie, is that you?" Avery asked, stunned.

Rosie's snout twitched as she stood on her hind legs,

raising a paw, as though saying hello to her old friend, Avery.

Turns out, the love and affection Avery wanted from a dog, she had right under her nose all along.

Acknowledgments

Many thanks to Cindy Bullard of Birch Literary and Kiri Jorgensen of Chicken Scratch Books for believing in this story.

Also, endless appreciation to my mom, Kory, Onion, and Cadence, for their support and inspiration.

About The Author

Prim Pawn

Since Prim Pawn could hold a crayon, she's been writing plays, poems, and short stories. She grew up on the shores of Lake Superior, where she spent summers swimming and fishing, and winters cross-country skiing, writing, and dancing ballet. While living aboard a motor trawler on Lake Michigan with her husband, yellow Labrador, and Persian cat, she developed the idea for her middle-grade novel inspired by the beauty and adventure of the Great Lakes. She presently lives on land in Calgary, Alberta, Canada.

Chicken Scratch Reading School

Avery the Dogless Orphan and the Interdimensional Stray

www.chickenscratchbooks.com/courses

Join us at Chicken Scratch Reading School for your choice of 2 different online Novel Study Courses for Avery the Dogless Orphan and the Interdimensional Stray. Created by certified teachers with extensive curriculum design experience, these offerings are 4 or 6-week courses of study for 4th- 8th grade students. They include reading study focus, interviews, quizzes, vocabulary work, thematic and character analysis, a written essay, and culmination project. The courses include a mix of online and on-paper work, highlighted by instructional videos from the instructors, Julie DenOuden and Kiri Jorgensen, and the author, Prim Pawn.

Chicken Scratch Books creates online novel study courses for every book we publish.

Our goal is to teach our readers to appreciate strong new traditional literature.

At Chicken Scratch Books,
Traditional Literature is all we do.

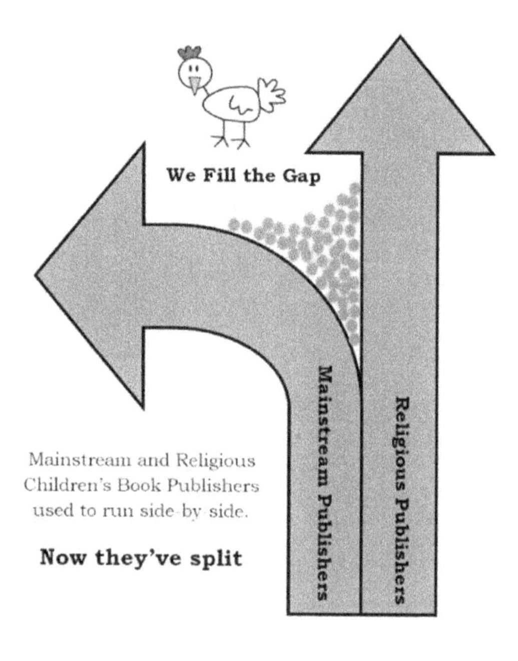

CPSIA information can be obtained
at www.ICGtesting.com
Printed in the USA
LVHW041736220323
742314LV00025B/472